TRUST NO ONE

When Michael Benasque was approached by the editor of *Outspeak* to write a feature on the transporting of rare gems, he had no idea he'd be plunging into the most dangerous adventure of his life.

Sure, the money was good, and he was intrigued when he met Christine Andress, the beautiful and mysterious courier with whom he was to travel. He'd even been introduced to the charming and sophisticated Sir Arthur Belder, their suspected criminal adversary, so he was not unaware that there were risks.

But when Christine strapped three of the world's most valuable diamonds to his crotch, Michael knew he had taken on more than he bargained for.

Other Avon books by
Alan Caillou

ASSAULT ON AIMATA	27086	$1.50
ASSAULT ON FELLAWI	28969	1.50
ASSAULT ON KOLCHAK	28191	1.50
ASSAULT ON MING	27565	1.50

ALAN CAILLOU

DIAMONDS WILD

AVON
PUBLISHERS OF BARD, CAMELOT AND DISCUS BOOKS

DIAMONDS WILD is an original publication of Avon Books. This work has never before appeared in book form.

AVON BOOKS
A division of
The Hearst Corporation
959 Eighth Avenue
New York, New York 10019

Published by arrangement with the author.
Library of Congress Catalog Card Number: 78-65318
ISBN: 0-380-43588-8

First Avon Printing, April, 1979

Printed in the U.S.A.

Chapter One

Goddammit, I was out of work again, and so broke that it was hurting, with nothing coming up over the horizon either. I was out of rent money, and grocery money, and even liquor money.

Some twenty-one hundred years ago, Isaiah the son of Amoz, an aristocrat from Jerusalem who decided to become a prophet, said—prefacing his comment with a "Ho!" if you please—"Everyone that thirsteth, come ye and buy wine without money. . . . "

But he had to be crazy.

My own experience is that if you go into a liquor store and let them know they just canceled your Diner's for nonpayment, they are more likely to tell you: *Get the hell outa here.*

But it's also my experience that when things are so bad they can't get any worse, something turns up out of the blue sky, just in the nick of time. The Greeks used to call it *Deus ex machina,* though why they chose to speak Latin I can't recall.

And true to form, while the nice man from the telephone company was actually standing there with a screwdriver in his hand, the phone rang, and it was my old friend and mortal enemy, Harry Slewsey.

You have to know about Harry.

He runs a very special kind of magazine that finds its way onto almost every important desk in almost every capital of the world. It's called the *Outspeak,* and it's largely political. But if there's a particularly fancy species of crime going on, Harry will leap in there and somehow find a way to make a fortune out of it, a sort of crusading evangelist in the world of information. He is smooth, and devious, and the nicest guy you ever met—on the surface.

When he wants something done he just starts writing very large checks, and if your acceptance of them means that you're probably going to get killed off—maybe—then all Harry will do is shrug it off without ever losing that wide, friendly grin.

And there he was on the phone; he *always* knows when I'm broke.

He said, in that exaggerated British accent he likes to put on to impress the *mujiks*: "Michael! How are you, dear boy? It's been a long time. It's not good for friends to drift apart like this."

I said: "Uh-huh," and he went on: "I hear on the grapevine that you're doing fabulously well, but if you can find the time, would you be interested in doing a small job for me? You'll probably find it a bit dull, but the money's good, and if you're at a loose end . . . I'd greatly appreciate it, Michael."

He really is a sonofabitch.

I said: "Well, I've got this article for *Viva* to do, and a layout for *Vogue*, and *Playboy*'s been calling me practically every day . . . "

He said: "Oh do shut up, Michael. There'll be a messenger round at your place any minute now, if she hasn't already arrived, with a package for you. I've booked a table at the Méditerranée for eight o'clock tomorrow night. Do try and be there on time."

The Méditerranée? I thought I knew all the restaurants in San Francisco, which is where Harry operates from these days. He's English, all right, but have you noticed? All the smart brains from England are Stateside these days. I said: "That's, uh, on Market Street somewhere?"

"No, Michael, don't be obtuse. It's on Place de l'Odéon. I'm calling from Paris." And he rang off.

Goddamn his eyes.

I could see nothing but trouble ahead. I put down the phone, and looked at the nice man standing there full of sympathy, and said: "Okay, do what you have to do; it looks like I'm getting the hell out of here anyway."

It was a rented apartment on Fountain, in Hollywood, with a kind of art nouveau decor and a pool that no one ever used, and a lot of phony-looking tropicals everywhere, the pots full of those goddamn geramiums, I said: "Christ, I'll be glad to get out of this dump!"

He really was a nice guy. He said: "Any special calls you want to make, Mr. Benasque, before I perform the mandatory surgery? I mean like maybe there's a girl someplace who's gonna wonder why she can't reach you?"

"Mandatory surgery? That's a hell of a way to talk."

"Before I cut the umbilical cord. Because that's what the phone is. Our lifeline to everything we hold dear."

He was about six foot three, towering over me and very muscular, a young black man with an Afro that practically hit the ceiling. He grinned and said: "There's always one call you just have to make."

Frankly, the idea had not occurred to me, but when I thought about it for a moment . . . I picked up the dying phone and dialed, and said: "Marcie? Michael. I'm going to Paris. You want to come with me?"

It was four in the afternoon, and she was still half asleep. Marcie Prendergast, a very good young actress who'd never really made it, though God knows, she tried hard enough. She was also a singer with possibly the world's worst sense of rhythm, a dancer who fell over her own ankles, and a model of ho-hum success. She was a girl of remarkable sagacity, who had learned, the easy way, how to look out for herself above all things, and very attractive. She had long golden hair and innocent blue eyes, and the tiniest nipples in history.

She said: "Michael . . . What time is it?"

"Four o'clock, more or less."

And you know you're not supposed to call me before six . . . " But then the voice changed, quite abruptly, and there was a note of expectation there. "Paris? You don't mean Paris, Arkansas, do you?"

"No Marcie, I don't."

"Or Paris, Idaho? Texas, perhaps?"

"Not even Tennessee. The original, one and only, Paris."

Now the expectation went, and the caution took over. "Do we seem to have money in the bank, Michael?"

I said apologetically: "Not quite. But it's on its way to me."

"This is Hollywood, Michael. You don't count your money before it's actually laying eggs."

"But it's practically a commitment, Marcie . . . "

Oh how sweet she was! She said plaintively: "Then why don't you give me a call when you actually get it? I mean, we really do have to be *sure*, don't we?"

I put the phone down, but I was too late; I heard the click at the other end a beat ahead of me. I looked at the telephone man and shrugged. "Well, that was the call I had to make."

We finished off the last three bottles of beer in the fridge before he went, and at five o'clock in the evening, the messenger arrived.

She was a skinny little thing who looked like she was still in school, with scraggly hair and thick glasses, and she had a heavy manila envelope for me, and she said, her voice high-pitched and squeaky: "If you'll just sign here, Mr. Benasque . . . " She wore jeans and a tank top, and she looked like hell.

I opened the envelope and saw that there was another inside it, roughly the shape of hundred-dollar bills and very thick. There was also a first-class ticket from L.A. to Paris, and a brief note from Harry:

> "I can't tell you how good it is that we're working together again, Michael. Maud will drive you to the airport. In haste, Harry."

I looked at the scraggly girl. "Maud?"

She nodded. "That's me. I have a car downstairs. And there's not a great deal of time. I mean, with the traffic and all. And I was told that you probably wouldn't want to pack anything, anything at all."

I held up the envelope. "This is all I need. Are you coming to Paris too?"

"Oh no. I have to get back to San Francisco. Mrs. Bentley's away. I have to look after the office."

"Mrs. Bentley? You mean she's still around?"

She said earnestly: "Of course. The operation wouldn't be the same without her, would it?"

"What operation is that, Maud?"

"Oh . . . just things in general."

"All right then." I started opening up the inner envelope and said: "I just have to square things with the landlord. I'm a bit behind with the rent."

She shook her head vehemently, and her glasses nearly fell off. She pushed them back up on her nose and said: "No, no, I'll take care of it when I've got you safely on the airplane. If you'll give me the key . . . "

I gave it to her. "No car key. I got rid of the car. I was tired of it."

She said casually: "Yes, we even heard about that," and I thought: "Goddamn your eyes, Harry Slewsey; why don't you mind your own goddamn business?" But that thick, thick envelope was a great panacea.

She was already in the kitchen alcove, turning off the gas under the kettle, looking the place over with a sharply efficient eye. She went into the bathroom, and I heard her jiggle the toilet, and when she came out she said severely: "Your tank is running. We're not supposed to waste water these days." She went to the kitchen again, looked briefly in the fridge, and nodded and said: "Well, everything seems to be all right. Shall we go?"

She had a little Pinto down there on the street; and she drove fast and expertly to the airport, and we made it in thirty-two minutes. Three quarters of an hour later, I was airborne, and a very attractive young stewardess was placing three Bloody Marys on the tray and smiling delightedly, and saying, as she lined them up carefully: "And pretty maids all in a row."

The timing was perfect.

There was a Citroën-Maserati to meet me at Paris' Orly Airport, driven by a young French-American who said his name was Bruce. He had a look of wry good humor on his face, with a very virile beard and moustache, and dark, intelligent eyes. At eight o'clock almost on the dot, we pulled up outside the Méditerranée on Place de l'Odéon.

In spite of everything, it was good to see Harry again. That's the kind of man he is; he'll happily drive a knife into your ribs, preferably from behind, and when you're half asleep; and still, next time, you're just glad he's around.

He was installed in a corner with a bottle of champagne

in a silver cooler on the immaculate linen, rising to his feet and coming to meet me, with the widest TV smile you ever saw. He thumped me on the back and shook hands, and put his arms around me, hugging me like a long-lost brother, and said: "It's good, good, good to see you, and you never looked better in your life. Are you hungry? I hope you are."

I said: "I'm thirsty, Harry."

"Of course. Come and sit down; we have to celebrate this happy reunion."

The waiter, beaming at all the goodwill, was poised, and Harry said in his near-perfect French: *"Deux choppes, en étain, s'il vous plaît . . . "*

It isn't everyone who prefers to drink vintage champagne out of pewter tankards, but I was glad Harry remembered. And the waiter didn't bat an eyelid, though the *sommelier* had a downturn of the lips when he came to pour it. I said: "What's it all about, Harry?"

He gestured vaguely. "Oh, there's time, Michael, plenty of time. We'll stroll down the riverbank after dinner, and we can chat. You're going to love it, just love it. But first, we'll have some oysters, and then a really first-rate dinner."

It's all a question of euphoria, of course. Or, if you prefer it, the softening-up process.

Fill a man's gut with Bollinger '69; a dozen of the little blue *Marennes* oysters; a lobster cooked in cognac and wine, with chervil and tarragon and shallots; a not-too-old Chateau Olivier from Leognan; a damn great plate of cheeses, washed down with Chateauneuf Du Pape; and three or four glasses of Camus cognac—in case he's still not satisfied—and that man, I assure you, is ready to be talked into *anything*.

This is the way Harry has always worked. Soften them up first and then hit them. I knew it. But it was so long since I'd had anything but junk food that I just didn't give a damn until it was all too late and I was hooked.

We wandered slowly up Rue Racine to the Boulevard and went on up to the Pont St. Michel and over onto the Island, and in the bright moonlight and the cool breeze it was more beautiful than I'd ever known it. But all I wanted to do was get into a bed and sleep. I was going to have the world's worst hangover in the morning.

Harry said: "Do you know anything about diamonds, Michael?"

We were crossing the other branch of the river already, heading for the Right Bank. I said: "No more than most people."

"Well, it doesn't really matter. There'll be experts around to keep you on the track."

"On the track of what, Harry?"

He didn't answer for a while. I was beginning to wish I hadn't accepted that third glass of cognac. He said at last: "There's a charming woman I want you to meet. Her name's Christine Andress, and you'll fall head-over-heels in love with her the moment you meet her. She's a professional diamond-courier."

"A what?"

"She carries diamonds from point A to point B. That's the way she makes her living. And a damn good living it is, too, if you don't mind the risks." He threw me a sidelong glance, to make sure, no doubt, that the euphoria was still there; it was, with a few stomach-rumblings playing counterpoint to it.

I said: "That sounds more like a job for a man. A retired cop."

"Once, it was, exclusively. Not any more. Nowadays, the association prefers to use women. They seem to be better at it. Part of that devious feminine mystique, no doubt."

"What association would that be, Harry?"

"The Diamond Brokers' Protective Association. Let's sit here for a while."

We perched ourselves on the low granite wall, with our legs dangling, and watched the play of the moonlight on the water. A solitary tug was moving by, its white wake rippling.

He said earnestly: "I never try to hide anything from you, Michael, and I won't now either. There is, I imagine, just a tinge of difficulty ahead of you, but nothing to worry about, no cause for alarm at all . . . "

I said, interrupting him: "You mean I'm not likely to get shot at this time?"

My last job for Harry, I'd spent most of my waking hours dodging bullets, and I'm not really cut out for that kind of excitement.

He waved an airy hand. "No, I don't imagine so, nothing like that. But you have to remember two things about good diamonds. First of all, they are immensely expensive and the most compact form of great wealth. Secondly, though they are safe in their impregnable vaults, when they are taken out to be sent somewhere else, they immediately become very vulnerable. Because every Tom, Dick, and Harry in the diamond-thieving business is busting his gut to get at them."

"Gun in hand, no doubt. I still say it's no job for a woman."

"No, you are quite wrong."

He thought about it for a moment. "It's a strange thing. Last year over four million dollars' worth of diamonds were stolen in transit, eight or nine different cases, and almost nobody got killed."

"*Almost* nobody?"

"Well . . . " He sounded apologetic. "There *was* one courier, a man, in this case, who didn't know how to size up the opposition correctly, and got . . . rambunctious. It was a mistake, the kind they don't often make. At least, not the good ones."

"And Christine what's-her-name is one of the good ones."

"Oh yes indeed. The best in the business." He said earnestly: "Let me tell you about her. Everyone knows her name is Christine, if it really is. Almost nobody knows about the Andress. Or where she lives, or how old she is, or where she buys her groceries, or what she does for a living. Her concierge takes it for granted that she's some kind of high-priced call girl and gets mad because she can never catch her at it. She has an apartment in St. Cloud, a small villa in Positano, and another on the Greek island of Hydra. But where she spends her time when she's not working, *nobody* knows. No one knows *anything* about her. When she's wanted, the word gets out, and she turns up at the right place and the right time. She picks up her little bag of diamonds, takes them where they have to go, and disappears again till the next time. She makes five or six deliveries a year and gets a flat fee of twenty-five thousand dollars each time, regardless of the cost of the merchandise."

"Even if it's only a fifty-thousand-dollar diamond? Doesn't make sense, Harry."

He was grinning broadly. "For that kind of trifle, they wouldn't call in Christine. She's at the top of her profession, and she deals only in top-quality merchandise. Museum quality." He was excited about her. He went on:

"She was born in Lausanne in Switzerland, brought up in France and England, and then the States. She speaks seven languages with equal fluency . . . " He broke off, and then said earnestly: "You and I, Michael, we're at home in English, and French, and Italian, maybe a few more of the civilized languages, but the way that woman tosses idioms around . . . you won't believe it. She changes her languages the way she changes her clothes, the right dress for the right occasion. It's depressing the way some people seem to have that ability. And she's gorgeous, a living doll. But with claws."

"And I think you said no one knows anything about her."

He thumped me on the back, a thing he's prone to. "You know me, Michael! The guiding light of my business is correct and continuing information."

It was two o'clock in the morning, and a tiny donkey was clop-clopping by, pulling a minuscule cart loaded down with boxes of produce, the driver bundled up in his overcoat and fast asleep with a pipe in his mouth.

I said: "Just where do I come into this, Harry? Or am I not going to be told until it's too late to wiggle out of it?"

He thumped my back again, nearly knocking me off the wall. "That's funny, Michael, I love it."

He was suddenly very serious again. "Every diamond-courier in the trade has what is called a CA, a Covering Agent, it's one of their regulations. The CA's job is simply to make sure that nothing untoward happens to the courier, or—more importantly—to the delivery. The really good CAs can be counted on the fingers of three hands, and they're all well-known in the business, ex-Pinkerton or Brinks' men, or retired officers from the FBI or the Sûreté, and they're pretty damn good as a rule. But we have to remember—they are *known*. And therefore, they attract attention. There's a major delivery scheduled, perhaps the delivery of the century, and obviously, this is a job for Christine, no one else. The question of her CA cropped up . . . "

He broke off, swung his legs round, and slipped off the wall. "That granite's damp, dammit; it's bad for my arthritis. Let's walk."

I just sat there. I said: "Harry, two things. First of all, I am not a retired Pinkerton man. Second, it sounds to me like the hazards might be more considerable than you pretend . . . "

He was beaming. "And third, you feel, therefore, that you ought to return all those hundred-dollar bills to me, a matter of conscience. Come off it, Michael."

They were strapped around my waist, under my belt at the back, and they felt very comforting. I said: "Well, you've got a point there."

He got a little didactic.

He said, laboring the point: "I am about to publish an exposé of the whole world of the professional diamond thief. I've done a hell of a lot of research on it. Now I want to learn at firsthand just how they operate, and for that I don't need a goddamn detective. I need a first-class investigative reporter, a bloody good one, which, like it or not, is what you are. And if it's the money you're worrying about . . . Have you counted it?"

"As a matter of fact, I haven't."

"Somehow, I imagined that. When you do, you'll be impressed. And if you want more, you can have it."

"I was worrying about *almost* nobody getting killed."

He raised his eyebrows. "It's never happened to you before, Michael. Now, has it? Well then."

The remains of the lobsters were rumbling again, and I said: "Goddammit, I haven't even found a hotel yet."

He pointed, smiling. "Just up the road. I've booked you in at the Hôtel des Pyramides. Just like old times. I thought you'd like that."

"I would indeed. You've got a long memory, Harry."

He was preening himself like a peacock. "Yes, I have indeed. I pride myself on it."

It must have been seven or eight years ago that I fell

so desperately in love for the tenth or twelfth—and yet the first and last—time. I woke up one morning after two weeks of unbelievable excitement, and she was gone. There was just a lipstick scrawl on the mirror: *"See you, Michael. It was great."* It was at the Hôtel des Pyramides.

I slid off the wall and joined him, and we walked up to Rue de Rivoli and moved slowly along under the fine old colonnade. There were very few people around now, just a few tourists, mostly American, looking for some action in quite the wrong place. But the lights in the store windows were still on, and the Louvre was floodlit, looking splendid against the dark sky.

I said: "So now I'm bodyguard to a woman no one knows anything about. Well, anything to make a buck."

He shook his head vigorously. "No. Not a bodyguard. Think of the end result. I want to know how these people operate. When a man makes up his mind to steal several million dollars' worth of diamonds, what is the first thing he does? What's the second, the third, the fourth, all the way down the line? I want to know every step he takes along the way. Stuff that *nobody* knows."

"There's an awful lot of the nobody-knows in this, isn't there?"

"And between us, we bring it all out into the light of public scrutiny. That's my boy . . . "

"Okay. When do I go to work?"

He shrugged. "Sooner or later. God knows when the delivery takes place . . . "

He broke off, and said: "Correction. Only God and Christine know, and the greater of these is Christine. In this business, it's the courier who calls the shots, every one of them. When she travels, how she travels, just what security measures have to be taken. When she's ready, she'll let us know. And her new CA will be standing by."

"A tough job for a living doll. Even with claws."

He said, musing: "There was a time, only a few years ago, when they called in some tough, young ex-cop, gave him a steel box to padlock to his wrist, gave him detailed instructions, and sent him on his way. Not any more. The steel box became too much of a target, every minor hood in town realizing that there was something there worth stealing and planning to do just that. But nowadays they don't hire a messenger boy and pay him a few bucks for his trouble. It's all moved into the big time, and an interesting thing has happened. It's moved from muscle to wit. To *cunning,* if you like. So now, they call in a real pro. With a brain."

I was hooked already, and he knew it; so he could afford to drop the easy-as-pie bit for a moment or two. He said, putting on his gravest, evangelical look: "The dangers are not great, Michael, but it wouldn't be fair if I tried to hide them from you."

"And you always were a very fair man, Harry."

He really thought I meant it. He nodded. "Yes, indeed I am."

He thought for a moment and said: "Three years ago, Kennedy Airport in New York. A courier named Arturo Bonsanto, a good man, was carrying a relatively small cargo to Manhattan, his safe-box handcuffed to his wrist. His cab got forced into the curb. Four minor hoods slugged him and the driver and tried to cut through the cuffs. They couldn't make it. So they chopped his hand off. The box was booby-trapped with a phial of gelignite, and one of them got killed when he tried to force it open with a power saw."

He was looking at me obliquely as we strolled, making sure I was taking all this in and still not running away.

He said, shrugging: "They all have their own tricks, the couriers. Bonsanto's safe-box was filled with paste. The real diamonds had been sent on a day ahead, his girl friend carrying them in her overnight bag. Delivery had already been made when this happened, but ever since then . . . no more handcuffed steel boxes."

"And the unfortunate Signor Bonsanto?"

The overly casual shrug again. "The association gave him half a million dollars. They're more liberal with their money than I am. He lives in Sardinia now, runs a small restaurant. I'm told it's excellent."

"Well, as long as the delivery was made . . . "

He was smiling again. "That's the spirit, Michael! I always had such great trust in you."

There was a tingling in my own wrist—nerves, I guess. I thought of that bundle of money pressing into my back.

That was almost the only nice thing about Harry. You

never had to count his money. In fact, in all the times I've worked for him, we'd never even talked about remuneration. He'd just drop by casually and drop a fat wad of cash somewhere. It's a very endearing talent.

When we reached the Pyramides, he looked at his watch and took my hand, a firm man-to-man sort of grip, and clapped my back again, and said cheerfully: "Well, I've got to run. I'm on the morning plane to London."

Unaccountably, there was a moment of alarm, as if I were all alone to face those minimal dangers, and I suppose I must have shown it. He said happily: "But don't worry, we'll be in touch, and meanwhile, Mrs. Bentley will fill you in."

I said blankly: "Mrs. Bentley . . . ?"

He nodded. "She's waiting for you in your room. She'll brief you on what has to be done."

"Oh God . . . "

"Come now, you love her, and you know it."

"All I want to do, Harry, is sleep off some of that dinner."

"It won't take long. Anything you want to know, just ask her. She has a room at the Meurice, so call her any time, day or night, and she'll be there to hold your hand." He grabbed both my shoulders, looked me right in the eyes, and said, smiling broadly: "I just can't tell you how happy you've made me. I'll see you soon."

He turned and began to walk away, and I said: "Oh Harry . . . ?"

He stopped and held his head back a little, looking at me quizzically, as though he knew what was coming. He probably did, too.

I said: "Just exactly what is your stake in all this?"

His eyes were wide and frank. "I told you, Michael: You're going to get me a story."

"You went to the association and just told them that?"

He shook his head. "I have a friend with them. He came to me for help in finding a good man. I thought I'd kill two birds with one stone. It's very simple, it really is."

I knew there was a great deal he didn't want to tell me. I said: "Harry, to get the kind of story you're after, you need someone on the other side of the fence."

He shook his head and said emphatically: "No, Michael. If you want to learn about cats, you ask the mice."

I didn't think that was a particularly happy analogy, but he went on: "You're not suggesting, I hope, that I pay you to consort with professional thieves? That just might lead to all kinds of illegalities. And it would be quite impossible to pull off."

Well, at least he was fairly frank there. Harry doesn't have the greatest respect in the world for the law, though he'd be highly indignant if I suggested that to him. But he doesn't like it to get in his way if he's after a story that he really feels has to be told. It's just that he's so damn devious and stubborn that he'll go to *extraordinary* lengths to find out what he wants to know; and if that means bending the law to the breaking point, he'll justify it righteously—even piously—in the name of what he likes to call "public scrutiny."

I'm really very fond of him, and I even admire him. Perhaps it's because he doesn't have the scruples and hang-ups that most of us are stuck with.

That's precisely the word for him: Unscrupulous. But essentially *good*. He'd lay down his life for you, and when he woke up in Hell he'd say: "My God, whatever persuaded me to do a damn fool thing like that?"

He said, looking at me quizzically: "Good-night, Michael."

He stalked off, as spry and fresh as the morning dew. He hadn't aged much since I'd last seen him, just a little more gray around the temples. He was still an extraordinarily handsome man.

The lobsters were complaining again, and I went up to my room to face the formidable Mrs. Bentley.

Chapter Two

When I saw her sitting there, demure but very agreeable to look at, I wondered why it was the word *formidable* that had first come to my mind.

She was sitting on, rather than in, the red-velour-and-gilt armchair by the little antique desk in the corner of the room, her long legs crossed, a pile of papers on her knee. She wore a medium-gray skirt of very fine wool—a little longer than I thought necessary—with a jacket of the same material, and a blouse of some ivory-colored stuff, all buttoned up to the throat. Her hair was piled up on top of her head, not quite as full as I'd remembered it, and her makeup was applied so carefully that she looked, posed as she was, as though she were waiting for the camera to start clicking for a fashion layout—for slightly more mature people. I suppose she couldn't have been a day older than forty, but she contrived to look not a day younger, either. And still, very satisfying to the eye of a susceptible man.

She got to her feet as I came in and came to meet me with a smile of pure delight on her face, and said: "Mr. Benasque . . . "

Oh Christ.

It had taken me four years to get her to call me Michael, and there we were starting all over. "I hope your flight was not too uncomfortable?"

I said: "It was great, just great. I got plastered."

"Oh."

"And how are you, Mrs. Bentley? You look lovely."

She actually blushed, and that's a nice old-fashioned thing to do. "Well, thank you."

There was a bright patch of blue, or rather of two blues, on the bed—a pair of pyjamas and a robe. She saw my instinctive glance at them and said smoothly: "Mr. Slewsey thought you would be traveling with almost no baggage . . . "

"None at all, the only way to fly . . . "

"So I went out and bought you a few things we thought you might need. I wasn't sure that you would not have added a little weight, but he said no, and he was right, wasn't he?"

"Harry is always right, and it's good to see you again. Will you join me in a glass of cognac?"

"No, thank you. There are a few things we have to talk about. It won't take long. I expect you must be tired."

"Slowly beginning to wake up again."

"It's only ten hours on the plane these days, but it seems like an eternity, doesn't it?"

"All you have to do is keep saying: 'Another Bloody Mary, please.' "

"Yes, I suppose so."

"Do you mind if I take off my jacket? I mean, it won't bother you?"

"Not in the least."

"Good." I slipped out of it and took it to the huge, ornate wardrobe, all covered with inlaid ivory; this really is a very satisfying hotel. There was a tuxedo in there, a rather too-neat gray suit, a dark blue blazer, a pair of light-gray slacks, and three pairs of shoes lined up on the floor with mathematical precision—one pair had *tassels* on them. I took the suit out and looked at it glumly, and said: "It's going to make me look like a Parisian banker."

She ignored it completely. "First, there's the matter of the schedule . . . " She pronounced it *shedule,* in the English fashion, though I happen to know that she comes from somewhere in Illinois. "Tomorrow, Mr. Slewsey thought you might like to rest up for the day or just wander around and do nothing. But tomorrow night, there's a party at half-past eight in the evening on board a small yacht moored on the river at the Quai d'Orsay, the *Marigold* . . . "

"What a hell of a name for a yacht."

She said, momentarily startled: "Yes, it is, isn't it? I hadn't thought about it. Anyway, it's semiformal, but you might like to wear your tuxedo."

"I'll look like one of the waiters."

She said smoothly: "Then I'm sure the gray suit will be perfectly acceptable. Our host is a man named Fouchon, Giles Fouchon. He collects antiques."

"Our host?"

The blush again. "Mr. Slewsey thought that perhaps I should accompany you."

"Ah yes. He said something about having you hold my hand. Well, that's nice. What does Giles Fouchon have to do with us?"

There was the slightest hesitation. Then: "There just might be someone there you'd like to meet."

"Or *ought* to meet?"

"Exactly."

She was frowning, correcting the kind of mistake she didn't like to make. "Perhaps I should say 'take a look at' rather than 'meet.' In fact, we'd both prefer that you did not actually meet her, though that might be hard to avoid. There probably won't be very many people there. Fifty or so. And she tends to take a lot of interest in . . . what she might think of as eligible men."

"I automatically want to meet any woman who thinks of me as eligible. Who is she?"

She sighed. She pulled an eight-by-ten photograph out of the file on her knee and handed it to me; there was a sheet of paper stapled to it, like an actress' resume. She said: "Her name is Veronica Verignana, and she represents the opposition we are facing, just a part of it, but a very important part."

The photograph was of a startlingly beautiful woman in her early thirties perhaps, with dark and somber eyes and a very petulant look to her mouth; it was the face of a spoiled Madonna, a young woman who always wanted her own way and was going to sulk interminably if she didn't get it. The features were fine and delicate, and the longer I studied them, the more aware I became of a certain imperious intelligence there, and of something else too . . . Was it *cruelty*? I didn't think she was a woman I could get very fond of, in spite of that really remarkable beauty.

I flipped over the closely-typed sheet, and it began:

"Veronica Verignana, alias Claire Aprise, alias Dorotea Respighi, born Florence, Italy, 1947. Sir Arthur's mistress since 1971, currently residing at the Villa d'Arcy, Juan les Pins. . . . "

I said: "Who is Sir Arthur?"

"Sir Arthur Helder, an Englishman who also collects antiques."

"And he'll be at the party too, presumably?"

"No, we think not. We believe she will be there to arrange the preliminaries for a deal they are probably making. The idea is that you should at least take a look at this woman and make, if you like, some sort of snap judgment of her capabilities."

She didn't seem to want to talk about Sir Arthur for the moment—everything in its proper order—so I let it pass. "A list of aliases presupposes what? A criminal record?"

"She has none. Those are just the names she uses when she's tired of her own."

"And when you say she represents the opposition, what does that mean, exactly?"

It's a strange thing about Mrs. Bentley. She's caught, from long association with Harry, the habit of telling you nothing at all and still expecting you to *know*. It's part of what Harry calls his "find-out-for-yourself philosophy." He likes to give you a problem to worry about, and then, if you come up with the same answer he already has, he's sure it's the right one, and he can feel he still hasn't influenced your thinking. It's a system that seems to work, but it's frustrating.

I said: "Sooner or later, love, you're going to have to tell me."

She sighed. She pulled another eight-by-ten from the file and handed it to me. No résumé this time, just a photo. A most dignified and alert-looking man in his late fifties, a small, highly amused smile on his face, an almost mischievous air about him. Gray hair expensively styled (a lot of it), bright, sharp, even shrewd eyes, and an overall look about him that seemed to suggest . . . if you were having a dull time at a party, this was the kind of man you'd look for to liven up the evening.

And yet . . . There was something *wrong*, horribly wrong about it. I was just thinking: *What an attractive couple they make*, when it hit me. There was the same look of latent cruelty there, better disguised in his case than in hers, but just as strong. This was not a man who was easily going to be crossed and ever forgive . . .

And Mrs. Bentley was saying, very slowly and carefully: "Sir Arthur Helder is without any doubt the number-one diamond thief in Europe—which means in the whole world. He's charming, suave, witty, and delightful. And the most dangerous man you could ever wish to avoid. He specializes in cut stones, particularly famous stones. In fact, he won't touch anything else; it's a matter of his personal prestige."

I looked at her.

She said: "The really good diamond thieves are all specialists in one way or another. Some handle only uncut stones, which are easy to dispose of, and they are at the bottom, so to speak, of the social scale. Some handle both cut and uncut, and they're not thought very highly of either. Then there are the ones who steal only the very valuable cut stones, and now, the respect for them is rising. Then, at the top, there are the aristocrats of the business, the few who go only for the famous, easily recognizable gems for a specialized market of collectors. And when I say aristocrats, I mean just that. The really good experts number about ten or twelve, and we are not concerned here with the ordinary thief who'll steal anything of value. We are concerned only with the cream off the top of the milk."

"And he's the cream of the cream?"

"The *crème doublée*. Recognized worldwide, and respected as the number-one professional. He, too, lives in the south of France, and one of the reasons which prompted the association . . . " She broke off. "You know about the association?"

"Harry told me. Not enough, I'm sure."

"The association is a combination of the FBI, the CIA, and the Mafia. When you meet them, as you will, you *must* try not to tangle with them. They are very competent and utterly ruthless. Anyway, their Intelligence Division found out that Veronica Verignana had turned up in Paris, which is where the delivery starts. It was enough. They're convinced that Sir Arthur is planning . . . I think it's called a heist."

I said politely: "The correct word." I looked at the photo again and wondered if this were the kind of man who could calmly cut off your hand to make things easier. That mischievous smile seemed to have taken on a sardonic look. I said: "Will I get to meet him too?"

"Probably not. Frankly, I hope not. He gives me the shudders. There's never ever been a single shred of evidence against him; and yet, it's common knowledge in the trade that he grossed over seven million dollars the year before last, in stolen diamonds. He's never cracked open a safe in his life; he doesn't have to. He goes for the couriers."

There was a message there somewhere, and I wanted to know what it was. "And last year?"

She was smiling slightly. "Last year, he made nothing. The association's intelligence men decided to kill him, because he was costing them just too much money. They tried twice, and they failed; he was hiding out somewhere. He's still hiding from them."

"Vigilante justice?"

"They refer to it as dollars and cents. As a result of Sir Arthur's previous successes, the insurance rates were almost tripled last year. That hurt them badly; it was already a matter of millions of dollars."

"So they decided to knock him off, just like that."

"I did mention their ruthlessness, I believe."

"So you did."

I flipped the photo at her. "How come he doesn't merit a few lines of typing? A nice little résumé on the lovely Veronica, nothing on the boss?"

"Oh, but there is." That smug smile was there again. She picked up the rest of the file and handed it to me. "Everything known about him. Everything there is to know. And I must ask you not to leave the room with it. I will pick it up in the morning."

"I may want to read it while I stroll in the gardens of the Tuileries."

She was suddenly very alarmed. "No! It must not leave your room!"

"Okay, if you say so."

"There's also a pamphlet there, the condensed version of the association's rules and regulations for their CAs." She shrugged, very nonchalantly. "It's marked 'Eyes Only,' and when a document with that connotation is out of the safe, two people are supposed to be with it at all times."

"Well, in that case . . . it seems you have to stay with me tonight. Good."

"In this case, we are stretching a point. But please read it carefully. That, and the file on Sir Arthur. It shouldn't take you more than a few hours to memorize the salient points."

"I was planning on sleeping far into the foreseeable future."

She sighed. "Please give me a call when you've finished with it. I'm at the Meurice, Room 78. And the pamphlet stays here, please, in your room, all the time."

"Well, all right. How long before the delivery is made?"

"We don't know that. Christine will tell us that when the time comes, and she isn't even here yet; she's in Greece, I believe. She never likes to arrive at the starting-point until . . . really, just a few hours before the delivery is to be made."

I said: "Harry talked about the delivery of the century. What's its value?"

She hesitated, and for a moment I thought she was going to weaken and actually tell me. But she said instead: "It's very, very considerable, the biggest for many years. Three cut stones from Armand and Company in Paris, to Vasileos and Company in Athens. That much, I can tell you."

I just waited, and she sighed and said at last: "All right. The intermediate stone, the one of middle value, is the Thai Queen. I happen to know that the British Museum values it at three and a half million dollars. The Louvre puts it a little higher."

"And that's the intermediate?"

"Yes."

"And one woman, by herself, is going to carry them halfway across Europe?"

"Not by herself, Mr. Benasque." She said with a touch

of malice, I thought: "You will be there to hold *her* hand while you get the story."

"Uh-huh."

"And don't sell her short, either. Christine Andress has more skill, more wile, and more . . . just plain guts than you, Mr. Slewsey, and I put together. If anyone can move that merchandise—which has been debated at great length, I'd have you know—she is the one to do it."

"So tell me who debated what?"

"Someone suggested that the delivery should be made by the French military, and they almost agreed. But then, the minister himself intervened and said no. It seems they got involved once before and lost the cargo . . . "

"Also to Sir Arthur?"

"Yes indeed. No one knows how he pulled it off, but he did. The broker sued the army and won his case. They had to pay out a great deal of money. So, this time, the merchants are on their own."

"Well. It promises to be exciting, to say the least. Not a dull moment in sight. I can't wait to meet the redoubtable Christine. When?"

"We wait until she is ready."

She got to her feet and looked at the file as though reluctant to leave it with me. I said: "Don't worry. It's in good hands."

She nodded. The smooth, friendly smile was there again, just a little reserved and distant, because you have to watch out for the animals when it's three o'clock in the morning and the bed looks inviting. She shot out a hand and said: "If there's anything you need, anything at all . . . "

I held on to the hand. I said: "Well, right now I'm going to soak in a good hot tub for a couple of hours. If you'd like to scrub my back for me?"

"No, I don't quite think so."

"Why don't we have that glass of cognac before you go?"

"Not that, either."

I went to the door to open it for her, always the perfect gentleman. It was locked, and Mrs. Bentley came up and tapped on it twice. I heard the key turn in the lock, it opened, and Bruce was there. He grinned at me as he held the door open, and she said: "Thank you, Bruce . . . "

She looked at me and said, apologetically: "Mr. Slewsey's idea, not mine. Just to make sure nothing mars your stay here. Good-night, Mr. Benasque."

She was gone. Bruce looked at me and grinned again, a very cheerful young man, and closed the door. I heard the key in the lock and thought: "Oh what the hell; it's nice to be taken care of, after all."

And then I had another thought, not quite so comforting; I was wondering about the extent of that opposition, and why I needed a tough and muscular young bodyguard to watch over me while I took a bath. I thought that perhaps I knew the answer to that worrisome question.

They were throwing me to the lions. Again.

There could scarcely have been a half hour of the night left when I clambered between the cool white sheets, the most comfortable bed I'd slept in since that time long ago in this same hotel.

I thought: Goddammit, you sonofabitch, Sleasy Slewsey, it's even the same room. How did you even *know*? It was hard to concentrate on the pages, and I kept remembering the last time.

I couldn't even remember her name.

I fought the nostalgia and studied Sir Arthur. He was a phony, it seemed. His father was not a knight at all, but a garage mechanic from Brighton, England. His mother had worked in the local post office, and Arthur himself had never finished secondary school; he'd been expelled for seducing the janitor's daughter in the headmaster's office. But at age twenty-two, he had suddenly decided to get himself an education and had gone first to the London School of Economics, then across half the world to Berkeley in California, and then to the Sorbonne in France, where he had earned considerable kudos for what was apparently a remarkable thesis on the inevitability of corruption in a liberal society.

He had gambled on the stock market and had won. At the casinos, he had lost, very heavily. He had acquired a trail of mistresses, each more lovely than the last, and now he was the *patron* and protector of the gorgeous Veronica Verignana, who seemed to be taking him for everything he had, which was considerable. He had also acquired a laudible fluency in French and Italian, and a taste for all the good things in life, which seemed to mean things material. He never lived for long in one place, moving every few years and selling his previous properties at huge profits.

There was so much detail there! I learned about his passion for scrambled eggs for breakfast, and that he smoked only after dark (a pipe—Balkan Sobranie tobacco). He drank nothing but white wine, and in modest quantities. (Veronica, on the other hand, drank anything she could lay her hands on and could safely be called a lush.) He liked dogs, but not cats. He was an indifferent horseman, and a fine tennis player. He drove his cars (a Bentley and a Ferrari) very fast and rather carelessly; he had twice walked away from accidents that ought to have been fatal. He was physically very powerful and seemed to spend a lot of his time getting more so, doing pushups and lifting barbells, and all the other things that people do when they want to look like Mr. Universe; fifty-two years old and still a muscle-man, as hard as nails.

I found it more important that he had a remarkable talent for judging the people around him; this little idiosyncrasy cropped up time and time again:

> " . . . long before this happened, Helder had become aware that he was being cheated. . . . "

> " . . . but already, he had taken pains to protect himself against just such an eventuality. . . . "

> " . . . she was surprised to find out that he had foreseen exactly this possibility, already knowing that such a weakness was one of her prime characteristics. . . . "

It was all in keeping with an extraordinary phrase I had found in the manual that was included among the papers, a manual apparently dedicated to the instruction of up-and-coming CAs:

"The psychology of the subject must always be regarded as of more importance than his actions. Actions are frequently motivated by unexpected circumstances: psychological characteristics are inherent, and therefore constant."

I thought that reflected rather well on the association's sagacity.

Sleep kept trying to force itself on me, but I found the story of Sir Arthur's life fascinating, and I wondered if I would ever meet him; he seemed to have a penchant for operating in the background, for getting other people to do his work—hordes of them, sometimes. On one of his capers (which had been unsuccessful, incidentally) he had employed at various times no less than forty-seven people, with a fine administrative capability—some of the people for a few days at a time, some for only a few hours. There was even one temporary employee whose job had been merely to post a letter, for which he was paid twenty-five dollars—something to do with misleading fingerprints on the envelope.

It was after five in the morning, and it occurred to me that I should open the drapes, so that when the first pale grays appeared in the sky over the river, I could enjoy the benefits of the lovely Parisian morning, when everything is beginning to wake up, and the sound of the old-fashioned drayhorses comes up from the cobbled streets. They still have them here, and there's no sound in nature more satisfying.

I put down the pages, clambered out of bed, and walked across the deep-pile carpet to the window, and there was just the slightest noise out there . . .

I froze. It had been a sort of scuffling sound, not quite a footstep, but something very much like it.

And I was frightened.

I am not a violent sort of man, not even particularly athletic or *macho,* and I have to admit to a moment of pure panic.

And then, I remembered Bruce.

I went quickly and silently to the door, tapped on it twice, just as Mrs. Bentley had done. It was opened immediately, and Bruce was there again. I had a finger to my lips, knowing it wasn't at all necessary, and he nodded and slipped inside and closed the door silently. I indicated the window.

He nodded again and pointed to the open bathroom door, but I shook my head; whatever was going to happen now, I wanted to know what it would be. He grimaced, and there was a small smile on his face, and he made the kind of gesture that means: *okay, wait . . .*

He moved like a cat to the window and stood there by the heavy velour drapes for a moment, listening intently, then turned to me and nodded again. It couldn't have taken him more than a split second to get the window open; one moment his hand was on the drapes, just seeming to pause there, and then he was through them and had the window open in a flash. I heard the sound of a real scuffle, much more pronounced, and a sort of muffled cry, like someone wanting to swear but not being able to get the words out.

There was a scream, diminishing horribly, and then silence again. My heart was in my mouth as I waited, and the window opened again, its hinges creaking very slightly.

Thank God it was Bruce, and he was rubbing his ear, which was visibly swelling and turning red as he rubbed it. But he was grinning, and he transferred his attention to his right wrist and rubbed at it, flexing it painfully, as though he'd hit something rather too hard for comfort.

He said ruefully: "I goofed, didn't I?"

"How's that? What was it?"

He shrugged. "Just a man. I didn't think anyone could get up here. But he came down from the roof of the building next door. I didn't think it was possible. But it was." He was staring at the ground, frowning now. "I'm sorry, sir. It shouldn't have happened."

"Who was it, do you know?"

He shook his head. "Looked like an Algerian. Lots of them around in Paris, these days."

"And, uh, what happened to him? Where is he now?"

He looked up and stared at me. "Oh, he sort of fell down, onto the street. Poor bastard, he must have slipped or something." He was rubbing his wrist again.

I went to the window, pulled back the drapes, and

opened it up. It was still dark outside, with just the slightest sliver of silver-gray in the east, low over the rooftops, with heavy rain-clouds above it. Down below on the street, the body of a man was lying under the yellow light of the lamp, like a rag doll carelessly tossed aside. A young woman in a very short miniskirt and a sweater was hurrying toward him, and I saw her bend over him briefly and then scuttle away, not even looking up to see where he had come from. I closed the window and stepped back inside. Somehow, it hadn't seemed quite real.

Bruce said, a wry look on his face: "I'll be outside the door, of course, until I'm relieved, but . . . well, it was nice working for you, Mr. Benasque."

I suppose I looked puzzled. He shrugged and said: "You know Mr. Slewsey, sir, and I'm working for him now. He doesn't allow mistakes. One goof, and you're out. He's going to fire me for sure."

"I'll have a word with him, Bruce. Don't worry about it."

He nodded. "Well, that's real nice of you, and I appreciate it." He went to the door and opened it and looked back; he was grinning again. "But it won't do one bit of good."

I was suddenly very angry with Harry and his goddamn machinations. I said: "No? Well, we'll see about that."

It was half-past eleven before I finished studying the file, and by that time I felt I knew more about Sir Arthur than he probably did. I also thought it might amuse him —or make him violently angry—to know just how meticulously his likes and his dislikes, his vices and virtues, his weaknesses and his strengths, had all been laid out for the association to brood over. I tried to sleep for a while, but I was restless; I kept thinking about the mysterious Christine Andress that nobody knew, and she worried me. I wondered if she were really as good as they seemed to think.

I got up, showered and shaved (there was even a new shaver in the bathroom, with my favorite brand of lotion, soap, a toothbrush, and everything else a man might need —no shopping to do at all) and called Mrs. Bentley.

She was knocking at my door fifteen minutes later, and the first thing she said was, rather tightly: "I'm terribly sorry about what happened during the night."

I was surprised that she knew about it already; then, on reflection, I wasn't surprised any more. I said, shrugging it off and forgetting how scared I'd been: "No damage was done, except to the intruder. Who was he? Do we know?"

She shook her head. "Not yet, but we'll find out during the day. It could, of course, have been just a hotel thief."

"In the Pyramides? They'd never allow it."

She said again: "We will find out."

She looked very smart indeed this morning, in beige and brown—a little prim, perhaps, but quite delectable. I realized, with a touch of guilt, that I had a passionate longing to see her with nothing on; and I knew that I never would, which made it worse.

I said: "Bruce told you about it?"

"Yes, of course."

"He was afraid he'd be fired. I wouldn't like that."

A slight hesitation. Then: "Well, perhaps if you talk to Mr. Slewsey the next time you see him . . . "

The hidden message again. "Will he be?"

She was brushing an invisible speck of dust off her immaculate sleeve. "He is on his way back to America already. We have a better man now."

"Uh-huh. When do I see Harry again?"

"In the course of time, no doubt. Did you get some sleep?"

"An hour or two. It's enough."

"Good. Then I'll be on my way." She was slipping the bulky file into a shoulder-tote. "Remember, if there's anything you want . . . "

I said: "Only one thing, at the moment. I need Bruce's address in the States."

There was almost, but not quite, a kind of hostility there. I could hear the wheels turning over in her mind, running smoothly and efficiently and coming up with just the right answers. She said at last, her eyes on the carpet: "I don't think that would be a wise thing, somehow . . . "

"You said 'anything at all,' if you remember. So did Harry."

She held my look for a long time, and then she was suddenly smiling gently, as though there were pleasure for her in the game too. She took out a pad, wrote it down for me, and handed me the scrap of paper and said: "I'm afraid Mr. Slewsey's going to be very angry with me."

"But for how long. He's never angry with you for long, is he?"

"No, indeed he isn't. Have a good day."

"Would you care to have lunch with me?"

"No, thank you. I have work to do." She was still smiling when she left, a very secret sort of smile.

I went down to the street and found a bistro for a *café-calvados,* wandered over to the Eiffel Tower, took the elevator to the top, walked up to Montmartre, down to St.-Germain-des-Prés, strolled around Place Vendôme, and did some shopping with Harry's money. When the afternoon papers came out, there was a small notice in one of them, tucked away on an inside page with all the rest of the nothings:

> "André Gaston, a small-time hotel thief and a known member of the Cosmos Gang, age twenty-four, was killed this morning in the early hours when he fell from the fourth floor of the Hôtel des Pyramides, where he was trying to effect entry through the window. The body is in the morgue awaiting a claimant. . . ."

I thought: The hell with it. I walked over to the beautiful gardens of the Tuileries and pulled the little pamphlet from my pocket and read it for a while. I thought: I may as well learn something about this temporary trade I've been seduced into.

Some of it—not all—was quite illuminating. I read:

> "The CA must remember that at all times he is under the command of the courier. The courier's safety is second only to the safety of the merchandise, which must remain, constantly, the prime consideration motivating all the CA's actions. . . . He must always

abide by the laws of the country in which he is operating and refrain, except in the case of extreme urgency, from contacting the local authorities; should he be forced to do this, he must remember that the PS may possibly have access to those authorities, and that by this action he may, therefore, be jeopardizing the success of his mission. . . ."

I wondered what the hell a PS was but I didn't really care that much. There was another passage:

"The CA may on occasion be kept in complete ignorance of the courier's MO. It is the policy of the association to regard this factor as the courier's inalienable right. . . . "

For a moment or two of considerable pleasure, I wondered what would happen if I were to leave this document of such surpassing brilliance, all marked up with red stripes and the annotation "Eyes Only," lying on the bench I was sitting on. The urge to do so was almost insuperable. But I fought it with commendable determination, slipped it back into my pocket, instead, and went looking for another bistro.

I wondered about the party that was forthcoming a few hours later on. The Quai d'Orsay is one hell of a place to moor a yacht; I was sure it wasn't going to be twenty feet of decrepit tug. And the more I thought about it, the more I looked forward to it.

I picked up the boxes that were my shopping and wandered back to the hotel for a couple of hours' snooze before it all started.

Chapter Three

Mrs. Bentley was quite gorgeous when she came to fetch me.

She looked aghast. I was wearing the jeans I'd bought, four times the price they are back home and only a trifle more elegant, and I was sure she was going to ask me why I wasn't dressed already. But that expression came over her face that indicated she knew—a touch of disapproval, as though it were a personal affront.

I said: "No one dresses up any more, not even in Paris." She sighed and made the best of it.

She wore an exquisite white gown, still very hide-everything and demure, and she looked like a very elegant fashion model from the sixties—cool, and poised, and lovely.

The new young man drove us over to the Quai in the Citroën-Maserati, and I took an instant dislike to him. I didn't even bother to remember his name. He was small and wiry, about twenty-six years old, with quick, nervous movements and a permanent scowl on his face. He wasn't as good a driver as Bruce either.

The *Marigold* was brightly lit from stem to stern, shining like a billionaire's plaything in white paint and polished brass, a low and sleek-looking yacht that must have cost a fortune. Its deck, from the Quai, seemed to be crowded already, and a lot of people were drifting aboard, the women mostly in evening clothes, the men far less formal. A dozen parking-valets were taking care of the Rolls-Royces, the Mercedeses, the Alfas, Jags, and Jensens —not a Volkswagen among them—and there were four burly men in uncomfortable tuxedos by the gangplank, their eyes constantly moving, searching out any possible undesirables and ready, no doubt, to toss them down into the river. There's always the fine cutting edge of distinction between the haves and have-nots at a party like this, and I couldn't help thinking that if I'd passed this way only forty-eight hours ago, one of the hefty bouncers would have been eyeing me carefully to make sure I wasn't about to intrude upon the pleasures of the mighty.

An officer saluted and greeted us as we went aboard, and almost immediately there were champagne glasses in our hands, brought by a smiling young thing in a long yellow gown with nothing underneath it but her, with a tiny embroidered badge on her breast, top dead center, which said: "Jeanine." It was so small and neat that you really had to stare to make it out. There were a score of other long yellow gowns moving around with trays of drinks and canapés, the hired help, and it occurred to me that our host must have selected them largely for the way they jiggled.

He was a spry and bouncy sort of man in his sixties, very rotund and deeply tanned—with hardly any hair at all, except a snow-white fringe around his gleaming scalp—and he was smoking a cigar that seemed bigger than he was. He tossed the cigar over the side as he came to meet us and hugged Mrs. Bentley round the waist, his face in the well-covered cleft, shook my hand, and beamed at us both and said: "I'm Giles Fouchon, of course, and you are Mrs. Bentley and Mr. Benasque, and I am delighted that you could come."

I thanked him politely for inviting us, and he said: "We have blackjack downstairs if anyone is interested, and roulette, and we even have *les craps*. No one is going to introduce you to *anybody*, I scarcely know half the people here myself; so if you see anyone you think might be interesting, and I doubt it, just present yourself and all will be well. And please, I will be personally affronted if you don't both have a marvelous time . . ."

One of the yellow ladies was hovering with a tray, and he patted her rump affectionately, took a large fat shrimp on the end of a toothpick, and hurried off to greet someone else.

I had already finished my drink, but there was another one in my hand so fast that I couldn't believe it, and Mrs.

Bentley saw me looking approvingly at the décolleté and murmured: "Oh, you're going to have such a good time this evening, aren't you?"

I said: "Now, now, the appreciation of excellence is a very desirable quality." I wondered if she was determined to stay close beside me all night to see I didn't misbehave.

We wandered off together among the crowd, tightly packed and no one paying any attention to anyone else—all talking and no one listening. I heard English, French, and Italian, and either Russian or Polish, and of course the ubiquitous Arabic, and I told her: "You see? Not a tuxedo in sight. Except for the waiters and the bouncers."

Even our host, the sprightly Giles Fouchon, was wearing old-rose colored slacks and a pink cashmere sweater.

People were still coming aboard in droves; there must have been two or three hundred on the deck alone, and she took my arm and led me gently to the railing. We leaned over it and looked down into the dark water, with the bright lights of the Champs-Élysées thrown up into the sky over the rooftops, and she said quietly: "She just came aboard, the woman in the corset."

I said: "In the *what*?"

"The corset."

"I refuse to believe that anyone wears them. Present company excepted, of course."

She threw me a look. "I do not. And I suppose that strictly it is called a *corselette*. Yves Saint Laurent, in gold lamé. And you will no doubt think it is gorgeous."

"But you don't?"

"It's awful. The wrap is sable, and *that* is far too ostentatious too."

I was watching the twinkling lights in the water and thinking: My God, what a great way to live, all you need is that kind of a bankroll . . . I turned round and leaned back against the railing and looked across at the gangplank. I felt I wanted to gasp.

The photograph had not done her any justice at all; she was absolutely stunning. And it was indeed a kind of corset, modeled, I suppose, after the old hourglass type of figure. It was tight at the waist where the lacing began, and flared out as it went upward, sort of cupped at the top, so that her breasts seemed to be riding on it—half in and half out of their own particular receptacle—with the arms and shoulders and almost everything else bare, and a long black skirt tight around very smooth hips. I heard Mrs. Bentley murmur again: "Awful . . . " I didn't agree with her one bit.

Her hair was a very dark auburn, which caught the reflected light nicely, and it was shoulder length and sort of puffed out—the kind of hair you just naturally want to run through barefoot—and her eyes were larger than they had seemed in the photo, and a true green in color. Her nose was just a nose, but her lips were very full, with that slight downturn at the corners as though she hated everything in sight. And then a young man passed by her, very good-looking, and said something as he moved on, and she laughed suddenly, and it lit up her whole aspect. It was turned off again with remarkable rapidity, and the sullen, petulant look was back there again.

I heard Mrs. Bentley say drily: "You don't have to stare quite so obviously, you know . . . " But I just could not take my eyes off those breasts. They were like globules of cappucino-colored jellied mousse, just freshly out of the mold and still quivering.

I was conscious that she was looking across at me suddenly, with no change in her expression, just a cursory and quite disinterested kind of look that said nothing. A band struck up somewhere, and her huge eyes switched to the flying deck where the combo was, a bouzouki group with some Theodorakis music. She was shrugging off the sable wrap, and a waiter was there at once, taking it from her and bowing respectfully. When he moved off, she hardly looked at him.

And then, I saw that she was watching Giles Fouchon, a buoyant piece of blubber in pink. He was chatting, very animatedly, with a group of three young people and lighting up another cigar. He caught her eye and nodded almost imperceptibly, and it didn't really make sense; after all, he was her host and was rushing off to meet almost everyone who came aboard. He said something that made the others laugh, excused himself, and moved off, not to her but to the companionway, tossing the just-lighted cigar overboard again.

Mrs. Bentley said quietly: "Let's go below decks, shall we?"

It was an order; so I followed her dutifully, and we all came together halfway down the stairs. Giles turned and beamed at us and said: "Is it going to be a boring party? I do believe it is; we will all have to get drunk, won't we?"

I said: "What a splendid idea," and Mrs. Bentley shook her head: "I'm sure it never will be, and we're going to try our luck at *vingt-et-un*."

"In the room at the end of the corridor. Excuse me, won't you?" He had half opened the door to the first of the cabins, and he laughed and said: "I have to get my pills. One cannot keep young without pills; what a wonderfully chemical life we lead these days . . . "

We moved on, and as I opened the door at the end of the corridor for her, I looked back and saw that the gorgeous Veronica was following him into the cabin. We went inside and wandered among another crowd there, a far more noisy one this time.

Mrs. Bentley said, looking at me thoughtfully: "There's just no way we can overhear what they have to say to each other, is there?"

"Nope. None at all."

"Are you sure about that?"

"I am not going to climb into an air conditioner and hope that their voices will come over loud and clear. It doesn't work like that, you know. And a wine glass held to an adjoining wall is no good either."

"What a pity . . . "

"Besides which, there might be just *murmurings*. Little endearing noises, followed by grunts and groans."

"You really do have a disgusting mind, don't you?" She had not lost the smile.

I said: "Let's try one of the tables. I feel enormously lucky tonight."

"You know very well that I don't gamble."

"But I do. You can watch."

There were twenty or thirty people playing roulette, far too many at the crap table, and almost no one at the blackjack. So we sat there and played for half an hour. I stood on seventeen, which is the lazy man's way to break even if he's lucky, and I won nearly eight-thousand francs.

I cashed in my winnings, and we started wandering again —the after-cabin, where three or four couples were fondling and fumbling in semiobscurity; the forward lounge, where there was a huge buffet table laid out with all the food in a starving world; another smaller cabin, where a rather surprising movie was being shown (I heard Mrs. Bentley's disapproving sniff); and finally back to the main deck, where things were getting boisterous and very cheerful now. And for the next two hours, there was no sign at all of either Giles Fouchon or Veronica Verignana.

We were sitting together, a little apart from the others, right up in the pointed prow of the yacht, sipping our drinks quietly and enjoying the cool night air. She was still on her second glass, and I had switched to cognac, when I suddenly became aware that *someone* was watching us.

You know how it is; nothing overt happens, but you're just certain that there's someone out there, in the shadows, watching and waiting . . . for what? I held it for a moment or two, then turned to look, and I was right.

But it was only one of the yellow ladies. She had a tray of drinks in her hands and was indeed watching me, and as I caught her eye, she smiled and moved in, and she said: "I could not quite see if your glass was empty."

She leaned over and filled it carefully, and I watched her. A little older than the others, who were mostly kids, and perhaps a little more mature; the yellow lady-in-chief, perhaps. She had very long black hair that fell down over her shoulders, and less makeup than was normal. Attractive, in a plain-Jane sort of way, with a truly remarkable figure under that wisp of yellow knit. The badge on her breast said: "Leda," and to justify the fixed look, I said: "Almost nobody gets to be called Leda."

Her voice was very appealing. "It's a nice name. I like it." There was something very charming about her; so I made a moment of conversation: "What's the cognac?"

"Augiers Frères, M'sieur. If you would prefer another brand?"

"No, I love it."

"We have almost every kind of cognac there is. M'sieur Fouchon insists that you have everything you want."

"Augiers Frères happens to be my favorite."

"Good. I am so glad, M'sieur." She looked at Mrs. Bentley. "Madame?" There was just a quiet shake of the head and perhaps a disapproving look, the kind she would normally keep tucked away out of sight until a Fallen Woman passed by. The yellow lady was smiling, as though she were conscious of the disapproval.

She had put down the tray on the little wrought-iron table, and now she straightened and picked up the tray, and although I was watching her—what else?—I was aware that Mrs. Bentley had unobtrusively placed her evening purse right where the tray had been. There was just time to catch a glimpse of white paper against the white paint, so slight that I could easily have been mistaken.

The waitress was moving off, and when Mrs. Bentley picked up her purse again I was looking right at her. She knew that I'd seen; she *would* know, of course. So she took the slip of paper quite calmly, looked at it, put it into her purse, and said: "What was it you were saying?"

I thought: *What a bloody woman.*

I said: "I wasn't saying anything, as you well know, and what was all that about?"

She didn't hesitate. "We have an appointment at three o'clock, a little cafe on Rue Dauphine."

"Ah. I smell the devious hand of Harry Slewsey in there somewhere."

"And it will be very, very important, so please don't have any more to drink."

I remembered the instructions in the manual: "The CA must remember that at all times he is under the command of the courier," so I drained my glass, looked around, and the first of the lovelies was there again, in a flash, the delectable Jeanine. I told her: "Why don't you find me three glasses of this excellent cognac and line them all up on the table here?" I thought of the Air France stewardess and said: "Pretty maids all in a row."

She went off and came back with three more, and indeed lined them up, and saw that they were brimful, and jiggled off again.

Mrs. Bentley said nothing. She just looked.

And till two-fifteen in the morning, she gave me the

impression that she really didn't want to talk to me at all, not any more.

The cafe on Rue Dauphine was dark when we got there, and I said sourly: "Ha! They're going to open it up especially for us."

"No. You will see."

There was a big Rolls-Royce parked on the narrow, cobbled street, the Rolls limousine half on the sidewalk and still taking up most of the available space. We pulled up behind it in the Citroën, and the young man whose name I didn't care to remember opened the door for us and said: "Shall I wait?"

Mrs. Bentley nodded. "Yes, please. When we move off, follow us."

We went to the Rolls, and someone in the back threw open a door for us, and we climbed in and made ourselves comfortable. In the glow of the lamplight I saw that it was a slender, elegant, and very dignified-looking woman, quite young, with fair, almost yellow hair piled up high on her head—very expensively coiffed indeed—with a pair of long silver earrings set with tiny stones that I thought might be emeralds. She wore a fur coat, bundled up tightly around her throat, and she looked rather like one of those ads for champagne, the grande dame in her Rolls-Royce about to visit the charity ball. The dignity came off her in waves—not only dignity, but a kind of overpowering self-assurance, of competence even.

I was sure that I knew who she was; it could hardly have been anyone other than the legendary courier I'd been hearing so much about, and I waited for the introductions to be made. But as soon as the door closed, she looked at Mrs. Bentley and said: "We'll drive around for a while; there's no safer place to talk than in a moving car."

I said: "Oh my God . . . "

She turned to face me, looking at me quizzically.

The face had seemed somehow familiar, and I was sure I'd seen her on a stage somewhere, or perhaps on a TV screen. You know how it is. But when I heard the voice, I knew.

I said: "I really can't believe it. May I make sure?"

I leaned over and took hold of the collar of the fur coat and opened it gently; she didn't even move, and she was smiling. Underneath was the flimsy yellow gown with the badge on it that said "Leda," and she was almost laughing now.

She said: "My tart's dress. And I've never had to fight off so many determined men in my life. Apparently, we weren't really expected to fight very much . . . "

Mrs. Bentley said, making the introductions in her nice, old-fashioned way: "Christine, allow me to present Michael Benasque, who's to be your new CA. Mr. Benasque, I'd like you to meet Madame Christine Andress."

Her hand was warm and friendly. "A great pleasure, Mr. Benasque. I've heard a great deal about you."

I held onto the hand, liking the feel of it. "And I about you, Madame Andress. Are you as good as they say you are?" I couldn't resist it and hoped I hadn't offended her.

She said: "It's a very debatable point. Almost against my will, a sort of legend grew. I sometimes find it hard to live up to. Do you think we'll get along well together?"

"If you promise me you won't wear that god-awful black wig again."

She laughed. "It's a promise."

The Rolls moved off in absolute silence. I sat back in the deep leather seat and thought about the woman whose welfare, it seemed, was perhaps going to be in my hands for a while. (I wasn't too sure about that; that air of competence was extraordinary, and I felt it might well be the other way around.)

But whatever . . . I felt an instinctive liking for her, even though I was aware of . . . how shall I put it? Of a certain *untouchability*. I slewed round in the seat a little, so that I could see more of her face every time we passed a street lamp.

Her forehead was high, her nose fine and straight, her skin fresh looking and good. Her mouth was a little wide, and there were lines at the sides, as though she found it easy to smile. Her fingers, holding the collar up to her throat to hide that tart's dress, as she had called it, were unusually long and supple.

She threw me a glance, once, aware that I was studying her, accepting it and perhaps even amused by it. I settled back comfortably again and thought that I didn't really have much to go on, not yet.

I also thought, with a certain cautious reservation, perhaps: *Well, untouchable or not, I like her.* It's not easy to make up your mind on so short and nebulous an acquaintance, but if I was wrong, well, I was stuck with her anyway.

And I started thinking of her as I had seen her on the yacht, looking far, far more attainable.

I am really quite a respectable sort of man, and some people have even been known to call me "square." But once you've seen such a gorgeous body draped only in clinging wisps of nothing, no amount of fur coat and dignity is ever going to erase the memory of it. I wanted to tell her that I liked her so much better dressed up as she had been on the yacht, but what the hell . . . She was like an empress now. I remembered Harry's bit about the claws, and I just didn't want to see them unsheathed.

Not yet, anyway.

Chapter Four

The first little while of the conversation, the dullest part of it, was between the two ladies. I just sat there like a male-chauvinist asshole, saying nothing and wondering if this was the kind of Rolls that came equipped with a cocktail cabinet. But it was very dark in the back seat, and I couldn't be sure whether the highly-polished walnut just ahead of my knees, shining with a mellow yellow light, was the back of the jump seat or something more interesting.

Christine said: "Did you get a really good look at the Verignana woman?"

It was strange how Mrs. Bentley had suddenly become relegated to a secondary position. She nodded: "Yes, I did."

"And?"

There was a surprising note of animosity there: "A whore."

Christine was very gentle. "Yes, we must accept that. But we are really more concerned with her mind."

"The mind of a whore, then."

"I'm not quite sure what that means. I'm concerned with the degree of her intelligence."

A retraction now; one thing Mrs. Bentley always knew was when not to push an argument too far. She said carefully: "By that I mean . . . the Verignana woman will think at all times only of herself."

"Yes, of course, I see your point. Even though a really good whore is trained to think of other people." I could almost feel the bristles rising on Mrs. Bentley's scalp, but before she could reply, Madame Andress said smoothly: "Is she, or is she not the kind of woman we might be able to get to, one way or another, to work against her lover, Arthur Helder?"

"I think not."

"It's always been a possibility, you know. Helder's had a bad twelve months, financially, I mean . . . But no, I don't suppose it's feasible."

"I'm sure it isn't."

Christine turned to me. "And what do you think, Mr. Benasque?"

I said, very distinctly (those pretty maids all in a row were beginning to have their natural effect): "I think you are both absolutely right. If we can forget that fantastic figure for a moment, which isn't easy, and concentrate on her face . . . I'd say there's a kind of stubbornness there that would make her stick close to anything she started on. If a face can tell us anything at all, I don't think she'd easily fall for a gambit like that. And if she sold Helder to us . . . she'd be just as likely to sell *us* to *him*. And is that beautifully-polished walnut a jump seat or a cocktail cabinet?"

Christine was not even smiling, and I have to admit that a smile would have slaughtered me. She said, more concerned than anything else: "Yes, it's a cocktail cabinet, and I believe there's Scotch and Bourbon in there, and perhaps even cognac too. Do please help yourself . . . "

I did. There were four bottles, and four lead-crystal glasses, and I thought again: *What a great way to live . . .* I was really beginning to enjoy my new profession. I poured and sipped, and the girls went on their business.

Christine: "Giles Fouchon, of course, you know."

"Yes, I do, though only at second hand."

"And as far as I am concerned, their meeting together, which lasted for nearly two hours, is already justification enough of our suspicions."

Mrs. Bentley: "Not for me. They could have been trading in antiques. Unhappily, Mr. Benasque was of the opinion that there was no way we could listen in on their conversation."

"He was right, of course. It doesn't matter."

"Oh, but it does. One way or the other, it would have made a suspicion a certainty. I wish we could have done that."

"Yes, I know. But we have a recording."

"You do?" I was delighted with the note of absolute astonishment there.

"Of course, I haven't had a chance to hear it yet, but we'll have it very soon now."

"Well, that's a relief. How did you manage to get it?"

"The association wired his cabin, three days ago, when they first learned the Verignana woman was coming to Paris. It's been monitored ever since. How much does Mr. Benasque know about Helder?"

Before Mrs. Bentley could answer, I said: "Mr. Benasque knows everything there is to know about the phony Sir Arthur Helder. Provided, of course, that the association's report on him is not just a lot of god-awful bullshit, which it well might be, and probably is."

She did an astonishing thing, Christine Andress. She simply laid a hand on my thigh, which is all it was, just on my thigh. It was warm, and firm, and somehow . . . apologetic? Whoever heard of an apologetic hand on the thigh? But it was meant for just that, and it endeared her to me. She said: "I'm terribly sorry; I really am. Will you forgive me?"

"Uh-huh. I suppose I'll have to. There must be something about that in that goddamn manual."

She laughed so long I thought she'd never stop, and she said at last: "Yes, the manual . . . It was written by idiots, for other idiots to enjoy. It's a masterpiece of earnest stupidity, isn't it? But since you've answered the question, I won't ask it again. Just tell me what makes you think it might be bullshit?"

I had expected a rephrase, but there wasn't a bit of it, and I liked her a little more.

I said: "One thing stands out above everything else in that report. Helder is a very, very astute man. I'd like to know how much of the stuff the association has on him was deliberately fed to them."

There was a little silence. Then, from Mrs. Bentley: "Very little of it actually came from him, you know. And the people in the ID aren't fools, either."

"The ID?"

"The association's Intelligence Division."

"Ah yes. The boys from the Mafia."

"Well." It was Christine again. "Be that as it may, I

think Mr. Benasque has a very good point there, and perhaps we should reexamine that dossier in the light of his comment."

Her hand was still on my thigh, warm and comforting, but now she removed it, and she turned to me and said: "Do you know how the couriers operate? Did Harry Slewsey fill you in?"

"I'm told they call all the shots. Is that correct?"

"Absolutely." She shrugged, eloquently. "Oh, not at the lower levels, of course. If they're moving a couple of thousand dollars' worth of stones around, the courier usually does what he's told to do. Picks up the diamonds and takes them to where they have to go; it's as simple as that."

I noticed the *"he"*; but of course she was talking about the small fry. As if reading my thoughts, she went on: "When it's a delivery of this importance, yes, *we* call the shots, every one of them. We do indeed. And we won't stand for any nonsense from the brokers, or from the police, or even from the association itself." She was smiling again. "You're a newcomer to this business, so may I lecture you? Without offense?"

I said mildly: "If my present knowledge of your trade isn't improved pretty damn soon, I'm not really going to be much use to you."

She nodded. "It's a very recondite world of our own, the couriers' world, and we're a very secretive breed. We have to be. Almost nobody outside the business knows the way we work, or even that we exist." Illustrating her point, she said: "Eleven major thefts from couriers last year alone, and not one of them was reported in the newspapers. Simply because the association, all of us, have an almost psychotic need for the tightest possible security. Without that, we couldn't even begin to operate."

"Almost one a month? Isn't that a very high rate?"

"No. The number of deliveries, large and small, averages out at three hundred and forty a year." She shrugged. "That's including the small stuff that no one of any consequence is going to bother about. But when the stakes are as high as they are now . . . that's when the top-flight pros move in on us, with no holds barred."

"About which . . . no one seems to want me to know the value of this particular consignment."

There was no hesitation at all. "It's insured for twelve million dollars. There's the Thai Queen, the somewhat smaller but equally valuable Astra Para, and a stone that is called the Jonkers Number Four, which is remarkable for having fifty-seven facets, only twenty-four below the girdle, instead of the twenty-five one would expect from this particular cut. The man who cut it, in the year 1836, was Johannes Bricek, who had always been regarded as an indifferent cutter, though he was also a mathematical genius; he had to be. This stone made his reputation. It's just not possible to cut a diamond into fifty-seven facets like that. But he did it. And that's the one Giles Fouchon wants."

"You're carrying them from Paris to Athens. When?"

It was too dark to see her smile, but that's what she was doing. "As far as you and I are concerned, the operation starts on Sunday night, at nine o'clock. Only M'sieur Armand and a handful of his people know that. The rest of the staff—the controllers, the guards, the others—they've been alerted to open the vault thirteen and a half hours later, at ten thirty on Monday morning, which is when all the usual fuss will be made. And the fuss, this time, really is quite something."

"So Monday morning is a feint . . . "

"The association aways refers to these things as a BM, a Blind Move. They have a way with words, I'm afraid."

"I noticed."

"For the BM, Brett Howard will be there, the deputy chief of the ID, and he's known to the opposition, of course, and will therefore attract attention. There will also be a small contingent of the National Guard there, and this, I think, is a nice touch. We have to assume that Helder knows the French government was asked to help, because too many people would be involved in this sort of question, and it can't be kept very secret. It will have been reported to him also that they refused . . . But—and this is what I like—he *may* just believe that their refusal was deliberately fed to him and is therefore not true."

"It's a game, isn't it?"

"We play our cards, they play theirs. Yes, it's a poker game, with millions in the pot."

"Then who actually picks up what on Monday?"

She said promptly: "The girl. She's not exactly a double; I really wish she were. But she looks a little like me, wears my clothes, has my name on her passport, and in this instance will be accompanied by my guard-dog, a Doberman. Apart from the real stones, there are three sets of duplicates, what we call decoys. The girl will pick up one of them, with all the fuss and bother to advertise it and hopefully occupy Helder's attention. She'll take them to Athens, via Rome—also in the hope of drawing him off. We go directly to Athens."

"So the real delivery will be completed before she even starts out . . . "

"Precisely. It sounds complicated, perhaps, but it's not, really. We have to guard against a number of strike potentials. Helder is no fool, and he'll know there will be at least one set of decoys, possibly more. He won't make just one attempt to get them. He'll hit us, and hit us again and again—until he either has them, or they are safely in Vasileos' vault. We expect a strike in Paris itself, probably at the airport; in Athens; and, of course, anywhere along the way. And we have to remember, all the time, that although the stones are quite small, their value is so extraordinarily high that Helder, or anyone else for that matter, can afford to throw an army against us and still make a good profit."

I said: "I have a feeling I'm going to enjoy this assignment. Even if I do wind up in the morgue."

"We'll try and see that doesn't happen."

"Well, that's nice to know." I put a comforting hand on her thigh too; she lifted it up gently and removed it.

I had a feeling that Mrs. Bentley was being kept out of it, my revenge. Christine seemed to feel it too (we were beginning to think alike already!), and she turned to her and said: "Has the question of a gun been discussed with Mr. Benasque?"

"No. He doesn't normally carry one, but if you think he should . . . ?"

"I much prefer him to be unarmed. I'm convinced that guns simply complicate matters unduly, besides giving us a sense of security which is quite false. No, I'd rather he didn't have one."

Mrs. Bentley sounded dubious. "If you're sure about that, of course, I won't argue the point. He doesn't like to carry a gun anyway."

Oh God, here we were starting all over.

I said: "No, he doesn't. He's almost forgotten how to use one. But not quite, perhaps."

Christine was about to say something, but a car passed us just then, a big Peugeot, shooting past us at full speed then pulling in to the curb a couple of hundred yards ahead of us. Immediately, the Citroën-Maserati that was following us shot ahead of us and of him too, and the scowling young man was out of it with a gun in his hand. Christine calmly picked up the speaking tube—my God, a speaking tube!—and said quickly: "That's ours, Claude."

Our driver tapped his horn three times as we pulled up beside them, and all seemed well again.

A young woman stepped out of the Peugeot and came over to us—twentyish, nice looking rather than attractive, very bright eyed and alert, with a sharp, inquisitive sort of nose and hair falling all over her face. She wore denim pants and a long smock thing, and she spoke French with an American accent, rattling it off at the speed of machine-gun fire. She was holding out a little package, and she said: "The tapes, Madame Andress. Everything's there, just two of them, the third one had nothing on it of any consequence at all."

Christine took them from her. "You have copies?"

"Yes, of course."

"Tell Mr. Howard I'll need transcripts too."

"Oui, Madame . . ."

She was gone. I watched her slide into the Peugeot and drive off at a rather hair-raising speed, and Christine dropped the divider down and said: "Claude, put these on the stereo, please, and pipe them through to the rear speakers."

The glass slid silently up again, and we all leaned back to listen in comfort. We were driving down the Champs-Élysées now, almost deserted at this hour of the morning, and the voices came through as clear as a bell—good equipment.

First, there was the sound of the door closing, though we had not heard it open; the mikes, then, were activated by the door itself. Nice work. Then, almost immediately, Giles Fouchon's voice, fairly bubbling over with delight: "My darling Veronica, I just cannot tell you how good it is to see you. And you look truly marvelous." I could imagine his eager eyes on that jellied mousse.

And then a voice I had not heard before, though I knew it to be Veronica's: "Well, thank you, darling."

"The tactile temptations are almost insuperable . . . "

Tactile temptations, indeed! I thought it was a well-turned phrase.

She said sweetly: "But we are here to talk business, Giles. Very serious business."

"Yes, indeed we are. But you are making it very hard for me to concentrate on such a prosaic thing as money."

She said gently: *"A bas les pattes,"* which can be translated roughly as "down, boy." So he had succumbed to the temptation to touch, and I envied him.

I said: "Soon, all we're going to hear is the grunts, and the groans, and the heavy breathing."

Mrs. Bentley said: "Ssshhh . . . "

The voices went on, very quiet and confidential . . . Hers now: "The first thing we have to talk about is a guarantee."

He sounded shocked. "A guarantee?"

"Arthur would like a hundred thousand dollars in advance."

"Oh no! I'm sorry, but that's out of the question."

"This is becoming a very expensive operation, and he insists on some development money."

"Yes, but not a hundred thousand. Ten perhaps . . . "

"We already have twenty-three people on the payroll, and their number is growing daily."

"Well, it seems an awful lot of money. Would you like some cognac?"

"Please. Not too much."

We heard some ice dropping into glasses, and I said: "My God, are we dealing with a man who takes ice in his cognac?"

"Ssshhh . . ."

His voice was a little farther away now, but still clear: "And if you'd like to make yourself more comfortable . . . you could take off that beautiful dress, for example."

"If you don't mind, I'll keep it on."

He was giggling now. "On? It's half off already. I suppose I could go as much as twenty-five thousand." The voice was getting louder again as he moved back to her. *"Santé."*

"Santé." A pause. "Ah, that's nice."

Oh? What was he doing? But it was just the drink she was talking about: "What is it, it's marvelous."

"My private stock, from one of my own vineyards. A very small one, in the Charentes. It's very, very old. Yes, I'm sure I could manage twenty-five thousand, just to keep him happy."

"But that won't do at all. It has to be a hundred."

There was a long, long silence now, and he said at last: "No, why don't you sit here on the sofa . . . ? And look at it like this. There is always the very acute danger that I will be handed a piece of beautifully made paste and that just would not do, now would it?"

"Your experts will examine it; you can make all the tests you want. If it's not the real thing, you don't pay."

"And I'll be out twenty-five thousand dollars."

"It will not be paste."

"They are certain to be using decoys. Two or three, perhaps."

"Yes, of course we know that."

"And you know who the courier is, I presume?"

"Yes. Christine Andress."

"I've heard it said that she's a very remarkable lady. Right at the top of her rather demanding profession."

Very offhand: "She likes to think so."

I heard Christine murmur: "What a bitch . . ."

Giles Fouchon wouldn't let her get away with that either. "No, my information comes from a very good source indeed. She's a very devious woman."

"And we are devious people too. A hundred thousand, Giles. Or we find another market."

"At this late stage in the game? There aren't many collectors around who'll buy such a famous stone . . ."

"Four, to be exact . . . "

"Oh." He sounded disconcerted. Then, plaintively: "Fifty thousand."

"One hundred, my dear Giles. And you're really supposed not to touch, you know."

"Well, just a little bit . . . No, the lacing here . . . Yes, like that. Oh, that's beautiful. And did you know Interpol is aware of your presence here in Paris?"

She sounded very thoughtful, though not unduly upset. "You can't really be sure of that . . . Ouch, that hurts."

"Oh, my darling, I'm so sorry. Like that?"

"Ah, that's nice."

"I have a young man in the cipher department at Interpol. He told me."

"Well, the Antique Dealers' Exposition will account for that; I don't mind too much."

I've always liked people who can be so prosaic when they're making love. It shows a nice, casual approach.

"And do you know where Christine Andress is?"

"She left her villa in Positano two days ago, and we lost her for a few hours. We tracked her down in Greece. She is there now."

"Unless it's her double. You know about the double?"

"Giles! Of course we do; you think we are amateurs? But the dog is with her too, that terrifying dog she has. And there's just no one else who can handle it."

"Ah, how very astute of you . . . "

"No, wait, I don't want my skirt to get creased; let me put it somewhere . . . "

"I'll take it . . . There, is that better? And what a gorgeous tan you have! You must sunbathe in the nude. You know, I hate that absurd little triangle of white. I always find it disconcerting."

"Oh, but that isn't the tan, it's my natural skin color."

"Oh really? It's fascinating. Too dark for ivory, too brown for alabaster . . . I hardly know what to call it. Cinnamon?"

"No, I'm sure it's not . . . "

"I've got it! *Tawny*. That's the word exactly."

"Yes, I like *tawny*; it's a nice word."

"Let's move to the bed; it's much more comfortable, shall we?"

"All right."
A little silence then, and a change in the tone of the recording. She said: "Ooh . . . your sheets are so cold . . . "
"They're linen. They'll soon warm up. I like the feel of cold sheets when you first get into bed, don't you? And you've got the longest legs I ever saw; they're wonderful."
"Well, thank you."
"And those lovely little boobies . . . they're hard, and soft at the same time. Like ice and like a house on fire, all at once."
I said: "Poetic sonofabitch, isn't he?"
"Ssshhh . . . "
"And when you lie down, they don't flop, either . . . "
"Well, I should hope not."
"And *mon Dieu*! They taste like avocados."
She sounded very surprised. "They do? That's remarkable! That's what the cream I use is made from. Avocados."
"Delicious, just delicious . . . "
In a moment the grunts and groans began in earnest, and I looked at Christine and at Mrs. Bentley but could see very little in the darkness—just a look of determined disapproval from the good Mrs. B. I said: "If anyone listened in to me under these circumstances, I'd be mad as a March hare."
Christine eased herself in her seat. "Two things. First, you are not trying to steal my delivery. And second, you wouldn't know a thing about it if we were to do just that."
"And what you don't know can't hurt you?"
"Something like that."
"One of the rare clichés that are completely untrue."
She nodded. "And you know, you are absolutely right. This little episode is their first step to the jail. When, of course, we catch them, as we will."
It all went on for a very creditable length of time. There was a lot of satisfied sighing at the end of it, and then Veronica said, getting down to business with rather tasteless—and pointed—alacrity, I thought: "When shall I pick up the hundred thousand dollars? It has to be very soon."

"I'll have it delivered to you first thing in the morning. Where are you?"

"At the Georges Cinq. Under the name of Claire Aprise. Room 108."

"About ten o'clock then?"

"Good."

"And we must do this . . . " The tape ran out, and when Claude slipped in the second one, there was hardly a break in their conversation: " . . . some time. Some time soon."

"Perhaps. You're very, very good, Giles."

"Ah . . ." He must have been beaming, a very happy man. "So let's just rest for a while and see what happens, shall we?"

"All right. Only move your leg."

"Like that?"

"Yes, that's better. And could I have some more of that marvelous cognac?"

"Of course, my love . . . "

In the little silence that followed, I said: "I wonder if she's really enjoying this? Purely from an academic point of view, of course."

Mrs. Bentley said sharply: "That kind of woman, does it matter?"

She sounded angry, and I said: "I was thinking of the energy crisis . . . "

Christine turned to look at me. "She's a nymphomaniac, Mr. Benasque. But she enjoyed it nonetheless. She got what she came for. The hundred thousand dollars up front. And that's all that matters to her."

They were talking again, and Giles was saying: "You must know too that there's a detail of the *Garde Nationale* reporting to Armand and Company on Monday morning?"

"Yes, of course we know that."

"It does mean, doesn't it, that they're opening the vault for a major delivery?"

"You're fishing, Giles."

"Yes, I suppose I am. I just want to protect my investment."

"Leave these things to the experts. It's always the best way."

"Just tell me where and when."

I thought: My God, they're going to drop it all in our laps . . .

But she said firmly: "I can't do that. I won't do that."

"Athens?"

"If I tell you, I tell the whole world. I won't do it."

A few moments of silence, and then, from Giles: "It really does have fifty-seven facets? It's very hard to believe."

"All symmetrical, and all perfect; it's an incredible piece of work. It was on show in New York three years ago, and Arthur and I went over to look at it. We decided then that one day . . . one day we would steal it."

He sighed. "And when I get it, what am I going to do with it?"

Her voice was very gentle indeed. "You gloat over it, Giles, as you do with all the others."

"Yes, and it's really very satisfying . . . " He was laughing all of a sudden. "You know the Brueghel they stole from the Gemeente Museum at The Hague? When was it, four years ago?"

She sounded surprised. "You mean *Girl with Dog.*"

"Yes, that's the one. It's been at my villa in Nice for three years now. How about that? And you're the only person in the whole world, except for myself, who knows that now."

"That's very, very indiscreet. You see why I can't tell you anything?"

He was chagrined. "Well, I want to get rid of it anyway. I've had it long enough. Would Arthur be interested? I'll give him a very fair price."

"No, Arthur deals only in cut stones. You know that."

"Well, if he should hear of anybody. Move over a little, will you? No, like that . . . "

"What, already?"

"I like to keep myself in good shape . . . Yes, there . . . "

There was a little more small talk about nothing, and then they were at it again, and it seemed for an interminably long time. Some more useless chatter, and then a very delectable tidbit . . .

He said, sighing: "You're sure that Madame Andress is not going to foist some decoys onto you?"

And Veronica said quite clearly, dropping her guard: "We will get as many decoys as they have, Giles. But we'll get the real ones too. We're going for *all* of them."

I heard Christine and Mrs. Bentley do exactly the same thing; they both caught their breath, a tiny little gasp.

Fouchon said slowly: "Ah . . . I see what you mean by this being an expensive operation."

She really was giving her secrets away now, though not enough of them, in my opinion. "We really have to, you know. If we get the wrong ones . . . it will take us forever to be sure; you can't just put a diamond like the Number Four under a loupe and say yes or no. It has to be tested quite meticulously. And that takes a great deal of time."

"Yes, yes . . . Well, a hundred thousand it is. May I deliver it personally? Like that, you won't have to get out of bed and all dressed up, just to receive an anonymous messenger."

She was being coy now: "If you promise you won't wear me out altogether, Giles."

"I will make every effort to do so, my dear Veronica."

They talked about nothing for a few more moments, and then the tape ran out.

For a long time, none of us said a word. Each time we passed a street lamp, I could see the dark frown on Mrs. Bentley's face, and a sort of faraway look in Christine's thoughtful eyes.

I said at last: "Well, did we learn anything? Except that there's a lot of life in the old boy yet?"

Christine nodded. "Oh yes, we learned a great deal. Not the least of which is . . . if they should get away with it, which I doubt, at least we'll know where to recover one third of it, the Jonkers. In Giles Fouchon's villa in Nice."

"I think you're jumping to conclusions."

"Yes, I am. And that's something I'm very good at. But the secret room a collector keeps for his stolen valuables . . . it can't be just a *room*. It has to be a vault, and he'll only have one of them, I'm sure. In Nice. If they succeed, that's where the Number Four will be. Take my word for it. Oh yes, we learned a lot."

She picked up the tube again and told Claude to take us to the Hôtel des Pyramides, and all the way there—from way out by the Bois de Boulogne—nobody spoke.

It was nearly five o'clock in the morning when we pulled up at the hotel, close by the gilt statue of Joan of Arc, and when she said goodnight, I held her hand a little longer than was usual, and she said: "My phone numbers are Jasmine 27-92, and Jasmine 22-16. Please don't write them down, but if you need me, call either of those numbers. Don't identify yourself, just use the code numbers 3-3-7, and I'll be here in ten or fifteen minutes. Have you got the numbers?"

"I've got them. Coffee tomorrow morning? Or rather, later this morning?"

It seemed to surprise her. There was just a touch of hesitation. Then: "All right. About eleven? Where?"

"The brasserie on Rue Duphot."

"Good, I like it there. Out on the patio. It won't be crowded there. Sleep well, Mr. Benasque."

"You too, Madame Andress."

Mrs. Bentley was waiting, looking very resigned. I grinned at her and said: "Good-night, love. Keep in touch."

"Good-night, Michael."

Michael? Well, things were getting better all the time.

Bruce was waiting for me in the lounge.

He said, beaming: "Well, I don't know what it's all about, Mr. Benasque, but as soon as I got your cable I just turned round and came right back."

"I'm glad. There'll be someone prowling around outside my room no doubt. Your replacement. Can you get rid of him?"

"I already did that, sir. An educated guess, you might say."

"Well . . . I don't know what the financial arrangements were with Harry Slewsey, but just let me know what I owe you when . . . "

"And you're going to bed now?"

"For an hour or two."

"Then I'll see you to your door." As we waited for the elevator, he said: "And this time, you can sleep well. It's all been taken care of."

"I'm sure it has."

We rumbled our way on up to the fourth floor.

Chapter Five

I don't ever like to go to bed at five in the morning. I'm a soon-after-midnight man, and if it gets to be three or four, then I prefer not to bother with bed at all but to stay up all night and the hell with it. Because if I've only got two hours of sleep coming up, invariably, I dream. I suppose the word is nightmare.

And my God, I dreamed that I was climbing down a steep escarpment—and I'm terrified of heights—with absolutely no clothes on at all, and a naked lady perched on my shoulders, my hands gripping her ankles at my side, as we stumbled into a sort of dark and terrifying chute that ran from halfway up the cliff right down to the bottom. The chute was lined with lobster baskets. The baskets were all full, and the lobsters, cooked to a bright red, were squawking at me as I slid down over them.

There was someone waiting for me at the bottom, with a revolver in his hand, and I didn't know if it was a friend or an enemy, or even if it was a man or a woman; and then there were two of them down there, with a wide cave-mouth behind them, through which I caught a glimpse of sand and surf. And then I was slithering down out of the cave and swinging the naked lady down from my shoulders and cradling her in my arms. It was Christine Andress.

I was running fast with her down the beach, and someone was chasing me, and I came to a big refectory table set out with its legs in a few inches of water, and there was a silver bowl there with a severed hand in it, but I paid almost no attention to it at all. I laid her down gently on the big table, and whoever it was behind me with the gun had disappeared, and I climbed up on the table and lay down beside her, and she looked at me with a very somber expression on her face and said: "What time is it, Michael?"

And for no reason at all, I was suddenly racing down the beach, running away from her in some kind of desperation, and there was only the disembodied, floating voice behind me, following me as I ran and repeating over and over: "What time is it, Michael?"

I woke up then, and I had the little bedside clock in my hand, and I heard myself say, even though I was in that strange limbo between sleep and wakefulness: "It's a few minutes past seven o'clock in the morning." And it was.

I shook the sleep out of my eyes and took a shower. And it's true, a cold shower really works wonders.

I could hardly wait for eleven o'clock to come. I called room service for some coffee and a little tot of calvados to get the adrenalin working, and then went out and wandered around the boulevards looking into store windows, and what a pleasurable way to pass the time. . . . And at a quarter to eleven I was in the little patio of the brasserie on Rue Duphot, always one of my favored spots to pass an hour or two. It was chilly this morning and threatening rain from dark thunderclouds which I hoped were not ominous, and almost everyone was inside.

I ordered a *filtre-calvados* and waited, wondering what she would look like in the light of day; so very many lovely women look that way only after dark.

And at precisely one minute before eleven, Christine arrived, looking fantastic. She had a man in tow, a big, florid, thick-set man in a much too conservative plaid suit with a tie straight out of Sy Devore's, with close-cut hair and that shiny kind of face that men have who still use a blade to shave with. Somehow, I felt I wasn't going to like him very much, but then I realized that I felt that way merely because I'd been hoping for a tête-à-tête with her, and it wasn't fair, so I behaved myself very correctly.

There was only one other couple here—two young kids in a corner paying attention to nothing but themselves—but his cold, shrewd, very hard eyes were on them as she made the introductions, her voice very quiet: "Mr. Benasque, I'd like you to meet Mr. Brett Howard, deputy chief of the ID. This is Michael Benasque, Brett, who comes to us very highly recommended."

Well, she must have told him that—or something, at least—much earlier, so that qualification was for my benefit, and I thought that was a good thing. Or was she trying to persuade herself?

He finally transferred his attention to me and shot out a hand, and it was very gentle, like the grip of a man who knows he's powerful and doesn't want to hurt the weaklings.

I mumbled something, and said to Christine: "The hell with it. It suggests in the manual that I'm supposed to treat you with respect at all times, if not with awe. But I really have to call you Christine."

She smiled. "All right, Michael. I think that's a very good idea. As you say, the hell with it." And in the daylight, she looked superb. The straw-colored hair was very carelessly thrown around now, still up on top of her head; though it occurred to me that the careless look may have taken quite some time to get quite right.

She wore a Turkish-looking sort of blouse thing, with a lot of intricate embroidery on it, and very long and slightly-flared black pants. Some of that enormous self-assurance seemed to have dribbled away in the few hours since I'd last seen her, and she was far more down-to-earth; still not quite the girl next door, but far less untouchable.

Brett Howard was saying earnestly: "And call me Brett, Mike."

I positively hate people who call me Mike. They mostly do it only once, but that's enough. I said pleasantly: "Michael, if you don't mind," and he sat down before she or I did and looked at my glass and said: "I've been in France for three years now, and I've never been able to figure out why people drink applejack in the morning. Not good for you, Mike. Uh, Michael."

The waiter came, and I looked at Christine, and she said: "I'll have the same. And Brett would like American coffee."

When the waiter had gone, Brett leaned into me and said, his cold gray eyes on mine: "I understand, Michael, that you're new to this game?"

"Yes. Yes, I am indeed."

"Uh-huh. Well, the PS we're dealing with is the top man in this trade, and I have to tell you . . . "

"The PS?"

"That's Prime Suspect. I have to tell you that when this guy Harry Slewsey somehow talked the board into hiring an amateur CA, for the heaviest delivery we've had in Christ knows how many years . . . I have to tell you, I practically went into shock. Seems like he had some top-secret deal going with the Board, and Christ, I'm the deputy, and they wouldn't even tell me about it! We get an SD worth this kind of money, I want the top man we've got . . . "

"An SD?"

"Special Delivery. This kind of SD brings out the real pros, like Helder. Now, his MO is pretty well known to us . . . "

"Ah. MO is *Modus Operandi.*"

"Right. We know the way he works, and that's important, usually. Only in this case, he has a different MO each time, there's no pattern to it. And that makes it rough, especially on an inexperienced CA."

"And that's Covering Agent, I guess?"

He leaned in to me and said confidentially: "The last time our paths crossed, me and Helder, can you believe it? He *paid* the courier one half the value of the consignment just to deliver it to him, instead of where it was supposed to go, and that's what the guy did. Hell, that had to be the easiest heist on record. Of course, he couldn't have made that much on the deal—fifty percent to the courier . . . "

Christine said tightly: "A man named Malcolm Reevers."

His mood had changed, and he was delighted with the memory. "Right, Mal Reevers. Fifty percent to him, 60 percent of what was left to the fence, 10 percent to his hired help. Hell, there was no way he could make more than a couple of hundred grand."

I said: "I don't really believe you're just reminiscing. I've a feeling there's a point to your comment."

He was positively smug. "Well, I'm glad to hear it, because one thing we're pretty high on is *perception.*"

"They killed him," Christine said, and she was very angry.

Brett was unmoved. "No. Poor sonofabitch ran his car off the road in the Italian Alps. What a hell of a place to run a car off the road. Nearly a thousand feet down when the car blew up, and it took us like forever to get down there. But we got most of the money back. Some of it charred around the edges, but . . . he had it in a leather briefcase—didn't burn too good."

I said: "It's a charming story, do go on."

His eyes were little Arctic pools. "This time, an SD so important it even scares me, and what do we have? The best goddamn courier in the business, with a CA . . . we don't know too much about. Like just how far we can trust him."

Christine had laid a hand on his, and she was smiling gently: "Brett, I am convinced that Michael is not a thief."

He didn't take his cold eyes off me. "If Jesus Christ saw twelve million dollars there for the taking, he just might climb down off that pedestal for a while. That's a lot of spending money. Tax free."

The waiter arrived with the coffee, finally. And when I had recovered my habitual good nature, I said: "Why don't we change the subject? I've been warned. Okay, I accept it."

He was nodding, satisfied that he'd done his job. "Okay." He looked at Christine. "I understand he heard the Fouchon-Verignana tapes?"

"Yes, he did."

"And that was another mistake. Okay, it's done, and it can't be undone. We got other things to talk about. An item in the DIR . . . "

I said: "Don't tell me, let me guess. Daily Intelligence Report."

He had a look on his face that said, very clearly: *One more crack out of you, Buddy, and I'm going to break both your legs.* Just a look, but that's what it said. But under the table, Christine's hand was on my knee, not apologetic this time, just restraining, so I said: "Okay, Brett, I guess I'm just kind of short tempered this morning. I didn't get much sleep."

He grumbled. "If you're going to stay up till five in the

morning, drinking two-thousand glasses of cognac, you just have to expect that."

I thought that was a very interesting comment, but I said nothing.

Christine was frowning at him: "We're in the report today, Brett?"

"We sure as hell are. Public Enemy Number One just drove into town." She was staring at him, unsure, and I said: "Good. I like it."

She looked puzzled. "I don't know why you say that, Michael."

"Because I like to know where the opposition's at."

Brett Howard said, giving the man his due: "That's the first sensible remark you've made yet," and Christine, still frowning, came to my rescue: "Yes, of course, he's right. But we didn't expect that. Usually he likes to stay in the background."

Brett said: "That's right, he does," and I threw in my little bit: "But his MO is different every time, didn't you say? MO. That's *Modus Operandi*?"

He sipped his coffee without taking his deep-freeze eyes off me, and I found it disconcerting and even frightening.

But he went on: "He left his villa in the south yesterday morning, no suitcase, no nothing. He'd ordered a table for lunch at a restaurant up in Vence, and that's where he was heading. But the moment he hit Route 7, he just put his foot down and punched that Bentley he drives, and the agent following him lost him. Sonofabitch had a Fiat, no contest. But the guy watching Verignana in Paris turned in a report nine hours later. Helder had switched cars someplace, and his Ferrari was parked in the garage of the hotel, the Georges Cinq. At eight thirty-five, when she left for the party on Fouchon's boat, he was seen by a bellhop at the door of her room. And this morning, two people had been sleeping in her bed. So, he's in Paris for sure. And I have to tell you, I don't like it."

I thought it was time I helped out. I said to Christine: "Does it mean he's found out you're in here? If he knows you don't get into the act until the last minute . . . ?"

She nodded, deeply concerned. "Yes, that's probably

what it is. But dammit, he's supposed to be concentrating on the girl in Athens!"

"Twenty-three people on the payroll, remember, the number growing daily. That means he's watching *everybody*."

"Yes, you're right, I think."

"Veronica, to get the action started; but the boss, to take over when the action really starts. Veronica said on the tape: 'We will get as many decoys as they have, but we'll get the real ones too.' When he said 'decoy' he could have meant the real delivery, as well as the Monday morning one. In other words, it may be that he knows what we're up to."

Brett said abruptly: "I want to reschedule the whole thing. Sunday *and* Monday. Make it a couple of days later."

Christine was absolutely in control, and she was right. "No. It's bad for him to have to hang around for two days, or even a few hours. It's far worse for me. If we did that, we'd be asking for more trouble than we already have. But I want two more men on the Monday morning show. One on Rue de Rivoli, a hundred meters from Place Vendôme, and the other on the corner of Rue St. Roch, where he can watch the intersections. And let them be in position quite early, long before the National Guard gets there."

"Okay, okay, I'll see to it." He was getting smug again, trying to assert his own expertise, and they went on talking shop as if I weren't even there. He said: "You know where the real weakness is, don't you?"

Christine was pouring impossible amounts of sugar into her coffee. "The real weakness is Armand himself. I've always worried about him."

"Right. The profile says he talks too much. Especially to that broad he has over in Montparnasse."

"She left him nearly a month ago."

"That's right. And ever since, he's been trying to get her back."

"Armand will talk about *anything*. Provided it's not his livelihood. Diamonds."

"That's what the profile says. Me, I've never believed it. Psychologically, it doesn't make sense. If he's trying to get her back, and if somebody like Helder got to her . . . Believe me, he'll talk. It's the delivery of all time, and if he wants to make like the big shot to impress her, he's going to talk. Too much to drink one night, shacked up with her . . . He's sure as hell going to try and impress her with what an important guy he is."

Christine was very thoughtful. "It's a possibility, yes. It's just the kind of thing Helder might do. Is she under surveillance?"

Brett shook his head. "Hell, we can't keep tabs on everybody. They cut my budget by nearly 15 percent this year. Helder's got more men than I have, goddammit!"

"But you're watching *him*, presumably?"

"Sure. He's been round to her new apartment a couple of times. Each time, two hours, in the mornings. Just long enough to show her how great he is in bed."

"Mornings only?"

"Yeah."

"That kind of loose talk . . . doesn't it presuppose, well, nighttime? Too much of a good dinner, too much to drink?"

Grudgingly: "Well, maybe. But I still don't want to rule it out. A guy can loose-talk in the morning too."

"And I still want it for Sunday night, as scheduled."

"Okay, if you say so. I still think it's a mistake. And Mike will be with you, right?"

"Yes."

He took out a pair of glasses, horn rimmed, and put them on and looked at me, a deliberate gesture. He said: "Somehow, I just don't figure you as the kind of guy who'd know what to do in an emergency."

I said politely: "And the way you don't figure is absolutely right. But Madame Andress will be able to take care of it all, won't she?"

He held my look for a moment, with cold, hard eyes that I was getting to dislike more and more. *"They're pretty ruthless,"* Mrs. Bentley had said. *"Don't tangle with them . . ."*

He looked at his watch and got to his feet. "Well, I have to get back to the office and draft some reports." He looked at me again, and back to Christine, and said carefully: "I came along on this coffee break to kind of convince myself that we were doing the right thing taking this guy on for a real man's job."

She was very sweet. "And did you, Brett?"

He didn't answer. "See you, Madame Andress." He strode off, and Christine looked at me with a smile of pure delight on her face. "Don't let him get to you, Michael. Hidden under that apparent idiocy, there is a very shrewd mind. I sometimes think the idiocy is a put-on, just to mislead the opposition."

"So how about some more calvados?"

"I'd rather have another *filtre*."

I looked around for the waiter, standing in a corner there, looking very bored. He caught my eye and hurried over, and I said: "Another *filtre*, please, and a calvados for me."

"Toute de suite, M'sieur."

I turned back to Christine. She looked marvelous, her skin soft as a baby's behind. By a curious accident of angle, her head seemed to be framed by the vines that crept over the white-painted trelliswork, and I thought: Jesus, I'm falling in love with a woman I know nothing about . . . I was tempted to tell her about my dream, but I thought I'd better not. I said instead: "What happens now?"

"Until tonight . . . nothing. Perhaps we rest up for a while. There'll be a sleepless night ahead of us."

"What's the emergency Brett Howard was talking about?"

For a long time she didn't answer. Then, when at last the waiter had scurried up with my calvados and her coffee and had gone back to his corner, she said slowly:

"It's very seldom a bed of roses, this thing, and sometimes, even quite often . . . " She thought about it for a moment and went on: "Last August, for example, there was another broker further down on Rue de Rivoli. He was sending a single stone, not even a very good one, to Amsterdam for recutting. It was worth about three hundred thousand dollars, enough to bring out a few of the pros. The courier, an acquaintance of mine, though we don't really get to know each other much in this business, had arranged the collection for a Saturday afternoon. A

Saturday afternoon in mid-August? Paris was *empty*! Everybody on holiday. It was the same kind of casual affair which I always prefer, no fuss, no bother, no guards to attract attention—just the way we're doing it on Sunday. The moment she got back on the street, a car came by, spraying bullets everywhere. Three Algerians, amateurs . . . She wasn't killed, but she was very badly wounded, and she'll never walk again. They got her safe-box, but the stone in it was paste. A second courier, a young man she was breaking in, was taking the real thing three days later. She was a very good courier, on her way up. Now she's out of it forever, a cripple in a wheelchair. Her CA was right beside her, and if he'd acted a little faster . . . I don't know."

"In that kind of emergency, what the hell can you do?"

"There's not much you can do except think fast. In the case of an overt hit, like that one, you just hope they'll get the decoy. Almost always, they do, that's what decoys are for. But once in a while, there's an Arthur Helder in the background, as there is now. And then . . . anything can happen."

I said, wondering about it: "Tell me one thing. I can understand how it is that you know all about Sir Arthur Helder. After all, you've got the police, the Sûreté, every law-enforcement agency in the country to help out . . . "

She interrupted. "No, that's not true. In every major city in the world, we try to avoid the local authorities as much as possible. There's always the danger of inefficiency, or bureaucratic red tape, or corruption, or all three of them. Here, the locals are good. But in some countries . . . No, we stay away from the police. We get some help from Interpol, but mostly . . . we rely on the association. That's what they're there for."

"So how come Helder knows so much about you?"

She was lecturing again, but it was nice to hear her talk so confidentially; I felt it was drawing us together.

She said: "Among the thousands of professional diamond thieves in the world, there's a handful, right at the top, the really good ones who've made a wealthy and safe living out of it for a long, long time. These three or four run extensive intelligence operations of their own. There's an enormous amount of money involved, and they can well afford to. They have their agents everywhere. We learned on the tape last night they even have a man in the cipher department at Interpol H.Q. . . . which is already being investigated, I might say. So they know . . . *us*. And as far as is humanly possible, they watch us, every minute of the day. Three or four top thieves, three or four top couriers . . . the cats, and the mice. That's why I have the girl, currently standing in for me at my villa in Greece."

"With your alarming Doberman."

She smiled. "Yes. The girl has learned to handle her too."

Suddenly, she looked . . . how shall I put it? *Shamefaced*. She reached into her purse and brought out a wallet-size photo and showed it to me. "I have no children to show off, so I carry a picture of my dog around instead. Is that terrible?"

"No. Dogs are more rewarding than children ever are."

"I'm sure you don't mean that, but never mind."

It was the most fearsome-looking beast I'd ever set eyes on, a huge monster of a dog with bared fangs, and I thought: thank God it's not around here just now. I handed it back to her, and she slipped it into her purse again, and said: "I don't allow myself to get emotional very often, but . . . Her name is Mia, and she's five years old."

I wondered why so desirable a woman had nothing more than a goddamn dog to comfort her, but I kept quiet about that. I said instead: "Did you know that I brought Bruce back? Did you even know about Bruce?"

She laughed. "Yes, I know him. He's one of the best men we ever had. Harry Slewsey took him over and promptly fired him. I'm glad you did what you did; he's very good." She thought about it for a while, and said at last: "There's an extraordinary thing about that young man. He always seems to know more than he's told. He listens, and puts two and two together and knows exactly what he has to do, even if it's far beyond the periphery of his instructions. And when you most need him and least expect him, there he is. You don't even know how he got there, but he's been *thinking*. And the answers he comes up with are always right. Harry made a big mistake in firing him. And I'm very glad you rectified it. Men like Bruce don't exactly grow on trees. They're very hard to come by."

I was glad she agreed with me; anything that we could see eye to eye on was satisfying.

I said: "There was a man named André Gaston, a member of a thing called the Cosmos Gang. He tried to break into my room last night."

"Yes, I know about that. We still don't know if he was one of Helder's men or not, and we'll probably never know. It's possible that he really was trying to break into another room. There was a woman just below you who wore an awful lot of expensive jewelry. Perhaps he just chose the wrong balcony."

"But it's also possible he chose the right one."

"I'm glad you're thinking along those lines. But we are trying to convince ourselves that Helder knows nothing about you personally. After all, that's why you were chosen for this job. Brett's trying to find out. And there are only four people who know you're in on this: me, Brett, Harry Slewsey, and Mrs. Bentley. We can trust all of them implicitly. Of course there are the peripheral people . . . " She laughed suddenly. "I suppose Brett would call them the PPs . . . Bruce, and Claude, a handful of others. But they don't really know very much."

She had finished her coffee and looked at her watch. "I have to run in a moment . . . so, about tonight. You have to go to dinner at the Belle Aurore, you know where that is?"

"On Rue Gomboust."

"About five minutes' walk from your hotel. There's a nine o'clock reservation for you, in the name of *Monsieur Michel.* After you've had dinner, you leave there at exactly ten-thirty, turn the corner, and walk down Rue de la Sourdière. There'll be a man working on the engine of a baby Citroën, a red one, outside the wine shop halfway down the street on the left-hand side. He will already have seen you in the Belle Aurore, so he'll know you. As you approach him, he'll move off. You follow him, and he'll take you in to the Armand vaults through the back way. That's where we meet. We pick up the delivery, come out the same way, and a car will take us to where the plane is waiting."

"A commercial plane?"

"No. We have a charter. A charter is never as reliable as a commercial flight; so they won't be expecting us to use one."

"Pawn to Queen Four."

She was delighted: "Ah, you play chess. We must have a game or two one day. Yes. Pawn to Queen Four."

I said: "There's just one thing that perhaps I ought to say. I'll do my damnedest, of course, to make sure you don't get into any trouble. But . . . perhaps Brett is right, after all. Perhaps you really do need a more experienced man."

"I'm perfectly happy with things as they are, Michael. And so is the board. They must have checked you out back to the day you were born, and if they hadn't been convinced, all of Harry Slewsey's efforts to get you in on this would have meant nothing."

"Yes. And I'm wondering about that too. He wants a story, he says, and I'll buy that. What I find hard to understand is how he persuaded the association to go along with it."

"He is a very persuasive man, I'm told. I don't know him well enough to have found out about that for myself." She looked at her watch again, a minuscule thing, so small I wondered how she could read it. "I won't see you again until tonight."

"The time will drag, abominably." I held her hand, and it was soft and warm and friendly. She said, looking at the couple in the corner, still whispering to each other: "Let's not leave together. Give me a few moments. *Merci pour le café.*"

I fancied I could still smell her perfume. I wondered how I could find out what it was, so that I could go out and get her a bottle of it. But then I thought: With all that money of Harry's in my pocket, I could buy her a five-gallon cask of it, at a hundred and fifty dollars an ounce, and it still wouldn't mean anything very much. So I forgot about it. I had another calvados instead, and wandered off, finally, into the street.

Rue Duphot, just off the Madeleine, is in one of my favorite areas of the whole wide world. And right now, it was a marvelous place to be in.

Chapter Six

The dinner that night was splendid, though I had an uncomfortable feeling about the last meal of a man already condemned to perdition. But the feeling soon went when I studied the menu and smelled the scents coming from the kitchens; there's nothing in the world like really good food to set a man's soul in peace. Though I remembered that this was Harry Slewsey's philosophy too.

I decided against their famous *Poulet Belle Aurore*, because I'm basically a beef man; so I ordered the *tournedos* instead, broiled *au point* and served in a sauce of brandy and white wine, with buttered artichoke hearts and little slices of poached bone marrow. No dessert, and I didn't even eat the salad they gave me—Romaine and Iceberg lettuce dusted over with the yolks of hard-cooked eggs, the thing they call Mimosa. Not too much to drink either, just a bottle of Gevrey-Chambertin and some Chateauneuf Du Pape with the cheeses.

And, of course, a few glasses of cognac to while away the last fifteen minutes.

There was an elderly, rather fussy-looking man at the next table, dining with a sweet young girl who might have been his granddaughter, studying me intently from time to time. I wondered about the girl and realized that she was his quite unnecessary cover—a beginner, in spite of his age. He had a napkin tucked under his chin, and he called for his check and left, just as I ordered my final cognac. He embraced the young girl briefly and kissed her on both cheeks. She hurried off about her own business while he fussed with an overcoat and patted all his pockets to make sure he still had everything. I suddenly realized that he was breaking *her* in; I thought that was nice.

At exactly ten-thirty, I wandered off down Rue de la Sourdière, the Deaf Woman's Street, a narrow and rather dismal alley that leads down to the far livelier Rue St. Honoré. My dinner neighbor was tinkering with the motor of a little red Citroën as I drew near, and he slammed the tin hood down and moved off, not even looking at me. I followed him.

We crossed St. Honoré, and down St. Roch, and then made a right turn and two lefts—a rather roundabout route to make sure, I supposed, that we weren't being followed. I was about to walk up to him patiently and suggest it would be easier to just tell me where we were going, and I'd go there; but he disappeared all of a sudden.

I was only fifty feet behind him, and he just wasn't there any more. I moved on, rather cautiously now, expecting God knows what to pounce on me, but it was just a dark doorway there, half open, and I heard his voice, very low and conspiratorial: *"Par ici, M'sieur,* this way . . ."

He closed the door behind me and switched on the light, peering at me as though to make absolutely sure he had the right man, and I sighed and said: "Yes, it's me . . ."

He smiled, and bowed a little stiffly, and said: "I present myself, M'sieur. Jean Delgarde. I hope you had a good dinner?"

"Thank you. And you?"

"Quite excellent. The chicken was impeccable. Now, if you would be so good as to follow me through the cellars? And with great care, if you please. The steps are very old."

We went gingerly down an interminable stairway, into an ancient crypt, and through a tunnel that had once been used to carry water away, and when we came out of it, he said, still whispering, though I was sure there were only ghosts down here: "There used to be a church over our heads, but it was torn down a few years ago. In the middle of the fourteenth century, I believe." It was all very vast and impressive, with huge stone pillars everywhere, and curlicues and archways, and flat slabs of granite for a floor.

Another tunnel to crawl through, and we were in the sewers, quite dry here, and arched in dark and somber brickwork. He shone his flashlight around and said, pointing: "We could go along this old sewer all the way to the cellars under the Louvre. But we go this way. Come. With care."

It seemed the doors to be unlocked would never end. Some of them were incredibly ancient and heavy, but the last few were made of metal, and he smiled at me and whispered: "We are now on the property of M'sieur Armand, and all is well."

We walked on through a maze of corridors, all brightly lit now, and came to a polished steel door with a small trapdoor in its upper half. My guide pushed a button, looked at me and smiled again, and when the trapdoor opened, he held up a little punched card for close inspection by a fearsomely-bearded face, the door slid back and we went inside.

We were in the beginnings of the vaults. The guard opened another door for us, also of polished steel, then my guide held back. He stood aside, gestured, and said: "In there, M'sieur, if you would be so good."

I stepped inside, and when the door slid back behind me, I was alone in a sort of anteroom—blue-carpeted, nicely decorated, with the lens of a closed-circuit TV camera high in the wall in one corner.

I heard Christine's voice coming over the speaker: "The door to your right, Michael."

It was an elevator, and I went up one story in it and stepped out into the main vault. She was waiting for me there, smiling, with a small and eager-looking man in his sixties, very carefully dressed in a dark gray suit with a very white shirt and a maroon tie. He stepped toward me, holding out his hand, and said: "M'sieur Benasque, a great pleasure . . ."

Christine made the introductions: "M'sieur Benasque, Mr. Armand." There was one other man there, standing apart and not getting introduced, middle-aged and hard looking, carelessly dressed in a blazer and slacks, the pistol under his shoulder bulking large.

Armand looked at his watch and said: "All right, I think we can go in now." He produced two electronic keys and inserted them in coded locks set about six feet apart (impossible for one man to operate them alone, I noticed), checked his watch again, and murmured: "Mr. Benasque, if you would kindly turn the other key to the left when I give you the word . . . " He counted off the seconds and said: "Now, please," and we both turned our keys, and the center portion of the wall slid silently down into the floor.

The other man had a stopwatch in his hand, and Armand looked at him and said: "Now." He turned to me and said: "We have a programmed number of minutes to get our work done. In no less than eight minutes, and not more than twelve, the door must be closed again. Otherwise . . . *mon Dieu,* all hell breaks loose."

It was a very fancy strong room indeed. Ordinary in some respects, with slim steel bars and sliding steel drawers everywhere, a limited amount of modernistic furniture and a closed-circuit camera on a track that ran around the ceiling, but stationary now. There was a long row of very impressive-looking gadgetry along one wall —what I thought might be a spectroscope, an oscillograph (I think), five TV-type screens in a row, and more colored buttons than I could count.

Christine went to a switch and threw it, and a dozen lights came on all over the console. She sat down and slid back a tray and said: "Let me have the Alpha set first, please."

I looked up at the camera as Armand unlocked a drawer. "Who's watching us, Christine?"

She shook her head. "It's been turned off. Ostensibly for a maintenance schedule of thirty minutes. We have plenty of time."

Armand gave her a small steel box, opened and lined with red velvet, and she took out three diamonds—much smaller than I had somehow expected—and placed them on an opaque glass tray. She pushed a few buttons, and in a moment a sort of X-ray negative slid out from one of those god-awful machines. She placed it on the screen, lit it, and stared at it for a while and said at last: "I don't see the flaw on the Queen."

Armand said: "If you change its angle, Madame?"

She moved one of the stones and tried again, studied

the new negative a while and said: "Ah, yes, that's good. Time please?"

The man with the stopwatch said: "Six minutes and twelve seconds to eight minutes."

She turned a dial, and the center portion of the negative zoomed up into an enlargement, and she said: "Michael, just academic interest, but you might like to see this, it's really quite remarkable."

I saw where the flaw was, in this huge enlargement, right away. It looked like an almost-perfect etching of a face—an Oriental face, plump and smiling—and I just could not believe that it was an accident of nature. The slanting eyes were very easy to make out, a tiny chip of a nose, and a line underneath that looked exactly like a smiling mouth. Even Armand was peering at it excitedly, and Christine said:

"Can you believe that it's a *flaw*? So small it can hardly be seen at all. With most instrumentation it shows up as just that, a flaw, and nothing else. But that, my dear Michael, is the Queen herself. They say it even looks like her. And that is the source of its enormous value."

She started punching buttons again, and a readout appeared on one of the screens: A long list of formalized numbers in green light, flashing on and off. She studied them intently and said at last: "Facet count is correct . . . " Another button, more numbers, more lights . . . and a lot more study, and then she nodded and sat back. "All right, I'm satisfied. Let's deal with these first. The pouch, please."

Armand gave her a tiny chamois bag, on a piece of ordinary dacron cord, and she stood up and turned to me and said: "I'm sorry about this, Michael, but if you'll undo your belt and the top of your trousers?"

I said: "How's that again?"

"Please."

Well. I undid the belt and unzipped the top, and she tied the cord around my waist, knotted it carefully, tugged at it to make sure it was secure, and said: "Good. Now that goes down under your underpants, and behind your scrotum, up as tight as you can get it." She was cool, and practical, and very businesslike indeed, and I felt like an idiot fumbling there with Armand's eagle eyes on me, to say nothing of Christine's. He threw her a look which seemed to ask a question, and she said casually, very offhand indeed: "That's just till we get on the plane, M'sieur Armand. Ten minutes after takeoff they will be somewhere else."

He still looked worried. "It's just the thought, Madame, of my beautiful diamonds traveling anywhere in such . . . such a remarkable place."

She seemed to freeze, staring at him with a look as cold as the bottom of an iceberg, and he almost stammered and said: "Of course, I am not questioning your decisions."

She didn't answer him. She looked at me and said: "Now stand back please and turn around slowly." She examined the crucial area from all possible angles, nodded, and went back to her bench and said: "The Beta set, please."

Armand produced a second set of stones that looked to me to be precisely identical, and there were more photographs, more flashing lights. This time she referred to a little notebook and checked out some numbers, and at last she shook her head and said: "Really, it's quite incredible; they're awfully good. Who made them up?"

Armand seemed mollified. He was smiling broadly now. "Henkels made them for us, and the job he did on the Number Four is particularly good, I think. But you see what he did?"

"Yes. He made three of the facets a fraction oversize. It's still very hard to see, even under intense magnification."

"The human eye cannot see it at all. Only the computer sees it."

She went on, studying intently: "Really excellent . . . the flaw on the Queen won't stand much inspection, but the Astra's awfully good too. . . . In your opinion, how long would it take an expert to reach a decision on them?"

He said carefully: "There are only seven of these machines in the world. Vasileos has one, there are two in Amsterdam, I have the only one in France, and the other three are in America. With normal analysis, it would take a first-class man . . . oh, I'd say at least half a day to discount the Queen, because there's really no other way than ours to examine that flaw minutely. In any case, he'd probably go for the Jonkers for the first test, and with normal equipment . . . yes, the facet-count would be correct. That, and the Astra . . . it would take far longer."

"All right. You have the safe-boxes?"

He opened a cupboard and took out an ordinary-looking briefcase—except that it had the Gucci stripes on it—and then a very expensive-looking shoulder-tote, fitted with quite heavy brass locks. She put the three stones of what she had called the Beta set into a little steel box, picked up the briefcase and examined it carefully, and said: "What's the charge in it?"

"Twelve grams of fulminate of mercury. Not lethal, unless they're unlucky. Enough to blow their hands off if they try and open it."

The man with the stopwatch said: "Two minutes to eight minutes."

"Thank you." Christine showed me the briefcase. "This is how it works." She slipped the box into it, zipped it and unzipped it three times, and said: "Now, the charge is set. We close it . . . (she did) ". . . and now, if it is opened again, it detonates. Not as dangerous as it sounds, because opening it now needs a considerable amount of force; it's automatically locked. But if it *is* forced . . . well, you know what happens. This is yours from now on."

She gave it to me, and I tucked it under my arm. She sat down again and said: "Gamma set, please."

She went through the whole rigmarole with the X ray and the computers again, and said finally: "Yes, they're almost identical with the Betas, aren't they? He really is a very good man, Henkels." She left them on their little tray for a moment and emptied the tote-bag onto the table. "What have I got here?"

"Everything you ordered, Madame."

There was a compact, a purse stuffed with French currency, a small hairbrush of quite beautiful rosewood, a bunch of keys, a small wallet filled with credit cards, three pairs of pantyhose in a plastic package, a pair of dark glasses, a gold cigarette lighter . . . She examined the hairbrush meticulously, and when the stopwatch said "three minutes to the twelve mark," she shook her head and looked at Armand: "No, I can't find it."

He was delighted now. "Splendid. I was half afraid you would."

He took out a ball-point pen, and said: "May I . . . ?" She gave him the brush, and he parted the bristles with the point of the pen and pushed down on it and said: "Precisely . . . here. Quite a strong push is needed." There was a tiny black button there, among the bristles, slightly recessed, and as he pushed it home, there was the slightest possible click. He twisted the top of the brush, and it opened to disclose three little compartments. She placed the diamonds in them carefully, snapped it shut again, and put everything back into the tote. She said to Armand: "There's one final thing. If you would please explain the safety-check on the briefcase to M'sieur Benasque?"

He took it from me and ran a finger along one edge. "Here, if you feel carefully, you might find the wire that leads to the charge. It's not intended to be concealed too perfectly. It goes through both of the handles, and if you cut through one of the handles you will break the wire, and the case can then be safely opened. Otherwise . . . emphatically not."

He gave it back to me, and I said: "Great. Some enthusiastic customs officer at the airport is going to make me open it."

"Michael, you know better than that."

The stopwatch said stolidly: "One minute to the twelve mark." He began counting down now: "Fifty seconds, forty seconds, thirty seconds . . . " And by the time he reached ten, we were in the outer room and the door was sliding up into position again.

Armand shot out a hand to Christine. "Madame, all that is left for me to say is . . . *bonne chance*. I am convinced that my stones are in, er, very good hands." He was staring at my crotch, trying to see if the tiny little pouch were visible. I was sure it was not; it was cutting into me like hell.

He said ruefully: "And I have to go through all this rigmarole tomorrow . . . "

"Tomorrow it will be far more of a rigmarole. Let the

girl use all the instrumentation she wants, and I don't really mind how many of your staff are present."

"There will be eight of us."

"That's good. Brett Howard will handle the National Guard, but in this room, the girl must be in charge."

"Of course."

"Good-night, then."

We all shook Gallic hands again for good measure, and ten minutes later, Christine and I were in the big Rolls-Royce and heading south on Route 7. Christine put out a hand, touched mine, and said: "Michael, you've been wonderful."

It surprised me. I said: "But I've done absolutely nothing!"

"That is what is wonderful. A CA has a heavy responsibility, and so often . . . they just want to take over everything. Most of them still don't believe that this is a job for a woman. For any woman. And yes, you're accepting everything marvelously well."

I thought: What an agreeable girl this is. It was hard not to feel positively smug.

There was almost no traffic going south on Route 7. Everyone was coming back in the other direction from the weekend on the Riviera.

We turned off the main road just before we reached Fontainebleau, onto the Route Ronde, and then into the forest, over a gravel track that ran past the spectacular Gorges de Franchard, looming awesomely high above us in the moonlight. We found a little clearing, a few military huts no longer in use, and a single runway—right where no one would ever have thought of finding one.

A single work-light was burning there, and close by there was an alarmingly small plane, looking not much bigger than a toy. I said: "My God, we're going in *that?"* It'll never make it, for God's sake; it's twelve-hundred miles to Athens!"

She was laughing suddenly, as though an unexpected revelation had amused her. She said: "Don't tell me you don't like flying, Michael?"

"If the plane is as big as a good-sized hotel, I can put

up with it, I suppose. Those things bounce around too much for my liking. Are you sure it has the range?"

"Michael . . . " She leaned in to the driver. "Under the trees there, Claude."

The Rolls glided softly over the tarmac and onto the grass and came to a stop under the tall pines. Christine was staring out of the window, her eyes very alert, and she said: "Brett ought to be here. Where is he?" She checked her watch and said: "Well, we're a little early; we'll wait."

I said: "There."

He was hurrying to us from the shadows, and there was something in his gait that made him look even more than usually angry. He opened the door, climbed in, pulled down one of the jump seats, sat on it, and said: "We've got trouble. One hell of a lot of trouble."

I heard Christine draw her breath in sharply; it was impatience more than anything else. "What kind of trouble, Brett?"

He scowled. "The pilot, he's been hurt. I only just found out about it. He's been replaced by a man I don't know, a man I haven't enough time to check out."

"Hurt? What kind of hurt?"

"He rammed his little sports car into a truck. Broke a goddamn leg."

It seemed important to be sure. I said: "He rammed the truck, or the truck rammed him?"

"No, it looks like it was his fault all right, but goddammit, we can't be sure. Any kind of an automobile accident can be faked; there's nothing to it . . . "

Christine said: "And the replacement?"

"He's on board, wondering if I'm going to let him take off or not. And I don't think I am."

"A company man?"

"Sure he's a company man. They say he's one of their best or he wouldn't be flying for me—you know the way they talk."

"And the company is Air Trans-Alpes again?"

"Sure, just like always . . . "

"And we know they're reliable; so I don't quite see what the problem is."

He sounded cross. "The problem is we've never used

this particular pilot before, and I'm not letting you take off in a plane piloted by a guy I don't know who the hell he is."

"You've talked with him?"

He sighed. "He seems all right, but *seems* is never good enough. There's a feeling in my bones. I don't like it."

"How long has he been with Trans-Alpes?"

"Six years."

"Well then . . ."

"Well then my ass. In a case like this, I check out every guy connected with the operation down to how does he like his eggs, sunnyside or once over. The company called me just before I left the office. They said Hozier had broken a leg, and they were giving me a man called Colbert, and who the hell is Colbert? I wanted that Jewish kid, what's his name, Levy. At least I know I can trust him, but Levy's in Iceland with a party of politicians; so they gave me Colbert." He said again: "And who the hell is Colbert? I don't know this guy from Adam."

Christine shook her head. "He's got to be good, or he'd never have lasted six years with them. That's a pretty efficient company, the best in the country."

He said: "I want to slow you down by twelve hours, Christine. Give me time to check him out, but good."

"No."

"Yes."

"I am not sitting around with the merchandise for twelve hours without damn good reasons. And if the pilot is a Trans-Alpes man, if he's been with them for six years, if they gave him to the association . . . then we can have complete confidence in him."

"Six hours, then."

"No. We take off on schedule."

He said urgently: "Give me three hours, Christine. Time to find a pilot I personally know is okay."

"I think you're being overly suspicious . . ."

"You bet I'm suspicious . . ."

"And there's nothing wrong with that . . . If he'd come to Trans-Alpes just a few weeks ago, a few months even, then I wouldn't insist. But I do."

I didn't know it at the time, of course, but later, when

things started getting rough, I was to reflect about it and realize: This was the only mistake I'd ever known her to make. And I had to admit I also didn't want to hang around unnecessarily with twelve million dollars tucked between my legs, knowing that some pretty ruthless people would move heaven and earth, to say nothing of my scrotum, to get at them.

He gave up, at last, but not without another scowl at me. He said: "Now we got two people on the SD I want to know more about. Jesus . . . Okay, if that's the way you want it to be."

He said no more and just stalked off, not a good-bye or a good luck, or anything—not even to Christine. She murmured, sounding very resigned: "He's a hard man to cross . . ."

And four minutes later, we were airborne.

From inside, the plane looked even smaller, just the young kid up front in the pilot's seat, no co-pilot or navigator, and four quite comfortable chairs behind him. He turned and grinned at us as we sat down, and said: "Welcome aboard, Madame, M'sieur . . ." He had freckles, and they somehow reassured me; it didn't make much sense, but freckles and trouble never seem to go hand in hand very much.

I whispered to her: "Aren't we supposed to be hiding something somewhere?"

She looked at me in surprise and then remembered. She said, smiling: "That was for Mr. Armand's benefit. They stay right where they are, Michael."

"Oh." I felt like a new boy at school trying to take in the first lesson and she whispered: "It's such a ridiculously obvious place that no pro is ever going to use it."

We crossed over the huge blue-white *massif* of Mont Blanc just after midnight, a little paper plane tossing around in the dark sky above its eerie, moonlit glow; and by half past one in the morning we could make out the dark blue of the Adriatic Sea and the deeper greens, almost black from up here, of the Croatian forests. There was a white and brilliantly-lit cruise ship down there, a few miles off shore and heading south, to Dubrovnik, perhaps.

And that's where one of the engines started to cough.

I felt the left-side wing go down as we made a turn and headed toward the land.

The pilot with the freckles—the unknown replacement called Colbert—looked back at us and grinned again, and he said cheerfully: "Don't worry, just a little trouble in one engine. We'll put down at Vaganovo and take a look at it. Won't hardly hold us up at all."

The engine stopped coughing and gave out completely. For a moment, there was an alarming unsteadiness in our flight, and I had to resist the temptation to clutch at Christine's arm for assurance. And then he got her on an even keel again, and we began to lose altitude.

Christine said: "*Merde.* There go all our plans for Athens. I don't like being held up for even an hour. Security standing around there and attracting attention . . . " She said again: "*Merde!*"

I said glumly: "There's going to be a Bosnian bandit at the airport, disguised as a customs officer, and the first thing he's going to want is a look into my briefcase . . . "

She didn't answer for a while. Then: "No, perhaps not . . . Vaganovo's a long way from anywhere, not an international stopover. They probably don't even have a customs office there."

"I do have a sharp pocketknife, if you think we should slice through the handles."

There was the hand on my knee again, and it felt good. "No. You can do that, if you have to, right there. I don't quite know how, but in the can or somewhere . . . "

"If Vaganovo has a can . . . "

"I'm sure you won't have to. Let's wait and see."

Fifteen minutes later, Colbert was on the blower asking for lights and spelling out his problem. The runway lights came on, about three of them, and we glided in smoothly without so much as a single bump at touchdown.

Whatever else might have worried Brett Howard, Colbert was a damn good pilot.

Chapter Seven

They couldn't possibly have been nicer at Vaganovo.

I'd never heard of the place, and small wonder; there wasn't really very much to it. It turned out to be a little coastal resort some thirty miles northwest of Split, which is about a hundred miles northwest of Dubrovnik. It was tucked away in a small inlet, surrounded with mountains and forests.

There was indeed a Bosnian bandit-type waiting for us, a sleepy guard with the biggest moustache I'd ever seen, and a carbine over his shoulder, who spoke no known language and wouldn't let us move out of the tiny Arrivals Lounge. He gestured to us in signs that meant: Wait. But he was smiling, so it meant: *Wait please,* and that's what we did.

Colbert had decided to stay right there with the plane, which I thought showed a nice sense of propriety; so Christine and I wandered around and looked at the travel posters there, with no one to make sure we stayed put, except an elderly cleaning woman with a black scarf around her head, who was mopping up the plain concrete floor.

And when he came back he had a very handsome officer in tow, about thirty years old, and looking a bit like Errol Flynn in his earlier days, but darker. The moment he saw Christine he flashed his teeth and began preening himself, and I knew we weren't going to have much trouble.

His English was pretty good, though heavily accented, and he fell down on his words here and there, but he was a thoroughly nice guy, no doubt about it at all. There was a lot of five-o'clock shadow on his face, and he was a little self-conscious about it, but he shook hands with both of us, particularly with Christine, and said: "I understand it was some kind of failing motor, well, never mind it. We have the best mechanics in the country here; and soon, when they come to work, we will take your airplane to pieces and untrouble it. Meanwhile, we will take you to the hotel, really a very good hotel for rich people. You will be our guests; you have money, no?"

I said: "What time do your mechanics come to work?"

He shrugged. "Oh, eight o'clock, nine o'clock . . . but they fix very quickly, very good mechanics, no problem. You are pressed, perhaps?" He corrected himself: "No, you don't say pressed, do you? You are hurried?"

"We'd like to be on our way as soon as possible."

"To Athens?"

"Yes."

"Is a more better place Vaganovo. You like it here. You have the baggage? The trunks?"

I gestured with the briefcase, thinking: Ah well, here it comes . . . "Just a few papers."

"Then is very excellent. I take you to the hotel myself. They don't have no taxis here till nine o'clock too. I telephone already, tell them you come, they have room, good room. Is little bit expensive maybe, but I think this is not consequential, no?"

I said: "You're very kind. What about our passports?"

I saw Christine throw a look at me, but I didn't worry about it.

He gestured broadly. "You are from America, no? From England, perhaps?"

"England, America, France, all over." He waved a hand and said: "Is not necessary. You don't stay too long; we fix your airplane very quickly, you see. You go to hotel, take shower—they got showers there, everything—you sleep little bit, you have breakfast, swim in sea. Your plane ready already." He frowned. "Is correct, ready already? Maybe not, I learn English long time ago. Sometimes I am forgetting."

I said: "It's perfectly correct." I already had my passport out. "Just the entrance stamp. I would like to . . . to boast to my friends that we have visited Vaganovo."

He beamed. "Ah . . . then it will take only little minutes."

He took my passport and Christine's, fumbled around for keys and unlocked an office. While we waited, Christine said, not reprovingly exactly, but asking a question: "Now he will take a note of our names. *Someone* will find out we have been here, when *no one* ought to know."

I said: "Christine, two things. He'll want to get back to you so fast he won't bother with anything but putting his stamp there. Secondly, when you've bummed around foreign countries as much as I have—not just toured them, *bummed* around in them—you'll learn a golden rule: A stamp in your passport means you're in the country legally. And if you're not—you've no idea of the headaches that just might crop up. If anything goes wrong. Of course, in this case, nothing *will* go wrong, will it? But it's nice to obey the unwritten laws of wise travel."

She was looking at me very thoughtfully. She said at last: "Yes. I must admit that in my world the problem has never arisen, but you are right, absolutely right. And I'm glad you insisted."

"You see what a good CA I'm getting to be?"

The young officer was hurrying back with our passports. He said, smiling: "Now you can show all your friends you were in Vaganovo . . . Your pilot? He stay here, no?"

"Yes. He wants to work on the plane, speed things up for when the mechanics get in."

"Ah yes, is good. Then you come with me, please."

He led us out into the cold night air, and held open the door of a little Fiat for Christine, and I said: "This really is very good of you. And we don't even know your name."

He said, clicking heels: "My name is Bunic. Lieutenant Bunic, and anything I can do for you, you tell me, I will be happy." And ten minutes later, we were at the Hotel Sava, and he was driving back to his bed, waving a friendly hand to Christine.

It really was a delightful place, quite small, but very sumptuous indeed—long and low and hugging the beach, with the soft murmur of the Adriatic under a near-full moon shining nicely on it, and a small wooden wharf right outside its door, with two very good-looking yachts tied up there, and a number of smaller boats bobbing in the slight swell. The night was warm and pleasant, the air marvelously fresh and clean, heavily scented with jasmine.

The desk clerk was still a little bit sleepy, but he was extremely affable, and he said, handing over a key: "When the lieutenant phoned, he said you would want the best accommodation we had; so I have given you one of the bungalows on the beach. I'm sure you'll find it very comfortable." His English was immaculate, with the imperceptible accent of the professional hotelier. "I understand you will be leaving us soon, but the room is yours for as long as you like. At this time of the year . . ." He grimaced. "Your baggage?"

"On the plane. Our passports too—does that matter?"

"No. Since you were brought here by the lieutenant, I'm sure it will be all right. The kitchen is closed, but if you would like a few sandwiches?"

I said: "I'll settle for a bottle of white wine."

"Ah. We have an excellent Ljutomer here. I'll put some on ice immediately."

The bungalow was right on the beach, built of adobe and tile, and looking more Spanish than Croatian, with a tiny entrance hall, a good bathroom, a little kitchen alcove with a small stove and a refrigerator in it, and two bedrooms—one large and very luxurious, the other still good but much smaller. There were double beds in them, the bed in the smaller room almost filling it completely. The windows were wide and nicely draped, and they showed that the walls were nearly three feet thick—a nice old-fashioned way of building from the local clay.

Standing in the doorway, I said: "It looks like you have a rather nicer room than I do. Well, that's the way it should be, I suppose."

Her eyes were very calm. "If you would be more comfortable in here . . . I don't mind a small room."

"No. Confining walls will make my misery all the more satisfying."

"But I don't want you to be miserable."

"Besides, the small room is nearer the fridge, and I might need a drink during the night."

"If you'd rather, really . . . I've slept in far worse places. Have you tried the springs?"

"Not yet."

I moved in and pressed them up and down for no reason at all, and then went to the other room and did the same. She waited patiently while I wondered what to do next . . . And then, the desk clerk arrived with the wine in a silver cooler and two very fine glasses on a silver tray. He put them down, beamed at us, and bowed his way out with a discreet sort of silence.

I poured the wine and wondered if I should change the subject; I decided that perhaps I should. I said: "Athens is all screwed up, isn't it? Even if we're only held up for a few hours."

"Yes, I'm afraid it is. And there are some good reasons why we shouldn't call Athens and let them know we're delayed, but I'm afraid we have to. We'll just have to be very, very discreet. It's a blessing they don't know our names here."

She put down her glass and picked up the phone, and when at last someone answered, she said: "How long, please, to get a call through to Athens?" She listened for a while, then: "And how long will that take, do you suppose?" A silence again, a long one. "Thank you. Please let me know as soon as it's open again."

There was a long, drawn-out sigh. "Well, there goes Athens, all screwed up, as you say."

"What happened?"

"A landslide, thirty miles up in the mountains; the lines are down. They're out there now, fixing them. Well, we'll have to make the best of it."

We sat on the edge of the bed in the big room together and sipped our wine, and I said: "Three o'clock in the morning, it's hardly worthwhile even thinking of sleep, is it?"

"A few hours are better than none. I look like hell if I don't get at least some sleep."

"I'm sure you never look like hell."

She went and peered at herself in the mirror, not really wanting to see what was there but just feeling restless and impatient. She turned and looked at me and said: "I hate this sort of thing so much . . . If *someone* is trying to stop me from getting where I'm going . . . it's a challenge, an intellectual exercise, and I can cope with it. But when a goddamn airplane breaks down . . . *Merde* is all I can say. I hate just . . . marking time." She turned back to the mirror again. "And you're wrong, I look awful."

"There's only one bathroom. Will you shower first, or shall I?"

"I don't mind. Whichever you like."

"He said something about a swim in the morning, the dashing young lieutenant. I wonder what the water's like?"

"Sea water is always good. And he wasn't exactly dashing, you know. It was just all that curly hair."

"Oh, so you noticed the curly hair."

"Of course. It was expected of me."

Thinking of his five o'clock shadow, I said: "My God, I don't even have a shaver with me." I ran a hand over my chin and hated it. She came over and sat beside me, and just touched my stubble with the tips of her fingers. "Don't worry about it. My hair's a mess too."

"It's not a mess; it's gorgeous. Everything about you is gorgeous."

She was traveling in a denim suit, long tight pants, and a little short jacket with a very good-looking shirt and a little silk scarf around her throat. The shirt and jacket were open to the air, way down. I could see the curve of her breast, just a little of it, firm and golden colored and very enticing. She turned away and poured herself another glass of wine, and if I thought her hand was unsteady, it was probably wishful thinking. She poured one for me too, and I rather gulped it down, wishing I'd ordered brandy instead; they make a very good one in Yugoslavia, a certain analgesic potency to it.

She put down her glass and lay back on the bed, and then sat up again at once, as though lying down might be interpreted as inviting something she didn't want. I felt a flash of irritation, but it was only momentary. She picked up her glass again and finished it off, just like that, and said: "Well, perhaps I'll use the shower first, if you don't mind."

She went into the bathroom and turned on the shower, and in a moment I heard her lock the door.

I picked up the bottle and took it to the other room, got undressed, and lay down on the bed and waited, thinking very hard—an occupation I usually enjoy—but feeling miserable. And in a little while I heard the door open and she called out: "All clear. It's all yours, Michael."

I stalked in naked dignity to the bathroom—her door almost but not quite closed—and had a long and comforting hot shower, followed by a cold one. I put a towel round my waist—one of those enormous bath sheets they seem to have only in Europe, all sparkling white and crisp to the touch—went to the door of her room, knocked, and opened it without waiting for an answer.

She was lying in bed with the lamp still on, her shoulders bare above the white sheets, with her hair—that strange, not-quite-yellow color—lying very prettily over them; she looked absolutely enchanting. I stood there in the doorway, not taking a single step into her room. I said: "I just wanted to tell you good-night."

Her eyes were very solemn and composed, holding mine unwaveringly. "Good-night, Michael. Sleep well."

"Up fairly early in the morning?"

She nodded. "Yes, I think so."

"I still think I ought to sleep with you."

"No, Michael. No." Her eyes were still on mine.

"Are you sure? Are you absolutely sure?"

"Yes, yes, I am sure." But the eyes were sad now.

"Well . . . Anything you want before I turn in? There's a drop of wine left."

She shook her head slowly, the lovely eyes still not leaving mine. I thought: *Goddammit.* I said: "Well, good-night then. See you in the morning. Pleasant dreams."

I closed the door gently and went to my goddamn bed, lay down under the sheet, and stared up at the darkness—just the moonlight streaming in through the open window and the sound of the surf very gentle and soporific. I wondered if I should get up and go for a moonlight swim, and then thought the hell with it, the hell with all of it.

I turned over on my belly to get some sleep.

The light from her room streamed in as she opened the door, and I looked up and saw her standing there silhouetted against it, her legs long and slim, her body smooth as polished ivory, her hair streaming down over her white breasts, just as she had been in the dream when I'd carried her down that strange, obscure, and somehow frightening shaft in the cliff. For a moment, I wondered if I were dreaming again, and then she was slipping into bed beside me, her body warm and cool at the same time, so exciting to the touch that I found I was trembling.

Her arms were tight around me, and she was crying her heart out, the tears streaming down her face. I wasn't quite sure I knew what it was that made her cry, but I thought that perhaps I could guess at it and come up with an answer that wouldn't be too far off the mark.

I held her tight till the tears had gone, and it was really quite a long time before we made love; we just lay there in each other's arms, listening to the surf. But when we did, she was fierce, demanding and gentle as well—and quite relentless.

As for me, I was in delirium, for all those long, ecstatic hours of the early morning, becoming part of her, time and time again and never feeling satiated. I just wanted more and more and more till time ran out.

I woke up when the sun came streaming through the window and hit the bed, and I thought about John Donne for a while and realized he knew what he was talking about. I climbed out of bed, opened the door, and stood for a moment stretching my limbs and breathing in great gulps of marvelously fresh sea air, the kind we don't get a lot of these days.

It was only a quarter past eight, but there were already a few people out there—a couple waterskiing behind an outboard, three or four others in deck chairs on the sand, a very brown-skinned girl, in two pieces of string, taking a sunbath on a bright blue towel, catching the early rays and making the most of them. She was long and slender and lissome and alone, and I found I wasn't interested in her at all. A middle-aged couple were walking through the sand, one of the hotel staff carrying chairs and an umbrella for them. I closed the door and went to sit on the edge of the bed just looking at Christine, still fast asleep.

As though she knew, even sleeping, that I was watching her, she opened her eyes and smiled at me, and then reached out and took my hand and snuggled deeper into the feather mattress. Another thing you don't see much of these days—feather mattresses. They are about two feet thick, and you practically disappear when you lie down in them—great if you don't suffocate. I eased over to her a little and stroked the long hair where it half covered her breast, and she murmured: "What time is it, Michael?"

I remembered the dream, the same words exactly, and I thought of the severed hand in the silver dish, with her long and golden body beside it on the oak table. I pulled the sheet down gently, the better to look at her, and her hand tightened on mine. I said: "Nearly half-past eight."

She still didn't open her eyes. "Then we'd better call the airport, hadn't we?"

"The lines are down, remember?"

"They may have fixed them by now."

"They were going to call and let us know when that happened."

"Ah yes, I remember." She was still half asleep.

"We'll find a car and run over there as soon as you've had breakfast. It's still early for them."

"Mmmm . . . " I didn't know whether she meant me, or the thought of breakfast. I said: "What do you usually eat at this time of the morning? I feel I'll have to get to know about things like that."

"Yes, you'll have to know. Unless . . . " The eyes opened suddenly, staring at me, very wide and solemn. "Unless that was just . . . just to pass a dull evening. Is that what it was, Michael?"

"It wasn't that, and I'm sure you know it. I hope to God you know it."

"Are you sure, Michael?"

"Sure as I've ever been in my life, of *anything*."

"Don't be afraid of making me feel . . . cheap. I won't, I promise you. I've been . . . bruised before."

"And that doesn't fit your character either."

"Either?" She was puzzled.

"Why were you crying when you came to me last night?"

For a moment, I thought I'd hurt her with the memory of it, but then there was an inexplicable smile spreading over her face. She was almost laughing. "You don't know very much about women, do you? I like that."

"I don't suppose any man does, really. But up till that

moment . . . somehow, I could never have imagined you in tears."

She was suddenly serious again. "Tears don't always mean sadness, Michael. Quite often they're an expression of . . . of relief."

"Relief? From what?"

Those lovely eyes were seeking inspiration in the sheet around her hips. She said slowly: "Everybody knows me as a very tough and competent woman, completely in control of everything, including my emotions, which a legend is not supposed to have. And yes, I know I'm a legend. Perhaps it's my own fault, merely because I'm good at what I do. But in a phrase like that, it's very easy to lose sight of the essential word."

"And the essential word is *woman* . . . "

"Yes, my darling. With all of a woman's sensitivities, and foibles, anl yes, goddammit, weaknesses."

"So why don't you tell me what your weakness is at breakfast time?"

"And I'm very resilient."

"Sausages? Waffles? I hope it's not kippers."

She sighed and sat up, looking superb, and tossed her head to get the hair back over her shoulders. She leaned forward and dumped her clasped hands in her lap, the sheet all bunched up around her waist. She said: "I like a large bowl, not just a cup, of coffee, and hot milk with froth on the top of it, and lots of sugar, and three croissants with plenty of butter, and about half a kilo of strawberry jam."

"My God."

"And you?"

"Coffee, black, no sugar. And a tot of something to get the adrenalin moving. How in hell do you keep that figure, with all that sugar and flour inside you?"

"I use up a lot of energy."

"Yes, I have to agree with you there. Go take a shower, and I'll rustle up breakfast and a car."

"If they don't have strawberry jam, raspberry will do. Or even orange marmalade. In fact, I think I'd like that better this morning. Orange marmalade. The chunky kind."

"And three croissants."

"Make it four. Preferably fresh out of the oven."

"I'll see to it, even if I have to bake them myself."

I put on some clothes, reluctantly, and went over to the main building to talk to the right people. Yes, they had croissants, just out of the oven an hour ago; yes, they had chunky orange marmalade, imported from Scotland; yes, they would be happy to serve the *café au lait* in a large bowl . . .

And yes, they had a car I could rent. It was a strange looking little toy called a *Citroën deux-cheveaux,* just two horsepower, but a car of intriguing character and commendable maneuverability. Not exactly the kind of thing to go drag racing in, but quite singular. And at nine-fifteen we drove over to the airport to find out what Colbert was up to.

He was still out on the field; so someone went to fetch him. Meanwhile we persuaded the airport manager, an elderly man with an enormous paunch, to let us use the airport radio. Christine printed out a short note:

Delayed in Yugoslavia, but all well. Will inform you later. Maintain present arrangements.

She said: "The first thing they'll do is check back. They'll know when we're leaving as soon as we do. And I'm still not convinced we're right in advertising our whereabouts."

"Good people there?"

She made a wiggling gesture with her hand, which means, in Europe, so-so. "This kind of accident works both ways, you know. It's difficult to reschedule all that unobtrusive security, but it can be done. But if Helder's men are waiting for us, they have to hang around for several hours too, and it's infinitely more discomforting for them. Every extra minute they spend on the job means an added chance of detection."

My diamonds had been put back in their very uncomfortable hiding place again; I reflected that during the night they had been tossed unceremoniously onto the floor —twelve million dollars lying around ignominiously. I was still clutching the briefcase, and Christine still had her tote-bag; but the hazard of it never entered my mind. It seemed so safe and peaceful here.

We found Colbert at work on the plane, with half a dozen bearded Bosnian bandits swarming all over it, and I said: "Have you located the trouble?"

He'd found a grease monkey's overalls, and they hung on him like a tent. He said apologetically: "Dirty oil; I just can't imagine how it happened. Got everything all gummed up."

"How long to fix it?"

"I'm afraid there's a lot of cleaning to be done. Two, three more hours. Four at the outside."

Christine said: "Then the question is, do we radio Paris for another plane?"

He thought about if for a while, frowning and wiping grease off his forehead. "If we do that, the chances are that it will get here an hour after we've taken off."

I said: "Is that common sense or professional pride? Suppose it takes all day?"

He grinned cheerfully: "Yes, I suppose professional pride comes into it somewhere. I hate not to finish a job I started. But common sense too. Maximum four hours, and it could be a great deal less. We just can't get a replacement here in that time."

Christine looked at me and I said: "Then we'll go back to the hotel and wait. If the phones aren't back in by then, grab a taxi and come out to the Hotel Sava to pick us up. Will you do that?"

"I'll be glad to. And I'm sorry about the delay. I feel personally responsible."

He was a nice kid, open faced and friendly. I said: "You won't have had any sleep; does that matter a lot?"

He shrugged. "Athens is less than two hours from here, no problem. I'll sleep when I get there." He looked at Christine. "I assure you, Madame, I am not the kind of man to fall asleep at the controls of an aircraft."

She nodded. "I'm sure of it. Then we'll leave you to it."

We drove back in the funny little car, parked it on the gravel strip at the side of the bungalow, went inside and made love again, bought swimsuits in the hotel shop and had a quick swim (she was wonderfully competent in the water), and at last we went into the main building looking for a bar. It was almost exactly midday, and Colbert was just about due.

You can always find the bar easily in any hotel all over the world. Whether it's Croatian, Czech, French, German, or Outer Mongolian, when it comes to a *Bar* it always says just that, in English. We went through a quite spacious lounge, dotted here and there with indoor plants in big ceramic planters. A young boy, about ten years old, all dressed up in a starched white jacket, was going from one to the other and spraying the leaves.

The chairs and sofas were all of leather, shining nicely and looking very comfortable, and there was a big Russian TV set on a stand in one corner, turned off now. The front of the lounge was almost all window overlooking the beach, with attractive gold drapes hanging at the sides, and the ceiling was thick with heavy timber beams—a very satisfying room.

There were half a dozen people sitting around with drinks at their elbows; a young couple, who looked Scandinavian, in tennis shorts; an agreeable-looking young woman in a red halter-top dress with a small boy in tow; a pair of elegantly-trousered legs sticking out from under a newspaper; and two very young girls who were playing backgammon very seriously. A waiter was going from table to table with a silver coffee jug, and cream and sugar on a tray, another was standing idly at the entrance to the bar.

I felt Christine's hand tighten on my arm. Not just an affectionate gesture, but a sudden grip like a steel clamp; I couldn't believe she was so strong. I looked at her, startled, but she was just looking toward the bar, a slight smile on her face that looked a bit phony.

I looked around the room, as unobtrusively as possible —nothing I hadn't already seen. We were close by the carved wooden entrance to the bar, and as we went inside —her hand still incredibly tight on my biceps—I looked back once and saw him.

The man with the elegant pants had lowered his newspaper slightly, and it was Sir Arthur Helder. There was no mistaking, even in this half-glimpse, the fine, aristocratic features, the thick gray hair so carefully styled.

The look on the face that was of sheer triumph—and cruelty. His eyes were on my briefcase.

We had passed through the portal already and were in a long narrow room with the bar down one side, highly-polished teak and gleaming brass, with a very creditable array of bottles lined up on mirrored shelves behind it; a few teak tables and red leather armchairs were arranged down the other side, lit with amber-shaded lamps. It was quite dark after the brilliant sunshine on the beach.

Christine barely checked her movements. She said to the red-jacketed barman: "Is there another way out of here, please? Not through the lounge?"

He had a thick Switzer-Deutsch accent, a cheerful young man with an amused look in his eyes. "Oh yes, Madame. Around the corner there." I felt he wanted to say: *We're ready here for any emergency, like the wrong wives being seen with the wrong husbands,* but there was just an amused and tolerant look in his eyes that said it all.

We hurried on around the corner, and there was a notice that said Rest Rooms in four languages. We went through them and found a way to the outside, and a moment later we were in the brilliant sunshine of the patio at the back.

Christine leaned back against the door, as I closed it, and took a long, shuddering breath. She said furiously: "I should have known it! I should have *guessed*! Did you see him?"

"I saw him. I still don't believe it. For God's sake, how did he get here so fast? How did he ever *know*?"

"He didn't get here as fast as all that. I've a suspicion that he would have been here last night if it hadn't been for all that mud. There were slides all over the place."

"My God, if he'd hit us then . . . Do you realize that . . . How shall I put it? In my extreme urgency, I tossed those damn stones onto the bedroom floor? And Colbert?"

She sounded bitter. "Brett was right. Damn his eyes; he always is. I should have listened to him. Do you have the keys to the car?"

"In the bungalow. But wait a minute . . . "

"Helder arranged it, Michael, you must listen to me! I know about these things!"

"Okay, okay, keep your shirt on . . . "

"I'm sorry." She sighed. "And the telephone too."

"*That* was a landslide . . . "

"I'll bet you anything you like that the landslide was purely fortuitous—that the lines have been cut in half a dozen places, and all of them inaccessible, where it will take them hours to fix. Thank God we still have the car."

"He probably knows that too."

"Yes, I'm sure of it. So what do we do, Michael? This is where we have to think very hard." She said bitterly: "The honeymoon is over, isn't it?"

I said: "No. That will never be over. There are people on the beach, twenty or thirty of them now, all within sight of the car and the bungalow. In public, there's not really much he can do. Not in broad daylight, anyway."

"How much gas do we have in the car?"

"In a tank that size? Must be all of three gallons."

"At least we can reach the highway."

"Where there won't be so many people around to offer us some kind of safety."

She nodded. "But we can't stay here indefinitely either, can we? Can we, Michael?"

"No, we can't. Let's run for it *now*."

She was suddenly furious again. "Christ, I should have guessed it!"

I said: "And so should I. So far, I haven't been much use to you, have I?"

She was still fuming. "And *how*, for God's sake? That engine really did break down; we could hear it!" She calmed down a little. "Well, I suppose that could be faked easily enough, couldn't it?"

"Yes. All he needs to do is pour some sugar in the gasoline."

The anger went quickly; she was smiling again, quite happy now. "And what do you mean, not much use to me? That's a hell of a thing to say. And I did tell you, didn't I? When *someone* is trying to screw me, I don't really mind too much. It's *things* breaking down that I can't cope with. All right, screw Helder too. Come on, let's get the car."

We hurried round the back through the little terraced garden, and she stopped suddenly and said: "I wonder why he let us see him? Does it make sense to you?"

"Yes. It means he wants us to run."

"That's what I thought. He'll know that's the way we'll reason; so he'll know we won't do it. So let's do it."

"And you got a bit screwed up there, too, somewhere."

"We hit the highway as fast as we can and look out for Arthur Helder en route."

We moved on cautiously toward the bungalow. I said, and I was whispering now: "If we can get to the airport, we could call on Lieutenant Bunic for help."

"No. That's one of the unwritten rules. It's far easier to get to a local cop than it is to . . . to a goddamn pilot of Air Trans-Alpes."

"And we don't have a gun between us."

"Let's hope we don't need one."

We reached the bungalow, and I felt like an idiot peering around the corner to make sure the coast was clear, with all those friendly people out there on the beach only a hundred yards away. I was holding onto her hand and feeling conspiratorial, and there was no sign of Arthur Helder or anyone else unfriendly.

I said: "Wait just one moment."

"What is it?"

"Don't go away."

I'm not much of a mechanic, but at least I know how a four-cylinder motor works. I lifted the hood of the ridiculous little car and peered into the engine compartment The ignition wires seemed to be in their right places. I took the cap off the distributor and found the rotor in its proper place. I even looked for carbon-pencil lines down the plugs, but there didn't seem to be any. I found a stick and poked it up the exhaust, but that wasn't blocked by a potato either. And I couldn't find any stray wires, or bundled-up sticks of dynamite, or any other crap which would really have worried me (and which I was looking for, to tell the truth, though I didn't want to admit it, even to myself).

In a moment of panic, I forgot where I'd left the keys. The *deux-cheveaux* had a steering-column lock, and there was just no way of hot-wiring it successfully. Then I remembered—in the drawer of the table by the bed.

I hurried back to Christine, and we sneaked around the corner and went inside, and as she closed the door I hurried to the little table and found the keys. With a sigh of relief, I held them up for Christine to see.

Then a man stepped out of the bathroom. A kid, not much more than twenty years old, very dapper and continental looking, dressed up in the kind of clothes a waterfront thug from Marseilles wears when he wants to impress all the girls.

He was holding a revolver, pointed straight at me, with a very nasty expression on his handsome, gangster's face.

Chapter Eight

I used to know a bit about handguns—not a lot, but enough to survive. And one of the things I learned was that a .22 is not really a gun at all, just a toy that can't hurt you too much. I was taught that you could take half a dozen two-two slugs, if you were even half lucky, and still have enough get-up-and-go left to run a mile—or clobber your assailant over the head if you got aggressive about it.

Not true.

In recent years, the silenced .22 has earned itself a certain notoriety as the new hit gun of the Mafia, and if you think about it, you realize that all it needs is good marksmanship. There are plenty of spots all over the body where an accurately made little hole, twenty-two millimeters across, is going to cause a lot of grief. The stomach is one of them—and there, it doesn't even have to be well aimed.

Somehow, this pretty young man had all the airs of competence. He was quite small, and slim, and he stood on the balls of his feet like a ballet dancer. He had a lot of brown hair held in place with spray, and very bright and alert eyes—a woman's eyes, really—with a straight and delicate nose, full lips, and a cute little cleft in his chin. I thought he must be hell with the ladies. The gun was the fancy one, the long-barreled Bayard, and it was fitted with a silencer.

Those big, fine eyes went to Christine, and then to me again, the gun unwavering, and he said, very quietly: "If anybody makes me nervous . . . Please don't move. I have orders not to kill you unless it becomes necessary."

I said: "Who's moving? Relax. No one's going to hurt

you, punk." His face went white, and Christine said tightly: "Michael, no heroics, please."

I said: "What heroics? If he fires one shot, we're all going to finish up dead, him included. He has to talk first; so let's hear what he has to say."

He said coldly: "Your reasoning is perfect. Now, drop your briefcase and kick it over here. Take off your jacket and drop it on the ground. Put your hands on your head and turn around slowly."

"In that order? Okay." I did as I was told, and I could feel his eyes on me as I turned, studying the contours. I said: "I don't have a gun. What the hell do you think I am, for Christ's sake?"

I was facing him again, and he said to Christine: "And you, Madame, empty your bag on the floor and drop it."

She opened up the heavy brass clips that fastened it, turned it upside down, and all the stuff fell out; I was surprised to see she'd added one more thing to it—a little chrome-plated pistol. He said: "Kick the gun over here, please."

Christine's foot shot out and sent it spinning over to him. It finished up neatly beside the briefcase, right at his feet, and he said politely: "Thank you. Now, if you will both lie down on the bed, on your backs."

Have you ever tried to get up off—or rather out of—a feather mattress in a hurry? He was way across the room, a very sensible place to be, but he was making doubly sure. It would have taken an eternity to get up and at him, even if I'd felt like risking it, which I didn't in the least.

We lay down side by side, and when we were good and settled in, he bent down and picked up the pistol, flipped out the clip with one hand like an expert, slid it home again, and dropped the gun into his hip pocket.

He picked up the briefcase, and he was smiling now. He said quietly: "I need both hands and both eyes for this, don't I? If you'd like to see how fast you can move . . ." He shrugged.

He put the tab of the zipper in his teeth and tugged at it, and I thought: *Ha! Just a little harder and you're going to get a few cavities to worry about . . .*

But he *knew*. He was tugging at it quite gently, and in a moment he said: "What is it, the Perelman look?"

No one answered him, and he said: "Oh well. And what's the charge in it?"

Christine said, very offhand: "Indelible dye. They won't let us use explosives any more."

"Yes, that's right, isn't it? The association's been getting into trouble over that lately. Well, it's nice to know you don't really want to hurt anyone."

He put the gun down now, close beside him on the little table there, looking at me with a kind of mockery, as though daring me to start moving; nothing was further from my mind. He ran his delicate hands—a woman's hands too—over the smooth leather, and smiled that smug smile again, and said: "What is it, fulminate of mercury? Or sodium nitrate?"

"We stick to the regulations; we have to. It's just a dye."

"With a wire running to it? Really, Madame."

He put the briefcase on the table, picked up the gun again, took some lengths of cord from his pocket, and tossed them onto the bed. He said: "You can turn over onto your stomach now, Mr. Benasque. Put your hands behind your back, with your thumbs together, and your little fingers together."

I didn't move, and Christine said urgently: "Please Michael . . . "

I turned over and heard him say: "Thumbs and little fingers, Madame—a clove hitch if you know how to make one. If not, any kind of knot will do as long as it's tight. Then the ankles."

I could feel her hands at work, and I heard him say: "Tighter, or I will be forced to find some other way to incapacitate him."

The ropes were biting into me, and he was chatting away without a care in the world: "Perhaps I should tell you that my own inclination was to kill you both, the easiest way in the long run. But it seems that . . . someone was in awe of the association's wrath. They'll hunt you down, he told me. . . . " I could almost hear the shrug. "So, we have to behave like schoolchildren. And it could have been so simple."

I rolled over half onto one side to see what he was up to. He had lit a cigarette, and the briefcase was there beside him on the table; the gun still in his hand. He said pleasantly: "Now, if you would please step over here, Madame? Please?"

I saw that the gun was aimed at her stomach again, and I had a horrible moment of terror. I started struggling like a maniac, but all he did was throw me a casual glance and then look back at her. She was moving toward him, hesitantly, and there was a look on her face that said she didn't know what was going to happen now. I could see her tensing herself. For what? I didn't know.

As she reached him and stopped, standing there with her head tilted back a little, her mouth half open, her eyes veiled, he made a movement so fast that I hardly saw it. He brought up his left fist and hit her hard on the side of the head, so hard that I imagined I heard the bone crack. It was an expert, cruelly efficient blow, and it could have only one result; she dropped to the ground like a log and lay still, and I struggled desperately, without doing any good at all.

And then he was moving over to me, dropping some more lengths of that damned cord onto the bed. He took hold of my hair and yanked up my head and said: "I do not much like to be called a punk."

He hit me just once, the same kind of a blow, and there were stars exploding in my head, pounding and throbbing like five-pound hammers on iron anvils, and he added some knots of his own to my wrists, put a cord around my neck and fastened it to the bed-posts, then roped my upper arms and my thighs together. When he was done, I could hardly move an inch, and the stars were still blasting away furiously. It was agony. There's no other word for it.

I squinted sideways and saw him pick Christine up. He dropped her down beside me and pulled a roll of adhesive tape from his pocket, prepared for everything like a cute little Rover cub. He tied her wrists and ankles, rolled me over onto my back, rolled her over on top of me, and wound that goddamn tape around our necks and our legs. It was the aluminum-coated cloth tape that sticks anything to anything, like the ad says, and when we were firmly fastened together, he stuck it over our mouths too —a double thickness of it.

I could hardly breathe, much less see what was going on. But through the stars, changing colors but not intensity now, I caught a glimpse of him moving the phone well away from the bed—as if we could have reached it! —and picking up the briefcase. He sauntered out of the room, and I heard the door close.

I couldn't move a muscle without tearing my throat out and worrying about doing the same to her too. So I lay still, with Christine on top of me, breast to breast and belly to belly, and thought hard and long—and got absolutely nowhere.

It was obvious that neither of us was going to move until someone came and found us.

Christine came round about half an hour later, and I heard her trying to mumble through two thicknesses of tape. I mumbled back at her, and she sized up the situation in five seconds flat and simply laid her face on mine and closed her eyes.

It was late afternoon before they found us.

I heard voices outside the door, hushed but quite angry —a language I thought would be Croatian, a lot of gutturals in it—a man, and a woman, and then another man as well. We both tried to make noises, but they didn't seem to be very loud.

There was a hesitant knock on the door, and then a louder one. I tried wiggling my body in the hope that the bed would make some sort of noise, but I only succeeded in tearing six inches of skin off my throat. Christine was making a high, whining sound through her nose; and it sounded awful, but at least it *sounded;* so I did the same, and it must have given the impression of a couple of warthogs mating.

Then, thank God, I heard the key in the lock and it opened, and Lieutenant Bunic was there, with the manager and one of the hotel maids behind him. Bunic was across the room in a flash, a very lethal-looking switchblade in his hand, cutting us free. And the manager, stammering, was holding up a card that said: Do Not Disturb in four languages, and saying lamely: "It was on the door; I didn't want to open it. . . ."

That damned sealing tape was the devil to get off, seeming to pull great strips of flesh with it. I was glad I didn't have a moustache; it must have been hell for Christine, and there was a terrible bruise on the side of her face where he'd hit her so savagely.

They were all waiting around to know what had happened, but I went and found a facecloth and some ice cubes, and laid it all on her face first, and Bunic shooed the others out and said: "It would be absurd, I think, to ask if you are all right, no? But are you hurt badly?"

Christine shook her head. "Nothing time won't cure."

The improvised ice bag fell off, and I put it carefully back in place again and said: "Just lie still, my darling."

She nodded, and I told Bunic: "A young Frenchman, with a gun, a long sleeve on the barrel . . . "

"A silencer."

"Yes, I thought it might be that. About twenty-three years old . . . "

"What kind of gun, do you know that?"

"No. I don't really know about guns, I'm just a journalist. He was very good looking, dark hair and eyes, a cleft in the chin . . . "

"What is *cleft*, please?"

I indicated: "A line here. He wore dark trousers, a blue sweater, a dark-blue blazer with silver buttons on it . . . "

He was nodding, and I broke off. He said: "Yes, that is the man."

There was a ray of hope there. "You saw him?"

"The plane was fully unbroken at ten o'clock, shortly after I am told you returned to the hotel. And at eleven-thirty, the man you have described came to the airport with the . . . the briefcase you had been carrying, and I thought: ah, a messenger from the charming lady and gentleman from America and everywhere else. And I took no notice, and I am guilty for it. While I was drinking my coffee a little minutes after, the airplane went by taxi to the runway, and I thought—with much pleasure, you understand, because I knew you were pressed—I thought, they make the testing now, and soon they will send to the hotel a message that all is well. But not so. The airplane lifted itself on its wings, without the clearance, and was gone. There was still no telephone because of the falling land; so I took my little Fiat, and I come here to see what is happening. It is a very serious offense for an airplane to take off without the clearance, you understand, and I was sure that there was some . . . some monkey affairs being performed."

"And very lucky you did, lieutenant. We could have been here all day."

He began to smile. "In this hotel, M'sieur, with a Do Not Disturb sign on the door, it could have been a week; it is a hotel very discreet."

The manager was peeking in, and he said, hesitantly: "I thought . . . I thought a steak would be the best thing."

He came in, and he was carrying a silver tray with a china plate on it, and the biggest and most luscious-looking steak I had ever seen. I wanted to say: You forgot the parsley, but said instead: "Ah yes, the best cure in the world for a black eye; the hell with all your medicines, and I thank you for it."

I took it from him, removed the ice bag, and laid the steak carefully over that livid bruise. Christine sighed and held my hand.

The lieutenant said: "Is it permitted to know what was in the stolen briefcase, M'sieur?"

I said: "I'm afraid he didn't get very much for his trouble. Just some personal papers, worthless to anyone else. But perhaps, since it was locked, he thought it might contain something more valuable. After all, it was all the baggage we were carrying."

It seemed to satisfy him. He said: "We are, of course, tracking the plane, is that the word? On radar. Unhappily, we are at the beach here, and in very little minutes he will be out of our territory. He was flying to the west, in the way of Italy; so we have telephoned to the Italian authorities."

The manager was still hovering, and Bunic spoke to him in Croatian, quite sharply, but he persisted and said awkwardly: "I assume, M'sieur, that you will naturally hold the hotel responsible for this . . . this *contretemps*? Shall we be hearing from your lawyers?"

Christine answered for me: "No, M'sieur. I'd as soon forget the whole thing. There will be no attempt to sue you."

"But the press, no doubt . . ."

"It will not find its way into the papers either."

"A thousand thanks, Madame. You are most generous. It could do irreparable damage to a fine hotel."

"Please think no more of it."

He beamed his way out, and I said to Bunic: "And I can't thank you enough, lieutenant. Without your perspicacity, we'd probably have been dead."

He was frowning: "Perspi . . . ?"

"Perspicacity. A new word for you? Your English is really excellent."

"And I am liking always new words. It means?"

"A sharp understanding."

"Please, if you would be so kind for the spelling." He had his notebook out already, and I spelled it for him, and he said: "Yes, a policeman must always be perspicacious."

There was a problem on my mind. I was beginning to like this young man very much, and he'd come to our rescue soon after we had gratuitously decided he wasn't to be trusted.

I said carefully: "Don't misunderstand me, lieutenant, but I feel we owe you our lives. It's not possible, ever, to put a price on a man's life, but . . . I would like to reward you personally, if you will allow me to."

He was already protesting: "M'sieur, I cannot accept a reward for doing my duty."

We argued for an interminable length of time, and at last I said: "It's an impolite question, but how much does a policeman earn in this part of the world?"

He said sadly: "In a year . . . a little more than you pay for one week at this hotel. But even so . . ."

I won out finally. He agreed that if he were to share it with his men, perhaps it would be all right. I gave him a fat bundle of Harry Slewsey's bills, and said: "There's not enough money in the world to take us out of your debt. And I propose to write to the police commission in Belgrade, mentioning your name, and asking them to thank you on my behalf."

Now he was happier. He stood up and saluted, and said: "Then if you will excuse me . . . Madame, M'sieur."

Christine took his hand and smiled, and he melted, and she said: "All I can do is thank you, Lieutenant Bunic."

When he had gone, it occurred to me there was an urgent problem to attend to. I said: "All right, that little bastard is probably landing in Italy right now. What happens when the police catch him and try to get my briefcase open? Some poor cop is going to get his hand blown off."

She shook her head. "No problem, Michael. There's not a hope in hell he'll be caught. He'll fly in under the radar and be gone before they even know he arrived. Take my word for it."

She seemed absolutely sure, so I did.

And as she had said long ago, it was always a question of counting the hours and the minutes.

She looked at her watch and said: "The plane took off at eleven thirty; they would have landed in Italy soon after twelve. Let's guess at a half hour, perhaps much more, for them to get to some sort of safe house, though they might have landed right beside it, up in the mountains somewhere. All right, some time after twelve. I don't believe they can get that case open, without detonating it, in less than an hour. One o'clock. Armand said it would take them half a day, even with good equipment, to find out they've got the decoys. Let's call it three hours. Four o'clock. And they'll need at least two hours to get back here and pick up the trail again. . . ."

"A phone call will do that in five minutes."

"If Helder is still here. But he won't be."

I thought about it. "All right, I agree. That makes it . . . let's say by half-past five or six; they're hot on the trail again. It's now nearly half-past four. We've got a head start of one and a half hours."

She nodded. "That should be enough if we leave at once. Are you up to driving?"

"My God, are you up to being driven?"

"Yes, I'm fine. Really, Michael, I am."

I took a few moments out to kiss her and went off to arrange things with the manager. I told him that since our plane had disappeared, we thought we'd drive around the countryside for a day or two, and I rented the car for a week. He was so delighted at not being sued that he wouldn't let me pay any bills and insisted on presenting me with a huge picnic basket for our journey—fifteen wasted minutes while the chef made sandwiches, but what could I do?

I got a good map of the area and gave the staff some money so that it wouldn't all be a total loss for them, and twenty minutes later were were pushing the little toy car for all it was worth over the dirt road that joined the mountain highway a little further up. The tiny tank was full of gas now, from a drum in the hotel garage—enough to last forever.

Christine, beside me, was studying the map intently. "Stay on Highway 3 till we cross the river. Then turn left at the first intersection, the road to Knin. There's a secondary airport there; so we can surely pick up a flight to Sarajevo, or Zagreb, or even Skopje. From there, it will be easy to find a plane to Athens."

"Should we stop off and call them?"

"Let's keep moving. When we find out about a plane."

She put her hand on my knee again and leaned over and kissed me. "I'm glad you got our passports stamped. There would have been problems. For all its charm, this is still a kind of . . . totalitarian state. It would not be easy to leave it if they didn't know how we got into it."

"People who bum their way around know all the tricks."

Another kiss.

The little car, my foot on the floor, was doing a little over sixty miles an hour on a road that was less than perfect. But it stuck to the gravel like a leech, and its front-wheel drive meant we didn't have to slow down even for the most dangerous hairpin bends.

There were forested mountains all around us now, with a deep, deep drop of a chasm below us on the left, a river rushing furiously by down there, a long slim waterfall. We bounced along over the ruts, crossed a stream over a wide wooden log bridge, and climbed higher and higher, hemmed in by hazel and pine trees, with narrow tracks leading through them here and there. Where to, I wondered?

We passed another waterfall, a huge one, with a rainbow arched across it, and Christine opened up the picnic basket. We ate some delicious sandwiches of cold roast beef on French bread still warm from the oven; it was all very rare and bloody, the way I like it, and I thought of the steak she had lain there with, pressed to her face, and I said: "How's the bruise coming along?"

She touched it gingerly. "It will look worse, and feel a lot better, tomorrow."

"The bastard. Nothing I'd like better than to catch up with him, gun or no gun."

"Can you manage a glass of wine while you drive?"

"You mean he gave us glasses too?"

"Nice ones, the perfect picnic basket. Or would it be easier to drink out of the bottle?"

"Not if it's good."

She sipped it, out of the bottle. "It's not bad at all."

"Then I'll have a glass."

It was impossible to drink with the car bouncing all over the place. Everything was leaving the ground except the wheels, glued there—one hell of a good car. But I got some of it down.

The road was winding high above us still, and we climbed it valiantly in second gear, and when we came to the top, the view was absolutely unbelievable. There were tall, fresh-looking trees around us, a dozen different kinds, another stream by the side of the road with another log bridge over it, an abandoned ox cart there with its shafts on the ground. Through the breaks in the trees, the mountains rolled on and on, and there was a wide green valley full of planted fields and tiny hamlets, and barns weathered to a lovely gray patina, and little black specks that were horses and cattle in the meadows.

We began to drop down the other side, a very steep hill indeed, a winding one with hairpin bends everywhere, and the great deep gorge dropping down perilously close beside us, first on the right and then on the left. There was a pretty little cottage further down the hill, half hidden by dense forest, a huge granite rock beside it, and yellow creepers all over its walls; it looked charming.

As we passed it—another stream, another log bridge—I saw that there was a very incongruous car standing by the open five-barred gate that led to it: A white convertible Bentley. There was a sudden lump in my throat.

Christine shouted: "Go, Michael, go . . . !"

I put my foot to the floor and coaxed another three miles an hour out of the little engine, and on the down-grade the speedo needle came to a rest against its maximum, which wasn't exactly fast. The road was winding crazily, the trees close by on both sides. I shouted: "Can we be sure?"

She shouted back: "For God's sake, Michael, how many white convertible Bentleys are there in this part of the world? It's Helder's car; it can't be anything else!" She had squirmed round in her seat and was looking through the rear window. "And here he comes. Oh God . . . "

I saw it in the rearview mirror, turning onto the road a mile or so behind us. I yelled at her: "Hang on tight and keep your fingers crossed." I coaxed another few miles an hour out of the two horses.

She stared: "You're not going to try and race a Bentley . . . in *this*?"

"That's exactly what I'm going to do. I've got front-wheel drive and a lot less width than he has. We can go places he can't even look at. Watch for a likely-looking track, either side, up or down; I don't give a damn."

We were yelling at each other over the furious sound of the little motor, banging away like Hephaestus with all his anvils lined up . . . We were on the steep downslope and probably hitting seventy-five or more, though the speedo couldn't tell me that; we were overrunning the needle.

The Bentley was almost alongside us when Christine yelled: "There . . . !"

It was hardly more than a tunnel, but the only choice we had, and I swung the wheel hard-over, rammed the little car into it, and crashed through some shrubbery that didn't begin to stop us. Then the path dropped down with alarming suddenness, and we bumped down over it and up a steep bank again, the front wheels pulling us over, and down again so sharply that we almost stood the car on its nose . . . But the tires stayed where they were supposed to stay, right down there in the mud, gripping with the surefootedness of a mountain goat.

Christine had still been holding the opened bottle of wine, and it was under my feet somewhere, spilling all over the place, and she was on her knees, her backside still on the seat, one leg stuck out at an awkward angle as she tried to retrieve it and scoop up the broken pieces of glass; it's not really the kind of car for gymnastics. She tossed the bits and pieces and the bottle into the back and slewed round and looked behind us and said, awed: "My God, did we come from up there?"

"And that's where he is still, wondering how he's ever going to catch us on foot. Because there's no way he can get his car down here."

She sighed. It was either relief or frustration. "And we'll never get back up there again either."

"Who wants to? This track has to lead somewhere."

It did.

It led us into a field of cattle that stared morosely at us as we lumbered along, slower now, giving the gutsy little engine a chance to cool off and get its breath. We came to an old-fashioned stile, two crosspieces of adze-cut lumber straddling the fence, and we followed the railing till we found an open gate, and went across a ploughed field, and I said: "I'd like to see him try this in a Bentley . . . "

Another wide-open meadow, and another forest ahead of us, and we found a footpath and drove along it, practically bulldozing the car in among the trees. And when we were four miles or more from the road, I rammed us in among some hazel saplings, and switched off, and we got out to stretch our cramped limbs.

Christine stood for a moment staring up at the mountain we had so dramatically left behind us. It was a long, long way off, and when she said: "Are we safe? Have we lost him?" I looked at the forest that lay between us and him, at the slope of the mountain that was more of a cliff than anything else, and marveled that we had made it at all in one piece. I said: "We've lost him; so let's do some thinking."

We lay down on the wet moss, with the map between us, and she ran a finger over it and said: "Here, this is where we are. No road within six miles of us except the one we left, and that curves down the mountain into the valley on the other side."

"Okay, we know where we are. Now tell me how come Helder knew we were coming this way?"

She said promptly: "He didn't. But he knew we had to make for an airport. The nearest one is at a little village here, called Biograd, only twenty miles up the coast from the hotel. That would be the logical place for us to go, so he'd rule it out at once, though he's almost certainly got a man on that road too. That leaves only Knin, where we were headed. Next question."

"He hasn't had time to get the briefcase open, or even if he has, he certainly hasn't had time to find out he's got paste. It's supposed to take him half a day to find that out, even with good equipment, which he can hardly be carrying around in the back of a Bentley."

She said thoughtfully: "That had me worried too. But I came up with a thought, no, two thoughts. First of all, he's going for the decoys too, remember? And second, he may just have decided that the overdressed little Frenchman got what he came for a little too easily. I was always aware of that, and . . . "

She broke off and sighed. "At one point, it seemed I should resist him more, but I thought that . . . if I encouraged you to fight over it . . . you might have been killed. So, I didn't."

We held hands for a while and said nothing; it seemed to make sense. I said at last: "So he's still just guessing."

"He will be until he's absolutely sure he's got the right stones."

"We have to agree that the briefcase was pretty damn obvious."

"No. Not in view of the fact that he's supposed to be watching the girl more than he is me. We *have* to be a little obvious; *we're* supposed to be the decoy, leading him off the track. What worries me is . . . how did he find out that the girl is not me? That really worries the hell out of me."

"Has he ever seen you, personally?"

"No, but he's bound to have photographs. Except that they won't be very good, telephoto sneak shots, that kind of thing. I avoid photographers like the plague, every courier does; they're a disaster for us."

"So maybe he still thinks you're the girl, and she's . . . Goddammit, doesn't she have a name?"

She was smiling up at the blue sky and the dark green treetops. "In the trade, she's known as "The Girl." But her name is Marie Abelard. And almost no one knows that."

"Almost no one in this business knows almost nothing. If you know what I mean."

"That the essence of my trade, Michael. Let them know nothing. But if they do find out something, make sure it's the *wrong* thing."

"We really do have to play some chess one day. Are you any good?"

"Yes, I am." She said, a little tartly, I thought: "As a matter of fact, I'm a Grand Master."

"Too good for me. And what about Arthur Helder? Is that really him up there? Or does he have a double too?"

"All Helder has working for him is a small army of savage young bastards like that one."

"Okay. What do we do now?"

She rolled over and looked at the map again, and I could almost hear the wheels turning over in her mind. She said, frowning: "We're safe here, I'm sure; so maybe we should stay here forever. . . ."

"Maybe that's not a bad idea, at that."

She ran a finger over the map. "There's only one way out of this little valley, this track here that joins the road . . . here. A village there called Drnis. From there, we still don't have too much of a choice; this country isn't exactly oversupplied with roads. We're in a trap, Michael."

"Abandon the car and walk out of it? Through the forest to . . . to somewhere?"

"I don't know. All I know is, Arthur Helder is bound to be waiting for us in Drnis. It's the only possible route out."

I said: "How sure are you about that, Christine?"

"I'm trying to read his mind. I'm pretty sure."

"Then we get up onto the main road again and take it from there."

"Back the way we came? We'll never get up there!"

"This little car will climb the side of a barn if you really want it to. We can make it."

She seemed enormously relieved. We got back aboard, and I pointed the car's nose in the right direction, and we just went, crawling along in low gear the moment we hit that horrendous slope. It had taken us no more than twenty minutes or so to get down to our hiding place, and it took us over an hour and a half to get back up again. But get back up we did.

There was just the final barrier, a deep ditch near the edge of the road that we'd jumped over at speed going down. Going up at two or three miles an hour it was more of a barrier, and the front wheels were almost on the road itself when the back end got stuck on a damned great rock, in there under the back axle. But the road, at least, was empty of Bentleys.

I got the jack out and started to use it, and Christine said suddenly, her voice hushed: "Michael . . . "

Kneeling in the mud, I looked up. A huge, darkly-bearded man in the dress of the local peasants, more or less, was stepping out from under cover on the other side of the road, slipping easily down a big gray boulder of granite that was all covered over with purple creeper. He had a machine pistol slung over his shoulder.

He must have been about six foot three, with a chest on him like a beer barrel, and he wore a dark khaki jacket and black woollen trousers, with a wide leather belt over everything, three hand grenades hanging from it. He carried two bandoliers, one of scruffy leather and one of cloth, and had a sheath knife about a foot long strapped to his boot. He looked like a rather wild pirate out of a Hollywood movie.

They still have bandits in these mountains, though they're called guerrillas nowadays, and my incongruous thought was: I wonder if he speaks a civilized language?

He just stood there, looking at us, and then he reached down to the trigger and fired two shots into the air, and I knew we were in trouble.

I took hold of Christine's hand, wondering if we could perhaps just sort of fall backward into the forest and try for a rapid getaway, though the chances didn't look too good; he was a mountain man.

I hardly saw the movement, it was so fast; the gun was suddenly pointing straight at us, and there was a look on his face that clearly said: Don't fool around. So we didn't.

We just stood there like idiots, waiting. And five minutes later the Bentley came silently round the bend in the road and pulled to a stop close by.

Sir Arthur Helder pushed open the door and stepped out.

Chapter Nine

At first, he was disarming, more than anything else.

He wasn't smiling or visibly angry; he just looked a little worried, as though he felt solicitous about our condition. He was staring at the mud all over my pants, and he said: "My, we are in a mess, aren't we? That was a neat maneuver, Mr. Benasque, and I take my hat off to you."

He switched his look to Christine, and said—and he was very courteous now: "I've long wanted to meet you, Madame Andress, I just wish it could have been under happier circumstances. But now that it's happened, I can't tell you how delighted I am. I'm Arthur Helder. But you know that, of course."

She said politely: "Sir Arthur . . . " We could have been making polite introductions at a cocktail party.

"Yes . . . And I've got to decide whether you really are Christine Andress, or just the girl. I've never been able to get a really good photograph of either of you. It's a little confusing to me that you've got Mr. Benasque traveling with you, because he's not a professional CA at all, is he?"

She said tartly: "If you know that much, Sir Arthur, you must know who I am."

He shook his head: "No, not really. The major source of my information is a very good source, except that it plays tricks on its own once in a while. Well, we'll find out, won't we? I have to ask you to come for a ride with me; would you mind very much?"

He was opening the doors of the Bentley, and he said: "I'd like for you to drive, Mr. Benasque, with Madame Andress beside you, and I'll sit in the back with Bluebeard here. Don't try to do anything silly, because he's itching to shoot somebody, and we can't allow that yet. He thinks I'm an officer from Scotland Yard working with the local police, and he thinks you two are high-priced smugglers, running diamonds. He wouldn't mind that in the least, except anything smuggled in these mountains belongs to him; that's his trade."

We all got in the car, and he said: "Do drive carefully, won't you? It's bad enough you have to get mud all over my upholstery; I don't like my car mistreated . . . "

Nobody spoke all the way back to the pretty little cottage, and when we got there, Bluebeard stepped out of the back seat, without even bothering about the door, and opened the gate for us, and we drove through and were shown into the house.

It was an ordinary peasant cottage, larger than most, with a huge sugarloaf stove built of ceramic tiles in one corner, about six feet square, with a wooden bench running around it to warm up the folks in the cold weather, and a pile of down comforters, the bed, on top of it. There was a tiny iron grill in the bottom, through which a handful of hazel roots would be smoldering, all day and all night, giving out a gentle warmth and providing enough oven heat for the day's supply of bread and meat. I've always wanted one of those stoves myself; they're great.

The walls were plastered and whitewashed, and there was a long pine table, scrubbed scrupulously clean, with benches beside it; an enormous and very beautiful dresser full of china; a stand in one corner with a jar of water on it; a large cupboard, also of pine; a deeply-stuffed sofa and two huge armchairs with sheepskins thrown over them; a big stone fireplace with a pile of logs beside it; a hand axe driven into one of them; and a very efficient-looking shortwave radio.

Bluebeard locked the door and put the key in his pocket, took up his post in one corner of the room, in a rocking chair, and just looked at us hard, and Helder said: "I understand neither of you has a gun, but I have to be sure. Just hold your hands out to your sides, Mr. Benasque."

He patted me under the armpits, and in the small of my back, and ran his hands carefully down the outsides of my legs, paying great attention to the area around the ankles.

He ran them just as carefully up the insides of my legs, and I was certain he was going to find what he wasn't even looking for, just like that . . . But he stopped with commendable delicacy just as the side of his hand hit my testicles, and then he said: "All right, go and sit on the sofa. Madame . . . perhaps I should apologize. I'm sure you realize it's necessary."

I sat down and watched him go to work on Christine—exactly the same procedure, patting her carefully all over and not missing a thing.

He was satisfied at last that neither of us was armed. He told her to sit next to me and said: "Not as comfortable a place as I would like, but we can't be too choosy, can we? I've rented this place for a while, and it was the best I could find in the right neighborhood. Would you care for something to drink? There's some rather harsh slivovitz in the cupboard there."

I shook my head, and Christine said: "I'd rather know what you propose to do with us."

He shrugged. "It's all in your own hands. Where are the diamonds?"

Christine said calmly: "You have them."

"The briefcase? Yes, it's a possibility, isn't it?"

"And there's another possibility, of course."

"Oh? What's that?"

"That they've already been delivered by the real Christine Andress to Athens."

He laughed. "Unhappily that's a ploy that's never going to work. The last I heard from Athens was that Vasileos is running around like a bear with a sore head. Not at all the way a man would behave who's just had twelve million dollars' worth of diamonds delivered to him. He's behaving like a madman, out of his mind with worry. And you might like to know that I discounted that Monday morning delivery altogether; I just didn't want to waste any time on it at all."

She said politely: "No? What a pity, Sir Arthur. Your Intelligence Service is falling apart, isn't it?"

He shook his head, and he was greatly amused. "No. The moment the National Guard got into the act, I knew it was just a red herring. I *know* that the government turned you down, so what's the Guard doing there? I'll tell you what they're doing there; they're holding out a carrot for me to snap at. Fortunately, I don't like carrots, and what's Mr. Benasque doing on this operation?"

"He is a journalist."

"I know that."

"He wants a story."

"I assumed that too. But the association doesn't easily get talked into that kind of thing. A journalist along on a delivery? It doesn't make sense."

"Then it should be proof enough for you that I am not making the delivery. That Christine is."

They were just fencing with each other, but I could sense a kind of angry impatience under his veneer of charm. Sooner or later, he was going to lose his temper; but not yet, and I pushed it home for him. I said: "Actually, I really wanted to go along on the real delivery. They practically threw me out of their office."

He looked at me very thoughtfully for a moment, and then back to Christine. He was getting hesitant now, wondering if he were on the wrong track after all.

I said: "Tell me how you knew we'd be on that road? We didn't even know ourselves."

That cold look again: "I just used my brains, if it's any of your damn business."

Back to Christine, more patient now: "All right, let's rationalize. I don't believe you'd carry them in a shoulder-tote, though we'll find out soon enough, and there aren't many other places they could be, are there? You remember that Polish courier, what was his name?"

"Branovski."

"Yes, Branovski."

He reached out a hand to Christine and said: "The bag, please." She gave it to him without a word, and he tipped everything out onto the table and examined the bag minutely, feeling the leather and the lining, looking closely at the heavy brass furnishings on it. He said, still working on it: "Branovski always had a broken arm, or a leg, and the stones were always in the cast—a very foolish man. He came to a sticky end, didn't he?"

"I know they murdered him."

"Yes, but that wasn't my operation. I would have just had both his legs broken to teach him to be more imaginative; there's nothing worse than hunting an idiot. Besides, he didn't ever carry my sort of stones."

He walked over to where Bluebeard was stolidly sitting, took the knife out of its sheath, and went back to perch himself on the table. He pried off the brass fittings and let them drop, and said: "And Charlie Fenner, he used to swallow them, what a disgusting business that must have been."

He gave up on the tote and examined the little compact, and said: "Then there's Hazel Rathbone, that crazy American woman. You know her?"

Christine's voice was very tight. "I know her."

"When she's carrying just a couple of stones or so, you know where she always hides them?"

"I'd rather not talk about it, if you don't mind."

"It must be very painful for her."

He gave up on the compact and picked up the hairbrush and peered at it. He said: "I don't have a nurse available, Madame Andress, not even a doctor."

"I told you, I'm not Madame Andress."

He was enormously interested in the hairbrush. He held it up sideways and looked at it, and said: "Nearly an inch thick, hand-carved rosewood, beautifully made, a craftsman. How do I get the back off?"

"It doesn't come off. It's just a brush."

"We'll see."

He looked at Christine long and thoughtfully. He said, finally: "It's going to embarrass me a lot more than it is you, you know. I haven't played doctor since I was ten years old. I was a very nasty little boy. Even stripping you both naked is going to discomfort me a little. And what about you, Mr. Benasque? You're happy to share her bed, but you don't mind sitting by and watching the indelicate things I have to do with her?"

It was the opportunity I'd been waiting for and was sure would never come. But I had to play it carefully. I said, as angrily as I could: "You lay a hand on her, Helder, and one way or another I'm going to kill you. In spite of your goddamn goon there."

He said sourly: "Let's put that down to wishful thinking, Mr. Benasque. Just make it easy for me, and for both of you. Tell me where they are."

"Go to hell, Helder."

He looked at me for a moment, and said to Bluebeard, in Italian: "Beat up on him, just a little."

He was grinning like a maniac, the outsized oaf. He put down his gun (which Arthur Helder promptly picked up) and came over to me. He took hold of the cloth at the front of my jacket, shirt, and half of my chest as well, picked me up, and rammed a fist into my gut so hard that it literally sent me sprawling across the floor to finish up against the wall without an atom of breath in my body. I've been hit once or twice before, but I just couldn't believe that a single blow could be so powerful. I lay there gasping, and then vomited, and I heard Christine scream.

Out of the corner of my eye, I saw through the haze that she had rushed at Helder and was clawing at him savagely. They were the claws Harry had mentioned, in full measure. She was raking them down his face and drawing blood, and somehow also contriving to grab at the gun and wrestle it away from him. He hit her once in the stomach, and when she doubled up, he pulled the gun out of her grasp, and dropped it to the floor and put a solid foot on it for safety, and then took hold of a handful of her hair and yanked her head up quite savagely. He had a forearm over her throat and was pulling it in tight with his other hand, and she just hung there, her screaming cut off now, and her lovely face turning purple . . .

I could hardly move, but I saw the big sonofabitch draw back his boot to kick me in the head, and Helder shouted: "*Basta!* Enough!"

No particular concern for my health, I was convinced; he just didn't want me dead yet.

I was gasping for breath, and as I rolled over onto my stomach, I saw him simply thrust Christine away from him, back onto the sofa. She lay there, breathing painfully, a hand to her throat, and Helder picked up the gun and casually tossed it to Bluebeard.

And I knew exactly what I had to do now.

I waited a moment or two to make sure I could move, and then threw myself across the floor, grabbed the hairbrush off the table, and crashed through the window with it. I hadn't gone ten feet before Bluebeard grabbed me.

He simply held one giant hand on my neck and squeezed, then lifted me up, and tossed me back through the window again. I landed with a terrible thud on the floor, and he clambered in and stood over me, grinning that crazy grin of his, and then leaned down and took the hairbrush from my hand and gave it to Arthur Helder.

I staggered over to the jug of water in the corner and splashed myself more or less clean. The pain in my gut was appalling, and I collapsed beside Christine and just lay there, still trying to get some air inside me.

Helder placed the hairbrush on an upturned log, took the axe, and went at it like a madman. It took him three hard blows to sever the rosewood in two, and there the diamonds were, the Gamma set, scattering over the floor.

There was one more thing to do, to be certain about . . . Bluebeard was standing over me, the maniacal grin gone now, just a stolid look of patience on his face, and I looked at him and said, in English and very clearly: "Water, I need water to drink."

He looked at Helder for a translation, and Helder said casually: *"Darlo acqua da bere* . . . Give him a drink."

And I chalked up a piece of knowledge.

Helder was positively bubbling over with pleasure. He said: "Amateur or not, Mr. Benasque, you're a good man. What is it the manual says? 'The prime concern of the CA must be the merchandise, over and above the safety of the courier he's shacking up with'? Not those exact words, perhaps, but more or less, something like that . . . "

He was examining the stones minutely, and he took out a jeweler's loupe and peered at them for nearly five minutes, saying nothing. And then the little red light on the radio was flashing. He put the stones into his pocket and picked up the mike, held a headset to his ear, and said: "Come in, Hawk, this is Nightingale."

He listened for a long time and said at last: "I think you're wrong, but it doesn't matter too much now. Get them over to the lab and run the tests on them. I think they're the decoys but let's be sure. Over and out."

He took out the diamonds again and played with them, and came over to stand beside us, looking down at Christine. He said: "Oh come on, I didn't really hurt you. And tell your boys, for God's sake, that fulminate of mercury doesn't worry us any more; we just explode it under sandbags."

He went to the cupboard and found a bottle and two glasses, poured drinks, and held them out to us. He said: "Drink this; you'll feel better."

Christine sipped hers in a sort of sullen silence that I thought was about right, and I gulped mine back and said: "Could I have another? Two or three more?"

He put the bottle down beside me, and he seemed truly solicitous now. "I'm sorry you got hurt, Mr. Benasque. You should have known you'd never get far. But it was a good try. And I think I'll join you in a glass of slivovitz. We really do have something to celebrate, don't we?"

He poured himself a drink and sipped it, watching Christine. He said: "You might like to know, Madame Andress—honor where honor is due, all that sort of thing—that you really had me confused for a while. For just a few moments I was almost convinced that you were the girl, that I was wasting all my precious time, my money too, on the wrong party. Does that please you? I saw all my plans crumbling, and I thought that for once in my life I'd made the wrong deduction. But I hadn't, and that pleases *me*; I was right again. But I must admit that you gave me a nasty moment there."

He looked lovingly at the diamonds again. "Fifty-seven facets; it's really unbelievable. How could they *do* that? And the Thai Queen is a masterpiece. Did you know the flaw can only be seen at certain angles? Yes, you must know that."

He sighed, the heartfelt sigh of a reluctant man who can't do something he'd dearly like . . . He said: "Do you know? I'm almost tempted to leave the Astra Para with you, a token of my regard for you. Unhappily, my expenses on this operation have been almost unbearable."

He rooted around in the cupboard again and came up with a glass jar of grapes. He tipped a handful of them out into a saucer and said: "They've been soaked for a year in the same slivovitz; they're very potent. I'm sure that if you eat a few of these, you'll both feel a lot better."

I was getting some breath back at last, not much, but enough to feed on, and I said, making conversation:

"You've got three of the finest stones in the world. You're never going to dispose of them."

"You're not really going to expect me to reply to a gambit like that, Mr. Benasque, now, are you?"

"It won't be easy to palm them off anywhere. They are too well documented."

"As a matter of fact, it's as difficult, if not more so, as getting them in the first place. Is this an interview?"

"Sort of."

"It's no good quoting me, you know. As far as the press is concerned, I'm in Kenya right now, and that's been well documented too. You'll have to call me Charlie Brown, or no one's going to believe you. What's your paper?"

"I am free-lance."

"Well, isn't that nice for you?"

He finished his drink and stood up, and said carefully: "Now, there's only one thing left that I have to say. Our bearded friend here believes that once I've got my hands on your smuggled diamonds, I'm taking them over to the provincial capital to . . . How did I put it? To report in. And that sooner or later I'll be back to pick you up. He is going to keep an eye on you, in return for which the local authorities are going to give him a blanket pardon for all the crimes he's wanted for—you see what an idiot he is? But he is convinced that you're very dangerous criminals, and when I don't turn up in the course of time . . . "

He broke off, musing. "I wonder how long before his bovine patience gives out? In any case, it will be long enough for me to do what I have to do, and at that time, I really don't know what action a man like him is going to take. He might let you go, or he might just cut your throats for the hell of it. I have really no idea. I've never delved very deeply into the philosophies that motivate the criminal classes. You are not allowed to leave this room at all, except to go to the bathroom, which is a hole in the ground outside, I'm afraid. When you have to do that, you go together, so that he can keep an eye on you both. You sleep tonight in this room, on the top of the stove, and he'll stay awake all night to make sure you stay there. If I know him as well as I think I do, this can go on for a week, and he still won't go to sleep. There's plenty of food and drink, and I've told him not to harm you unless you upset him. Is all that understood?"

I said: "Perfectly. I suppose you wouldn't like to leave a forwarding address?"

He smiled. "Then I'll say goodbye. It's been truly delightful." He seemed to swing from venom to charm with no difficulty at all.

He tied the stones into his pocket-handkerchief, stuffed them into his pocket, and came over to me and shot out a hand. To my surprise, I took it instinctively; we could have been old friends saying our farewells. He held out his hand for Christine, and I was sure he was going to kiss hers. She just stared at him with a look of absolute fury on her face, and I admired her for it.

He said soothingly: "I know just how you feel, Madame Andress. But defeat comes to all of us once in a while. Take pride in two things. You gave me a very considerable run for my money, and you almost fooled me. There are not many people around who can do either of those things."

She said nothing.

He looked at Bluebeard and said to him, in carefully simple Italian: "You know what has to be done. Just remember your orders. I may be gone quite a long time; so have patience, and don't let them out of your sight." He pulled a cute little trick of his own then. He said: "They've both killed before, so be careful."

I saw that maniacal grin begin to creep over Bluebeard's face. It was a cruel thing to say; I knew that we could both get ourselves knocked for no good reason at all.

Helder looked at us briefly and went out. A moment later we heard the crunching sound of the Bentley's tires on the gravel.

Christine did not move. She said quietly: "All right, it's obvious that he doesn't speak English; so let's decide what we have to do."

"We have to get out of here fast, before he finds out what he's got."

"It's more urgent than you think, Michael."

"How's that?"

"He's left fingerprints all over the place."

I didn't understand what she meant for a moment. And then I suddenly realized . . . I could feel my scalp crawling, and she went on: "For the really dirty work, he likes to get someone else."

There was a little silence. I got to my feet and consciously tried to ignore the hulk of muscle and violence sitting in his corner with the gun across his knee, scheduled to be killed too. He'd moved the chair over a little, close by the broken window. I could feel his eyes on me.

I said: "Yes. He can't afford a police investigation if we should manage to get out of here, can he? He's supposed to be in Africa, but . . . I can't believe it, Christine."

She said drily: "For twelve million dollars? That man wouldn't hesitate to kill this time. All he has to do is send that little Frenchman back here—a couple of hand grenades through the window and then a good fire."

"You really believe that?"

"Michael, his fingerprints are all over the place! What other possibility is there?"

I said: "Jesus Christ."

"If he does try something like that, he won't do it till he's safely out of the country. So we've got a few hours, at least."

"That's true. So let's put our heads together." I said again: "Jesus Christ."

Chapter Ten

I kept wandering around the room, throwing a covert glance at Bluebeard once in a while. There was absolutely no expression on his face at all, a robot.

Christine was sitting up now on the overstuffed sofa, her ankles crossed, her hands in her lap, just looking resigned to her fate.

I said: "And how long before he learns what it is he's really got?"

"A long time. I don't care how close by his equipment he is; we have one tremendous advantage now. He's got two sets of stones—the Beta and the Gamma—and they're almost, but not quite, identical. It's going to confuse him terribly, because normally, decoy stones aren't made up quite so expertly—or so expensively. He's going to think one set is the right one, the other the decoy, and he won't know which is which. It will take him a long, long time to find out the truth. But he may not wait for that to do what he has to do with us; so let's not count on too much time."

"And the crux of the matter is that we can't get out of this room in a hurry, except by one device."

"The outhouse."

"Yes."

"If we make a break for it outside, he's sure to get one of us. Probably you."

"Not if we do it intelligently. We reconnoiter first."

"Then let's do that now."

She got to her feet, picked up her purse, and looked at Bluebeard with that haughty expression on her face, and said clearly, in Italian: "I need to use the bathroom."

For a moment, he just stared at her, his eyes very hostile, his gun ready, and she said: *"La toiletta, il W.C."* In Italian, it comes out as *doubleh-veh-seh.*

He looked at me and grunted something or other, and

moved the gun in a gesture that obviously meant: You too, and he went over and unlocked the door and followed us outside, escorting the children to the can. One look at his face told me it was not going to be easy, now or at any time, to get away from him.

We went round to the back of the cottage, and there was the privvy, set under a very prolific apple tree, looking like any other privvy the world over. Christine went inside, and I sort of hung around and waited, with Bluebeard's hard eyes on me all the time. I took an apple and started biting into it to show how unconcerned I was.

She was in there an interminably long time—setting the pattern, I realized. When she came out, I went in and sat down and gave the place a thorough going-over.

It was very solidly built—what else? This was a woodsman's cottage—and there was no hope of getting through it any way except by the door. It was an ordinary, simple single-holer, with a crescent moon and some stars carefully cut into the door, a thick wad of cutup newspaper fastened with string to a nail, and a magazine picture of a prize bull pinned to one of the walls.

I waited a long time too, and at last he started hammering on the door; so I came out, zipping up, and made a gesture to him that meant—I hoped—that I had diarrhea, take it easy. He grunted, getting the message, perhaps, and shepherded us back into the house again.

He locked the door, took the slivovitz bottle and had a good long swig out of it, and started telling me something I didn't understand, until, with a lot of comic-opera gestures, it became apparent he was trying to say: *Don't think I'm going to get drunk.* I nodded wisely, and he took another swig and put the bottle down, then sat by the window and watched us.

I rooted around in the drawer of the table, with no reaction from him at all except a very wary look, and found a pack of cards and shuffled them, and we sat down at the table. I started playing patience while she watched me. We talked together quietly for a while.

She said: "Are you feeling all right now? I was afraid he must have at least broken a few ribs."

"We're both of us in the wars, aren't we?" The bruise

on her face was still there. "And I was afraid he'd break your neck holding you like that."

"Not my neck; it was just my Adam's apple that hurt."

"All right now?"

"It will be by tomorrow. How long do we have to wait before we go out again?"

"An hour, I'd say. Any less, he might get suspicious."

"I don't think so. He seemed to understand you were having a problem. And when we do?"

"I think the best thing is for you to go in there first, again, and I'll make a break for it . . . "

"No. The other way round."

"I know what you're thinking, but you're wrong."

"No, I'm not. He won't hesitate to start firing at you, and he won't miss. But with a woman? There's an old-fashioned respect for womanhood here. He won't shoot; he'll simply chase me. And he won't catch me. . . . "

"Oh yes, he will . . . "

She shook her head. "No. All I need is twenty yards start, and I'll get that while he's wondering what to do. No, Michael. You go in, and I make a break for it. Before he starts after me, he might just fire a burst or two at the outhouse to get you out of the way, so crouch down low on the floor the moment you get in there. There's not much room."

"It's a great idea, but it's still the other way round."

"No." She was adamant. "I'm in charge, remember?"

"And you're the woman I love."

"Michael . . . We could argue about this for weeks on end, but it's going to be my way, if only because it's the right way."

I sighed. "Okay. Maybe it's the best thing at that."

"Good, then that's settled. Can you find your way down to where we hid out with the car?"

"Parallel to the road for a mile or two, and there will be the tire-tracks in the mud, lots of them. Straight down from there."

"That's where we rendezvous. And we keep on running till we're sure we've lost him."

"I have a nasty feeling that I'll be the only one running. You'll be lying back here in a pool of blood."

"No, Michael. He'll try and catch me first; I'm sure of it."

"And he will."

"No." She was even smiling.

I put down the cards and found another bottle of slivovitz in the cupboard and picked up the corkscrew to open it. I was amazed at his instant reaction; he just swung the gun round in my direction and held it there, saying nothing but looking a lot.

I suppose a twisted four inches of chromed steel would make a good weapon if you were fast enough; and a quick jab at the throat would put a man out permanently. He wasn't taking any chances. I paid him no attention but took a long drink out of the bottle, put it down, and said loudly: *"Doubleh-veh-seh."*

I stalked to the door, a little unsteadily for good effect, and he came over like an obedient St. Bernard, unlocked the door, and took us both outside again. I saw Christine picking an apple, too, all red and shining, as I went in and shut the door.

I crouched down on the ground, as low as I could, and waited; there was precious little room, and I felt I wanted to shield my head with my hands against an onslaught I was sure was imminent. Somehow, I expected at least a shout first . . .

But why should he shout?

The first indication I had that Christine had taken off was exactly what she had predicted. A furious burst of machine-pistol fire practically cut the privvy in half, only inches above my head. Had I been sitting down in the normal posture for these matters, it would have sliced right across my chest. Only a short burst, but enough to put me out of the struggle forever, while he took off after her.

I didn't wait a moment. I felt the urgent need to confuse him while he was still within hearing range, and I thought incongruously about the baby that swallowed some lead shot, and the doctor who said give him a pint of castor oil, but don't point him at anybody. . . . And that's how I went out of there, fairly shooting out, low down on the ground and rolling over and over in the leafy humus, getting myself caught up in wild blackberry canes and all sorts of unpleasant things, and finding myself in a gully, where I got to my feet and just *ran.*

The forest was very dense here, and there was hardly an open space anywhere. I slowed down in ten minutes and then stopped altogether to get my breath back and to listen.

Nothing except the birds and the frogs and the wind rustling the leaves, no alien sound at all.

I took my bearing from the setting sun, turned to the east, and walked very quietly—trying not to force a way too noisily through the shrubbery—for another half hour before I found the tracks of the little Citroën going down the hill. I followed them down, down, for ever, deep into the valley, and found the huge, dead mimosa tree, close to which we had parked the last time we had felt safe. I saw where we had lain side by side on the moss, and I moved a few yards away and lay down in the bushes, covering myself with ferns and vines, and I waited.

I worried like hell about her, and every passing minute made it worse.

I heard her coming, at last, after I'd been there for nearly forty minutes, and it was almost dark. She was approaching stealthily, just a slight rustle here and there, and I fancied that it might not be her after all, but Bluebeard, instead; so I waited till I could see her, moving in behind a pine tree and looking all around. I ran to her then, and took her in my arms, and she said, whispering: "Oh God, I didn't think you had made it. I thought he'd killed you back there . . . "

I whispered back, holding her tight: "Yards over my head; are you all right?"

"Yes, just . . . out of breath."

"Then we can rest here for a while . . . "

"No. He might find the tracks of the car and put two and two together . . . "

"All right. This way then."

I took her arm and we crept out, walking further and further east. We went for miles, and it was getting dark, when we came to a deep gorge and slithered down into it. There was a slim and very high waterfall tumbling down the rocks into a pool. We lay on our bellies and drank from it, then sat close together and decided that we had finally lost him.

She said: "My God, I was so worried about you . . . "

"And me you. It couldn't have been easy."

"Much easier than I'd expected. I was lucky. I ran and got under cover in seconds, while he was firing, and made a turn to one side where the going was easier, and kept on running. He was behind me all the time, and I was afraid he might be catching up; it's not easy to run in shoes like these . . . So I hid, and just then there was an animal of some sort—I don't know, maybe a wild boar—crashing through the bushes close by, and I actually saw him take off after it. I waited a while, that's what held me up, and then went off very quietly in the opposite direction. For all I know he's still chasing that boar."

"And it's liable to lead him to Russia and back before he'll get near it. Good." I said again, groping for her: "Are you all right?"

She grimaced. "I tore the hell out of my pants; they weren't made for this sort of thing." She showed me a great rip along her thigh covered with blood. I made her take her pants off and tied my handkerchief around the deep cut to stanch the bleeding. As I worked on it, I said: "What about Athens now?"

She shook her head. "I don't know, Michael. I don't even know where we are or where we go from here."

"All we have to know is that the merchandise is still safe, and that we're in the clear."

"Yes, yes . . . " She was silent for a moment, frowning, and she said slowly: "I made the point, I remember, that the first time . . . they got what they were looking for too easily. Is that what . . . what prompted you to behave like a maniac back there? That business with the hairbrush?"

I loved her for the thought, and I kissed her again and felt very happy. I said: "Well, it paid off handsomely, didn't it?"

"You could have been killed."

Quoting Harry Slewsey, I said: "It's never happened to me yet . . . "

"That was a little bit *too* not-too-easy. But I love you for it."

"Poor old Vasileos. Running around like a bear with a sore head."

She was suddenly very angry. "Yes, damn his eyes! He ought to know they must be watching him and play his cards accordingly. I'll have to have a very serious talk with him when we get there."

The moss down here was unbelievably soft and thick and luscious, a yellow-green bed for lovers. The rocks were taking on a strange colored light as the last rays of the sun left them and they picked up the secondary light of the moon. She lay back, one arm thrown out, and I lay beside her and put a hand on her breast, a thigh across hers.

She said: "We're a thousand miles from where we're supposed to be, and God knows how far behind schedule, and all I can think of . . . At this moment, I don't need food, or shelter, or comfort, or even the absence of fear. All I need right now is a *comb*."

I said: "It so happens . . . " I suppose it's because I usually drive a convertible—unless the finance company has taken it away from me—that I've gotten into the habit of carrying a comb in my hip pocket. I gave it to her, and she sat up and shook her lovely hair loose, tugging at the tangles with a couple of bobby pins in her teeth. Somehow, it was an exquisite picture of femininity, and it was hard to reconcile it with the hazards we had left behind us such a short while ago.

The untangling was done, the hair hanging straight down over her shoulders now, and she looked at me and said somberly: "We can't really move from here till it's daylight, can we? What do you think?"

I said: "We can wander around a black forest in the black night and exhaust ourselves for nothing, but it doesn't seem to me to make any sense. I think we're safe here; I think we have to wait till it's light again and we can see what we're doing."

"He just might be a good tracker, follow our footsteps."

"Then we spend a couple of hours making sure he doesn't. The stream's only a few inches deep."

"All right."

We walked hand in hand along the bed of the stream, stepping delicately on water-worn pebbles, following its twisted course for more than four miles. We came at last to a huge, deep pool in the middle of some flat, smooth boulders that led us to a tiny grove, all covered over with sweet-smelling ferns. We made a bed from them, lay down together and made love, and slept like children, until the rising sun came over the top of the hill and woke us up to a new and different day.

It was a glorious morning, fresh and clear, and in spite of the huddled cold of the night, I felt great, shivering in the pale light of the new sun. We stepped over the flat boulders to the big pool, and she looked at the green water for a moment. I was afraid she was going to suggest taking a bath, and she did.

She stood up and said: "And now, I'm going to get cleaned up. Why don't you join me?"

The water looked as though it was coming straight down from the tops of snow-covered mountains; it gave me goose pimples just to look at it, and I said: "There's no way I'm going to get more than my face and hands wet. Maybe my feet, for about two seconds."

"Nonsense! It looks very refreshing . . . "

"Goddamit; it isn't even heated!"

"So much the better; it's invigorating."

"No way. You go ahead. I'll watch."

She was adamant. "There's a psychological disadvantage to waking up in the morning and being . . . smelly."

"You smell of Guerlain. Maybe I don't, but it's . . . it's *freezing*; you can tell by just looking at it."

It was.

I stood there up to my neck in it and froze to death, while she swam around happily for five minutes, and then, in answer to my pleading, we got out and found the sun to dry off in, and I was covered from head to foot in goose pimples, and all shriveled up and miserable.

She said: "Oh you poor darling," and put her arms around me and kissed me, but it didn't do any good at all. I thought I'd never warm up. As we got dressed, she said: "All right, what's the next step? Where do we go from here?"

I wished we still had the map, but there was only my memory to rely on. I said: "Well, we're out of danger for the moment; we have to go to Athens, so let's go there."

"Thank God for that little bit of nonsense at the airport. About the passport, I mean." For a moment, I had been worried about hers; mine was still in my pocket, and hers, it seemed, was in her purse.

I said: "It's all a matter of transportation, nothing else. That, in turn, means a main road. So let's find one and take it from there."

She sat down with just her shirt and her jacket on, and I redid the bandage around her thigh; there was no more bleeding now, just a gash wrinkled pink at the edges where the water had practically frozen it.

I said: "We have two alternatives. We can make for the notorious road at Drnis, just a few miles east of us. Or, we can head up again for the equally notorious Bentley road. I flatly refuse to believe that anyone will be waiting there for us again."

"And I agree. So let's do that."

I held her for a moment just to comfort myself, and we set off again, climbing now up the steep slope of the gorge. It wasn't too hard, really, though exhausting. We sat down to rest at the top for a few minutes, then moved on wearily till we came through the woods and out onto the road. It was the same one; not too many tarmac roads around here. We turned to the right and went on walking, not quite sure what we were both hoping for.

We heard the high-pitched roar of a fast car hurtling around the bends below us, the squeal of tires, and we took cover urgently, lying down together in the ditch at the side of the road. But it was a Mercedes with a young man at the wheel, a black-haired girl beside him, sweeping past at high speed. When it was gone we walked on again and kept on hoping.

In a little while, we heard the sound of a diesel truck laboring up far behind us, and we stopped and listened and I said: "I don't believe Helder's lumbering around the countryside in a diesel truck. It's more likely to be a farmer on his way to market."

"Giving Bluebeard a lift?"

"That would be stretching coincidence a little too far."

She nodded. "I think so too. Let's just be careful."

We stood by the side of the road and waited. The truck was an old and very delapidated Lancia. There was a steep slope beside us; and we were right on its edge, ready to fall backward and out of sight if the diesel's occupants looked in the least suspicious, ready to start the long running again. But the truck pulled to a stop, and the driver looked out at us, grinned cheerfully, and said something neither of us understood.

He was about twenty-two years old, with a week's growth of beard, and bright, penetrating eyes. He wore a sweater with the sleeves rolled up to show off his muscles for the pretty girl who sat beside him, not much more than seventeen years old and very sweet.

I spoke to him in Italian, the second language all over Yugoslavia's north: "We don't speak Croatian; how about Italian?"

The young man shook his head and looked at the girl. She said eagerly: "Yes, I do. I speak it very well, I think."

I said: "Thank God for that. We've had an accident with the car. Can you take us to the nearest town?"

"Where do you wish to go, *signore*?"

"Almost anywhere will do. We'd like to get to Mostar."

"That is a very long way, *signore*."

"So where are you headed?"

"We go to Sinj. We have a load of melons for the market there."

"Can you give us a lift?"

She spoke to the young man in Croatian, and he nodded vigorously and said something while she translated: "It will be a great pleasure, *signore*."

She started to climb into the back with the melons, to make more room for us, but I said: "No, please stay. I have to talk to the driver and you can translate."

She seemed a little surprised, but she nodded and squeezed over so that Christine had to sit on my knee. No problem. And off we went, the gears crashing abominably, the forest closing in on us as we climbed higher.

It's a remarkable thing about this part of the world. The forest has more than its habitual bucolic effect on you; it really seems a comfort as you drive through it, as though the denseness of its shrubbery is a shield against all kinds of evils. The mountains, too, seem to be standing guard against oppression. The Romans found out about that, and so did the Goths and the Visigoths and all the other would-be conquerors—right down to the Italians, who got the hides beaten off them in these narrow gorges.

There was comfort, too, in the presence of these two nice young people who weren't out to harm us, or to steal twelve million dollars' worth of diamonds, still tucked away behind what Christine, an eternity ago, had so clinically referred to as my scrotum. I thought: *My God, after all this hassle, they're still there. . . .*

I said to the girl: "Mostar is what? About a hundred kilometers from here?"

"A little more, I think."

"Suppose you were to take us all the way there in the truck? We would pay, of course."

She was startled. She spoke to the young man at length, and they seemed to have an argument; I had the impression that he didn't like the idea very much. When they were through, the girl said: "We can take you to Sinj, and there you will be able to find a train or a bus to Mostar that will take you more comfortably."

Her Italian was good, although a little hesitant at times. I changed the subject for the moment and asked her where she'd learned it. She was blushing. She said: "My mother has a friend who is Italian. My father died a long time ago—a truck driver. He had an accident. There is a shrine to him on the road."

Ah, those shrines . . . every hairpin bend you come to in these mountains—with thousand-foot drops down to the chasms below and no railings anywhere in sight—there are three or four tiny shrines, an image of the Virgin Mary, a few plastic flowers, a candle always kept burning. Communist or not, a lot of these people are still deeply religious.

I waited a reasonable time, and then said: "We do not have any Yugoslav currency, but we do have dollars. I would be willing to pay a fair price, even a very good price."

The conference again, and I was watching him. He was getting suspicious now, and I interrupted them and told the girl carefully: "Please tell your friend . . . explain to him that the lady and I . . . Well, her husband might be in Sinj, and it is not a very good place for us to go just now."

She stared at me wide eyed for a moment, then looked at Christine, and suddenly burst out laughing, delightedly and energetically, covering her mouth with her hand to try and hide the laughter. The young man was staring at her and saying something that obviously meant: What goes on?

He was already grinning, conscious that there was a huge joke coming up. When she told him, he started laughing too, a boyish laugh of pure mischief, and he shot out a hand and took mine and in his ecstasy nearly drove us off the road. He broke off in a moment and was serious again, even admonishing her. She turned to me and said, still giggling: "He wishes me to say we are sorry for laughing, but . . ."

"Yes, I know how it is. But as far as we are concerned, anything to avoid a fight with this man. He is very, very big, a boxer." I wondered if I were perhaps embellishing it a trifle but didn't really care too much; everything seemed so pleasant now.

They had a long, long discussion together, full of gesticulations and raised eyebrows, and she turned to me and said hesitantly: "There is one problem, *signore,* a very serious problem. We are not allowed to sell our melons in Mostar, only in Sinj—the regulations, you understand—and by the time we get back . . . maybe we will miss the best prices in the market."

She sounded embarrassed, as though she were asking for money and knew it wasn't the right thing to do.

I told her very carefully: "I do not know what your melons are worth, but . . . you must realize that we are tourists, and tourists always have plenty of money with them, a whole year's savings sometimes. We spend it on things we like, and then . . . " I shrugged. "What will you get for your melons in Sinj?"

Now she was really hesitant, even shy. "A very big sum of money, *signore*. Perhaps as much as five-hundred dinars."

I said: "I will happily pay five-hundred dinars for a ride to Mostar. For us, it is worth it." The embellishment again. "He really is a very big man, a very angry man."

She was laughing again suddenly, and it was agreed. I

thought: That probably represents several days' hard work for them.

The laughing had stopped as suddenly as it had begun. There was a look in her eyes that was almost sad—and quite devoid of envy. I knew what was in her mind. This is a country where private enterprise, to a very limited extent, is allowed, but still not really approved of. And five-hundred dinars, in highly-illegal foreign currency—very desirable, nonetheless—would be a fortune for them. Back home, it's about twenty-five dollars.

I said gently: "Some of us have more money than others. Perhaps it is not the way it should be, but . . . you know how it is."

She nodded vehemently. "Yes, I have seen tourists, in Split, a town on the coast where many tourists go. I have seen them spend more money on one meal than we earn in a week. I worked in a restaurant there once, just for the summer, and I saw. And sometimes they push the plate away with food still on it."

Her eyes were very bright again suddenly. "And where will you go with your lady when we get to Mostar?"

"There is an airport there?"

"Oh yes, a very good one."

"Then perhaps we will go to America."

She sighed. "Ah, America . . . "

We drove on in silence for a little while until we came to a bridge and a fork in the road. The young man swung the wheel over, with an explanation to the girl, and when she had translated, laughing again, we learned that he was bypassing Sinj altogether, to avoid any possibility of a chance encounter . . .

We were on very secondary roads now, dusty in some places and muddy in others, and at ten o'clock in the morning the girl produced some bread, onion, cheese, and sausage, cut it all up with her boyfriend's knife, and shared it out among the four of us.

I was thinking: *We'll be there soon after midday, and with any luck at all, a flight out to anywhere, anywhere we can pick up a connection for Athens. . . .* We had our passports; we had plenty of money. Even our patience was holding up and everything was going well.

And when everything seems to be just right, that's when it all starts going wrong.

We were coasting downhill at a fair turn of speed when we blew a front tire. The young man fought the wheel, as the truck aimed itself at the gorge and kept on going, and when I saw the muscles bulging in his arms, I thought the steering linkage would surely come apart; we had a lot of weight behind us. He pulled it back from the edge of the chasm just as I was getting ready to jump, yanking Christine and perhaps the young girl, as well, out with me. The truck skidded sideways, right on the verge, for a few yards—broadside on and leaning over horribly; and then, slowly, inexorably, it began to tip over.

We all threw our weight into the offside, but the melons were just too heavy for us, and the truck slammed down on its side and lay there—another piece of machinery gone wrong. But no one was hurt, apart from a few bruises and some ruffled nerves. We stood at the edge of the sheer drop for a moment and watched half a hundred big green melons bouncing their way down to the bottom, splitting open to show their scarlet innards, finding their way down to the river there. The driver was swearing and cursing at great and deliberate length, and then the two of them went to work.

The girl produced ropes and pulleys from the back, while he began cutting poles with a long, two-headed axe. Then we all lent a hand and bullied that damned truck back onto its wheels. To this day I'll never know how we managed it.

Not a solitary car or truck passed by in the six hours that we sweated there, straining at poles, hauling on ropes, with no one at all to give us a hand. But manage it we did, and then there was the long process of reloading all of the melons that were still good, of changing the wheel (the spare was down to the canvas), and filling up the radiator from a little spring that bubbled nearby. . . .

But we set off again, in good spirits once more. It was already half-past five, another day gone by and nothing achieved except our continued safety.

And as we limped into the old, historic town of Mostar, the bell in the fine old church was striking eight o'clock.

We got down in the middle of the town, a cobbled

market square, and I gave the young man quite a lot of money. The girl was still enjoying the joke and couldn't stop laughing. We shook hands all round, and I thought what a delightful couple they were—young, vibrant and ready to face anything that life might have to offer them. When they had driven off, I said to Christine: "We didn't even know their names."

She nodded. "It's a shame. But what's more important, they don't know ours, and they won't talk about this to anyone. That's black-market money they have in their pockets, a long spell in jail if they're caught."

"It's rough, isn't it?"

"Yes, it is. Nice people."

There was a taxi-rank in the square, and the first driver we approached, a grizzled old man with no teeth, explained laboriously that yes, he'd be happy to take us out to the airport, only it was closed for the night and wouldn't open again till seven in the morning. The railway station, then? Yes, there was a train that left Mostar at eleven o'clock, but it went back to the coast and was no use to us at all; inland, there were no more trains until tomorrow either. Could he perhaps drive us all the way to Sarajevo, a distance of some eighty miles or so?

He shook his head sadly. It was against the law for taxis to operate outside of their well-defined areas. He would be happy to help us, except that it would cost him his license. A rented car then? There were no cars for hire in Mostar, and besides, we would need the government *carnet* to get us past the checkposts that had been set up to control the smuggling of cigarettes.

It seemed that trucks and trains and planes and everything else mechanical were all conspiring to slow us down; to keep us here until the honest light of day, when we could begin our race for Athens all over.

Christine said philosophically: "We have to make the best of it, Michael. If we can find a plane in the morning, it will still be faster than driving through the mountains all night."

"Yes. Yes, I suppose so."

"And I'm still hungry."

"Let's go eat. It's hiatus time again."

We found a charming little restaurant, where the first

thing I did was order two bottles of Ljutomer Traminer, the wine they had given us in the hotel back there on the beach. We emptied the first bottle while we tried to make out what was on the menu.

My natural good spirits were returning fast. Christine had lost all of her makeup, and except for that bruise on the side of her face, looked all shiny and nice (even the bruise made her look more down-to-earth and less ethereal). There was a homely, appetizing look about the restaurant—neat white tablecloths, shining glasses. Apparently, by local standards, an expensive sort of place, it had a maître d'hôtel, which is usually a good sign. The whole ambiance was relaxing and inviting, and when she leaned over and placed her hand on mine, saying nothing but smiling that wonderful smile of hers, I couldn't help thinking to myself: Surely this is too good to last.

Of course, it was.

Chapter Eleven

The restaurant was obviously used to foreigners, but not too much so. I'm told that *Mostar* means Old Bridge in Serbo-Croatian. Quite a lot of tourists come here from all over the world to look at it and the famous Naretva Defile, which it spans, so we weren't overly conspicuous. Now there were no more than a dozen other diners.

The menu was in three languages, only one of which we could read, but it was enough. The waitress had a smattering of Italian, and the head waiter spoke tolerably good English; so we were in good shape.

We ordered a shish kebab of goat's meat, and peppers stuffed with rice and tomatoes and spices, with some very good wild mushrooms that grew in these parts—the kind they call *cèpes* in France—and a salad made mostly of dandelions. They were a little bit stringy, but quite delicious, and a very good plate of goat's cheese to follow.

We talked quietly, as we ate, about the options open to us now. There was only one, really: To get on the first plane out of there. There'd be no direct flight from here to Athens. But we could, no doubt, make a connection at either Sarajevo or Skopje, or even Belgrade if necessary. Ten minutes at the airport with the schedules would put us back on the beaten track once more.

But I was worried about Athens and the people waiting for us there.

I said: "Shouldn't we call and let them know what's happening?"

Christine shook her head vehemently. "Not now. It was always a risk back at the hotel when we thought we'd be taking off at any minute, but now . . . in this country, my darling, all phone calls over the border, any border, will undoubtedly be monitored. Some hired hand might just be monitoring the monitors. We don't want Helder, wherever he may be, getting a call from someone he's got in his pocket saying: 'They just called Athens from Mostar . . . ' "

"We can get a radio message through from the plane, once we're safely over the border."

"No, I don't think we even have to do that." She thought about it for a while, skewering little bits of roast goat, and said: "There's a lot of very overt security in Athens—all for the girl. Police outriders, an escort car, that sort of thing."

"And the girl must have arrived there long ago."

"Of course. They will all have stood down by now, the mission accomplished. But you and I . . . all we have is one man standing by. He'll come with us to Sounion, the last leg." She looked at me and smiled: "You've met him before; his name's Bruce."

"Oh really? Well, that's nice. And whose idea was that?"

"Mrs. Bentley suggested it, and I agreed at once. She seemed to think you regarded him very highly."

"Indeed I do. I'm glad about that."

"The pressing question is, how soon in the morning can we be on our way?"

"Maybe they have a schedule here."

The maître was a roly-poly man in his sixties who couldn't do enough for us. He had no airline schedules but he knew all about them anyway. He confirmed that the airport would reopen at seven in the morning and said there were daily flights to places like Ljubljana, Zagreb, and even Trieste and that there was a flight to Belgrade at half-past eleven.

Nobody mentioned Athens. We just talked in terms of international carriers, and we hinted vaguely at Milan. He beamed and said, yes, there was a service Athens-Belgrade-Milan, daily in each direction but he didn't know what time. Would we like him to find out?

We said no thank you, don't bother, we're in no hurry, and I asked him where to find a hotel for the night. He recommended the Ibar, just down the street, the second turning on the right, and should he call and make reservations?

I was about to say yes, but I felt Christine's warning kick at my ankle; so I said no, instead, and he went off to get her a piece of pie all mounded up with raspberries, whipped cream, and nuts, and what looked like honey dripping from it, that she'd seen at a nearby table. . . .

I said: "What was that all about? We've got to have somewhere to spend the night."

"Not a hotel, Michael. We'd have to hand in our passports; it's mandatory."

"Oh. So what do we do? Walk around all night? Till half-past eleven tomorrow morning?"

"I haunted the streets of Istanbul once for three nights in a row rather than let it be known I was there. I finished up in an all-night movie house, sleeping through seven performances of "I Love Lucy." That was last year. You think there's an all-night movie in Mostar?"

I said: "Somehow I doubt it. I don't suppose it's a very swinging sort of place. I wonder what time the bars close? We could go on an all-night pub crawl."

She didn't like that either. "I hate it. We're too vulnerable. Could we go to the airport and sleep in the lounge?"

"It's closed! Besides, how can I make love to you in the middle of an airport lounge? Quite apart from the fact that if anyone should be watching for us here, that's the most likely place for them to be. It's going to be tough enough getting a flight out without being seen, anyway."

"Yes, I suppose that's true enough. And I really could do with a good shower and a decent bed. But don't tempt me, Michael. You're not supposed to do that."

The waiter came with the biggest hunk of creamy pie I'd ever seen, and she tackled it with great vigor, while I had two glasses of an acquavitae that nearly burned my mouth and stomach raw. I said: "I hate sleeping in dark doorways; I've had to do it too often."

She said, eating happily: "Not a doorway. A hayloft, a barn. This is a very country sort of country, and there has to be a whole mess of barns within a mile or two of here. We just walk out of town till we find one. Have you ever slept in a hayloft before?"

"Uh-huh."

"I used to do it all the time when I was a child. In

Switzerland we have the most beautiful haystacks. I'd get up in the morning climb up to the very top, and then slide down the sides again. It was fun. It used to take forever to climb up. They make them very steep there because of the snow, and they're slippery. . . ." She was chattering away like a young child, and her mood was infectious.

She finished the huge plate of goo at last, and when the waiter came, there was the question of paying in dollars, the only currency we had. He insisted on fetching a bundle of forms for us to fill out for the currency board, but I just laid a twenty-dollar bill on the table and cheerfully said: "Why don't you take care of all that crap for me?"

He glanced quickly around the room to see if any of the other diners were looking our way and pocketed the bill so fast I couldn't believe it. He said quietly: "Thank you, M'sieur . . . " and began to move away, taking his forms with him. I stopped him: "Is there an all-night bar here, maître?"

He gestured. "Not exactly all night, M'sieur, but . . . they are staying open until everybody has gone home. Sometimes, it is very late."

"And exactly how do I find it?"

"Yes, yes indeed."

"Where?"

"Oh . . . " He gesticulated. "Go this way, then one street that way, little bit down you see a red light, is called Bar Vajevo, very nice place, only . . . " He looked at Christine and said, covering up: "Is very nice place if Madame is not minding too much. . . ."

"The girls have to have some place to hang out in."

"Indeed, M'sieur. They are not Yugoslav, you understand. From Austria and Czechoslovakia."

"I am quite sure Madame will not mind."

"Then is nice place. They are closing three o'clock, sometimes more later."

I laid a couple more twenties on the table and said quietly: "Could you give me some local currency for one of those?"

It made him very nervous. There was the quick look around the room again, and he said, his voice hoarse and conspiratorial now: "It is forbidden, M'sieur . . . "

"That's what the other twenty is for, maitre."

He was fidgeting with his hands, but I saw with a start that the bills had already gone. He said: "If M'sieur will wait one moment, I will bring him his change." He swept away and came back in a moment with a fistful of dinars on a plate, laid it on the table, and said bowing: "Good-night, Madame, M'sieur. May I say . . . I hope your meal was satisfactory."

I thanked him, pocketed the dinars, and we went to look for the bar, wandering off down the dark street in the cool night air. The moon was incredibly bright and there were cobbles under our feet and ancient arched stonework all around us—a most attractive place.

Christine said, thinking of me, no doubt: "Do you want to go straight to the bar, Michael? It will be open for a long time yet."

"Let's walk a little, would you like that?"

"I'd like to go take a look at the bridge, you know about it?"

"Ah yes, the famous one. Let's see if it deserves its reputation."

It was good to feel her beside me, the two of us casually strolling arm in arm like lovers forever. We found the bridge in no time at all, sixty feet above the river and looking splendid in the moonlight.

I remembered that the Turks had built it three or four hundred years ago, though some say it was built by the Romans and only repaired by the ubiquitous Turks several hundred years later.

We climbed up there and leaned on the parapet for a while, and stared down at the river below us—incredibly far below—neither of us saying anything or even feeling that talk was necessary. The silences between us were beginning to be important too. We walked through the park, one with walnut trees everywhere—the Mostar walnuts are perhaps the best in the world—found the main street again and started looking for the Vajevo.

We passed a fine old hotel, the lights above the door proclaiming it to be the Ibar, the one the maître had recommended, and I sort of stopped Christine for a moment and said: "Maybe we could slip the desk clerk a couple of bucks and hang onto our passports?"

She tugged at my arm. "Leave it to me, Michael, and I promise you the best hayloft you ever slept in."

"Okay."

We went on to the bar, finding it quite easily. It was just like any other bar in almost any part of Europe . . .

Very soft lights in amber and red, a lot of bottles on mirrored shelves, the sleepy barman in the obligatory red jacket, three quite attractive young ladies sitting together in one corner, and another two at tables with young men in their Sunday best, out for a night on the town, and a very discreet seminude of a reclining girl all covered over with carnations and grapes hanging on one wall.

We stayed there for perhaps an hour, drinking acquavitae, until Christine began to yawn a trifle obviously. I said: "All right, let's go find a bed for the night."

I paid the tab with some of the money the maître had given us, and out again into the night we went like lost souls.

We hadn't gone far when she stopped and said, "I believe we ought to be going in the other direction. It seems to be getting more built up here. What do you think?"

"So we go back past the hotel again—and I won't tempt you—and then on to the market square, and the road we came in on should lead us out of town in about five minutes."

"Yes, and there were barns all around us, remember?"

"No more than a couple of miles out. Yes, we have to go this way. We can take a shortcut through the alley."

It was dark and narrow with only the meager lights of the main street at the end of it. It ran along the back of the hotel and as we walked down it, she said: "If all goes well tomorrow, we're going to be two days late. Well, it's happened before, and it's sure to happen again. Once I was nearly three weeks late when my plane got hijacked and flown to Algeria."

Open gates were all over, leading to the backyards of the stores and the hotel. Through one I caught a glimpse of polished chrome and white paint and my heart missed a beat. But I had to be sure. We walked on for a brief moment, and I said to her: "Excuse me for half a minute. Don't go away."

She looked at me, mystified, and I said: "A dark corner I have to investigate."

"Oh. Why didn't you use the one in the bar?"

"Stay right there."

"I will."

I left her and hurried back. The gleaming chrome and shiny paint was the Bentley. I couldn't believe it. It was very dark in the narrow alley, and I studied the car for a while from the shadows, wondering just what to do. I waited a long, long time, worrying about Christine, but I wanted to make sure there was no one watching it. Then I crept silently to it and tried the hood. It was unlocked.

It had its own little lock, the kind almost no one bothers with. I opened it up silently and felt around in there for the distributor, pried it off, took out the rotor arm, put it in my pocket and thought: *Well, that's one item you're not going to replace easily in Mostar. . . .*

And as I straightened up and quietly closed the hood, the shouting started, alarmingly close and very loud. What he was shouting I don't know to this day, and I didn't wait to ask. It was just a loud and violent stream of yelling in a foreign language that meant nothing to me, except: *Run.*

And that's what I did. I went hurtling along the alley at great speed, grabbed Christine's arm as I ran, and practically lifted her off her feet as the shot rang out. I heard the bullet strike a wall and ricochet off, a most unpleasant whining sound. Then, as we rounded the corner into the street, another hit the mud only inches from my feet.

We ran into another alley, found it was a dead end, clambered awkwardly over a fence and into somebody's tomato patch. We knocked down their supports as we ran. We climbed over a wall and into another garden, across that one and over a wooden fence that gave way as I tried to climb it. Onto another street over a fence again, another two gardens, another two more walls, and finally onto a road that seemed to mark the beginning of a residential area—tall buildings four or five stories high were on both sides of us now. We ran down it till we found an open doorway that led into a modern apartment building and stood there in the darkness, frozen into immobility, trying to catch our breath.

There was only silence. . . .

We stood behind the open door, and Christine said at last, whispering: "What happened?"

I whispered: "Helder's here. Of all the goddamn places he could have gone to, this is where he came."

"Oh no . . . no!"

"Yes. His Bentley is parked at the back of the Ibar Hotel."

"And we nearly stayed there."

"I can picture the two of us, walking down to breakfast in the morning, and who's at the next table? For Christ's sake, that man must have second sight."

"He does, Michael. Let's not ever forget that."

We were whispering so quietly we could hardly hear each other, but she said: "Ssshhh . . ."

It was unnecessary; I'd heard it too, the quiet, hesitant steps of a man on the prowl. Through the open crack between the door and its jamb, where the hinges were, I could see him, a tall, gangling young man in a dark overcoat, a gun in his hand. I eased over silently to watch him as he moved on. He stopped as though he had heard a sound and looked back for a moment. I held my breath, balling up my fist with the knuckle of the second finger wedged there for a quick and frightened blow to the Adam's apple; and then, maybe, with luck, get his gun before running on again. I had a feeling we were going to need one before all this was over.

He turned back and moved off, the way he had come, passing the doorway and not even bothering with it—or was he? He reached the corner and whistled softly and I knew that he was calling for help. But from how many? Everybody had been busting a gut to impress upon me the fact that he had a small army to call on.

I took Christine's arm and silently pointed up. We tiptoed together up the stone stairway; after three flights the steps changed to wood for the last two. We found an unlocked door at the top, a heavy oak door with hinges that creaked horribly as we opened and closed it. We went out into the breeze, high up on a flat roof with steeply-sloping gables all around us on three sides; the fourth was guarded with a rusty iron railing. I crept over to peer down into the street below. Only five stories, but I can't even climb a ten-foot ladder without getting dizzy. . . . Now there were three men at the corner. They seemed to be huddled in a kind of conference; one was pointing to where the doorway was.

I went back to Christine and said quietly: "Now we have to do some mountaineering—up over the ridge there. We'll see what's on the other side of it."

There was no way of locking the rooftop door we'd come through, and there were no odd pieces of lumber lying around—or anything else we could wedge under the handle to give the impression, maybe, that the door was locked; so we got on our hands and knees and climbed carefully, silently upward. The moon was flooding the rooftops—and us too—with a clear, cold brilliance that exaggerated shadows everywhere.

I heard Christine mutter: "Goddammit, there go my pantyhose again." She still had her purse, and I took it from her and stuffed it into my pocket.

We reached the top, and for one alarming moment it seemed there was nothing on the other side save a steep drop down to the street below. I looked right and left, and we straddled the ridge at the top, and Christine pointed and said: "There, it joins up with another roof."

"Isn't that the roof of the hotel?"

"Oh. Yes, it might be . . . let's try the other way."

It was just too steep to try walking on, one foot on each side; so we straddled it and humped our way along, and every movement drove those damned diamonds deep into some very tender portions of my crotch. We could still see the door from up here, and I was watching it carefully, just knowing that sooner or later it was going to open, and we would be caught silhouetted against the sky. But we passed on across the big square block of the chimney stacks, and there was another roof, not nearly as steep. As we were wondering where it might lead, we heard that ominous squeaking sound I had been expecting; someone had opened the door.

We froze, and waited. Christine pointed silently down, and I couldn't for the life of me see what she was trying to indicate; there was nothing there except a stone chasm dropping down five flights to the tarmac.

Yes there was; there was a cluster of three iron pipes, very close to the edge of the roof, and she was scuttling down toward them and looking back to signal me to follow her. I was terrified, even before I knew what she had in mind. There was just a steep tiled slope that even the Citroën wouldn't have been able to climb, and then nothing, not even a guardrail, and the tiles were wet with the night's dew and slippery as hell. She was already crouched by the pipes, long before I gathered up enough courage to go down after her. And I never would have done that, except for one thing—someone was climbing the reverse side of the roof, leather-soled boots stomping their way up it.

I almost ran down to her. I felt an insuperable urge just to let go and fly, all the way down to the bottom, but Christine was locking her two hands together, the fingers intertwined, and gesturing with them to me, showing me what a good strong bond the hands made when they were locked together like that. I couldn't bear to look. I threw a glance over my shoulder to see if anyone's head was coming over the ridge, and when I looked back, she was already slipping over the edge, hanging onto her pipe with clenched hands around it.

I wanted to die right there. I closed my eyes, locked my hands, slipped them over one of the other pipes, and just rolled. They were about four inches across, the pipes, made of galvanized iron—right at the very edge. Vents, perhaps, for the bathrooms or the furnaces; I didn't care what they were.

Thank God we were in shadow here, and almost nothing of our hands would show. I just hung there like a sack of coals on the rope that was my arms, absolutely sure I'd never manage to get back up there again. I opened my eyes at last, and looked across at Christine; it was a selfish blessing to see that she looked good and scared *too,* and I wondered just how long we could hang there over a void that seemed to be tugging us down to its depths.

We could hear voices, just quiet murmurings that meant nothing to us, except that they were now on top of the ridge, and giving the view a good once-over. I wanted to sneeze.

We hung there, and we waited, and we went on waiting. The pain in my arms was excruciating, and again there was that urge to kick myself free from the wall where my feet were, let go, and go sailing out backward into eternity. Acrophobia is not a good thing to be stuck with.

Then at last, when my arms were at the breaking point, I heard them scuttling noisily down the other side. We waited for what seemed like five minutes, and then the sheer terror of it took over, and I started reaching up with one leg, trying to get it back onto the roof. I heard Christine whisper urgently: "Not yet, Michael . . . " But I couldn't have cared less at that moment; the only important thing in my life was to get away from that frightening edge. I rolled up over onto the roof. They were gone.

She was climbing up now too, and I even helped her. We scurried a few feet up like frightened rabbits. She pointed, and we eased our way along at an angle; we had not heard the sound of the door squeaking shut yet, and God alone knew where they were.

We half-crawled, half-slid, and half-stumbled around the corner of the roof, and on again halfway up its slope, still keeping the same angle of direction. Below us now was a wide flat roof with a few squat cubicles that might have been storerooms. We almost ran to them and then crouched down on the other side of the first, in relief.

We waited for a long time. At last I whispered: "Have they gone? I didn't hear the door . . . "

"We may not be able to hear it from here. I want to look over there . . . " She indicated the edge of the roof and moved off quietly to examine it, came back and whispered: "Can you jump about twelve feet, do you think? The top of the next building is a few feet lower; it should be very easy . . . "

I said: "Five flights up in the air? Good God, no! I don't think I could even do it on the ground, but up here . . . "

"I'm sure I can. And if I can, I'm just as sure you can too."

I said: "Christine, I'm terrified of heights; it's a phobia. If I get on top of a high building, I just want to make like a pigeon—fly off into space—I can't help it. And for people without wings, that just isn't a good thing to do."

She was hissing at me: "We're trapped up here. They're

still back there somewhere, and sooner or later they are going to find us. Unless we move on. Ssshhh . . . "

Her hand was tight on my arm. I dropped to my knees and put my face in the shadow and peered around the cubicle carefully. Just one man was there, standing high on the ridge, completely at ease and comfortable; his rifle was at the ready, across the front of his body. I wondered if my face were white enough to show up against the black tar of the roof. I watched for a moment, and then he turned and started moving away and I lost him.

We waited a moment again, and then Christine whispered: "All right, let's make it." I was about to protest again, but she had already slipped out of her shoes. She stood up, and with a shoe in each hand, ran fast across the intervening space and just took off. She went flying out like a bird, and I heard the muted thump as she landed, knowing for sure that *they* must have heard it too.

I didn't wait to make up my mind. I just charged across and jumped; as I flew through the air, a shot rang out. I heard the bullet smash into some brickwork on the other side. I let myself go limp as I fell but was on my feet again in commendable time, reaching for Christine's outstretched hand; we *ran*—again.

Almost everything seemed flat here, and we jumped over a gap that seemed twice as wide as the first. I had the swing of it now, as we climbed another steep ridge and down the other side. It seemed the chase would never end. But we were slowly losing them, perhaps because sheer fright was giving us the edge. A few more shots were fired; one was so close that a chip of shattered stone stung its way into my cheekbone. And then, there was a taller building between us, and we were out of their sight. We found a door that led below and had a bolt on the inside. We slammed the bolt home, ran down a single flight of stairs, stopped to take a breath, and then ran on down until we came to the ground level. The front door was locked, but we found a door at the back that was only bolted on the inside, top and bottom. We went out into the mandatory tomato patch and began fence-jumping again, keeping off the streets till we came to the very edge of the town.

Here the garden was hedged in, a field beyond it, and

we found a gate and went through, then along a stream ankle-deep in icy water. We crouched low so that our heads would not be seen. We didn't straighten up or stop worrying till we were more than two miles from town. We clambered out of the water and simply flopped down on the grass, lay on our backs, and tried to breathe again.

The stitch in my side was appalling, but in a moment I rolled over and propped myself up on one elbow, looked down at her, and touched her hair. "I'm forever asking you if you're all right . . . are you?"

"I'm glad we're on firm ground again. I don't like to be too high up either."

"Really? The way you went over the edge there, hanging on. . . ."

"Sheer terror, Michael. You can do anything if you're frightened enough and there's no other way out."

It was hard to talk, even. I said: "What have we got that I can bring you water in?"

"Nothing. We'll manage."

We staggered together back down the bank, and lay on our stomachs and sucked in water till we were bursting from it. Then we rested for a while again, neither of us saying anything. After a short time Christine got to her feet, straightened out her jacket and pants, and we wandered off to look for somewhere to sleep.

It took us less than an hour to find the ideal place. There were four or five barns within a half mile of us, but the first two we tried were locked, and we didn't feel like breaking in. Soon, however, we found a large haystack standing by itself in the middle of a meadow, partly cut open and with a tarpaulin draped over the cut. We lifted it and crawled inside; inside was a little hay-lined cavern about six feet square, big enough to stretch out in and smelling sweetly of the countryside.

We just lay on our backs very close together, quite exhausted, and I said to her, still whispering out of habit: "All we need now is a bottle of really good cognac."

She didn't answer. She was already fast asleep.

And in a couple of minutes, so was I.

Chapter Twelve

It was a long time since I'd last slept in a haystack.

I had a vague memory of when I was a kid, wandering all over the place, when haystacks were the best possible beds, if you only had enough money to buy bread and cheese and onions and a bottle of something or other once in a while. But now, I'd gotten out of the habit and my main impression was of loose ends of hay that kept finding their way into my nostrils, of sharp thistles sticking relentlessly into my flesh; and of hay fever.

I spent half the night sneezing, and every time I woke up, Christine was sleeping beside me like a long-leggeddy, soft-skinned baby. I spent quite a lot of time wide, wide awake, but it wasn't wasted; I was able to do quite a lot of thinking about the predicament we were in, and even how to get out of it.

The sun came up with admirable promptitude, right on time at six in the morning, and as soon as its first rays sneaked through the gap for air we'd left in the tarpaulin, Christine stirred lazily in her sleep, half opened her eyes, closed them at once and murmured: "Coffee, with lots of hot milk and sugar, some croissants, and strawberry jam," and went back to sleep again.

I pushed the tarpaulin away and slipped off the hay-cut to stretch my legs and look at our environment in the first light of day.

It was very different from what I'd expected. I had thought that we'd covered quite a few miles, but the tops of the town's higher buildings were still very visible through the trees—alarmingly close. On the other side of us though, there was a pleasing expanse of melon fields, with pasture beyond them, and in the far distance, a small herd of cattle was being driven by a very old man who was hobbling on a two-handled stick, looking, in this perspective, a little bit like Moses. There was the cheerful sound of birds, thousands of them, and some running water I hadn't even noticed in the stillness of the night—too damn tired to notice anything except the fact that we were temporarily safe.

I'm not usually awake till I have three or four strong cups of coffee inside me, but somehow, with the cold, impossibly fresh air, I was waking up faster than usual, and I went back to the hideout and woke Christine, and she said, exactly as I had expected: "What time is it?"

She was stretching her legs and pushing away whisps of hay and looking perfectly at home, just as if this were the only kind of bed she slept in, ever.

I said: "It's a little after six in the morning, and I told you that once before, I remember."

She had the disconcerting capacity that some people have of being wide awake the moment they open their eyes; I hate it. She said: "You told me that before? No, Michael, you never did. You must have been dreaming."

"As a matter of fact, I was. Immediately after our first meeting."

"You *dreamed* about me? That's sweet of you . . . "

"Not in the least. It was merely unrestrained desire raising its subconscious presence, and it was very frustrating."

I told her about the dream, about the long tunnel down to the table on the beach, about carrying her naked on my shoulders. She listened to me with great patience, just sitting there and forgetting entirely about all the deadly and urgent business at hand, as though this, just between the two of us, were more important by far. She was sitting up with her legs crossed, occasionally brushing away a whisp of hay and saying nothing, and when I'd finished, there was a strangely sad look in her eyes that I did not immediately understand.

She said: "And when you put me down on the table, you *ran away*?"

"That's what I did. Ran off down the beach with my feet in the water."

"Do you know why?"

"No, I don't."

She was frowning now. "It's an omen, my darling. It means that when this is all over, you're going to run away and leave me."

"Never."

"You will, you'll see. Dreams never lie."

It astonished me. "You really believe that, Christine?"

"Oh, I believe it. On a beach somewhere, when we're all finished with this, you'll just . . . leave me."

"You have to be absolutely crazy!"

"You'll see. Well . . . " She was suddenly a bundle of energy, slipping off the haystack and taking in the air, just as I had done, but with more vigor. She said firmly: "And we have to decide right now exactly what the next step is. We've a lot to do today. Like getting to Athens. Only how?"

I said: "I spent a restless night working it all out, and I'll be happy to tell you exactly what we are going to do."

"Good. I was rather hoping for something like that."

I said: "First of all, let's agree that we can't go back into Mostar, right?"

"Right. They'll be scouring the streets for us still, God knows how many of them."

"So the airport there is very definitely out. So, by the same token, is the train."

"Right."

"So . . . " I said carefully. "We keep moving *away* from Mostar. For the first several miles, under cover, in the fields, close by the hedges, whatever. When we're good and clear, in open country, we start watching the road, for a truck—a produce truck maybe, just like the last time, with the two nice kids on board. We're moving on foot already, in the direction of Sarajevo; that's where we pick up a plane. I'm still trying to visualize the map, and Sarajevo's quite a way. But there's another village about, oh, twenty miles up the road. I can't remember its name. The railway line goes through it; so we take the train from there all the way to Sarajevo."

She said: "Jablanica, I think it's called."

"Yes, Jablanica, something like that. So we hitchhike to Jablanica, get on the train to Sarajevo, take the plane from there to Athens, if there's a direct flight, or to Belgrade if there's not. How does it sound?"

She thought about it for a long time, almost counting the pros and cons on her fingers. At last she nodded: "I think it's the best possible thing we can do. Let's do it."

It wasn't quite like that; luck seemed to be on our side for a change.

We'd walked for maybe four miles and were close by the road, when a bus came creeping along, an old OM diesel, loaded down with passengers and its roof piled high with baskets of produce. The dilapidated sign over the cab said *Sarajevo,* and we decided on the change of plans without the slightest discussion.

We both started waving our arms at the bus, and it pulled onto the side of the road and stopped. We piled aboard and looked over the passengers quickly, and Christine smiled at the driver and said: "Sarajevo? How much?"

There was a slight delay. He understood the *Sarajevo,* but not much else; so I produced a handful of bills in the accepted manner of the bemused tourist, and he carefully took one of them and gave me some aluminum coins in change, and we found seats among the early-morning farmers on their way to the big city.

There were peasant women in black shawls, grizzled old men with flat cloth caps on their heads, bundles of who knows what lying in the aisles, some squawking chickens with their legs tied together, and a young goat, its legs trussed, lying on the lap of a very fat woman who smiled at us and tried to make conversation in Serbo-Croatian.

I said to the driver, trying Italian: "What time do we get to Sarajevo?"

He didn't understand, but one of the passengers came to our rescue, a middle-aged man with glasses as thick as beer-bottle bottoms. He told us, with great pride, that he was a schoolteacher who taught Italian to a group of unruly fifteen-year-olds, and English to adults in the evening, to add a little something to his income. He said happily: "In Sarajevo, we are arriving at six o'clock of the evening, is a very long way, no? But is very comfortable, a good bus of the People's Republic. We are stopping in Jablanica and at Krinjic where we are eating some food and at Sarajevo we are arriving at six o'clock, sometimes at seven or eight. I am making this journey once every week, to talk to my family, you understand?"

It was indeed a long way, over tortuous roads and through some of the most spectacular country I have ever seen. There were incredibly green high mountains all around us, some of them still covered with snow; dense forests of pine; deep ravines; great open fields, where sheep and cattle grazed; charming little houses here and there, all covered over with trelliswork and creeping vine; and enormously high bridges everywhere.

We stopped at a roadside cafe in Jablanica and had a quick aquavitae, and again in Kronjic, where they brought trout for us from the river that ran through the garden of the little bus-stop. We also were served a salad of dandelions and sorrel and tomatoes, with balls of goat's cheese in olive oil.

And when we were back on board the bus, I slept for a while with my head on Christine's friendly breast, and woke up with a start when I realized I was snoring, which I have always thought was an undignified thing to do in the presence of a lady. We looked at each other and realized that we looked like broken-down tramps, the both of us.

I said: "I wonder what time the stores close in Sarajevo?"

She shook her head. "I don't know . . . but it's a tourist town, quite a big tourist trade, so perhaps . . . I'd give my soul, if I had one, to be clean again. Just to wear some fresh clothes! But if there's a plane out tonight . . . we have to take it, you know."

"Yes, I know that, and maybe there is. But if not, no more sleeping in haystacks."

She sounded dubious: "Well . . . there are those hotels where you can take a girl for a few hours, no passport, just a few dollars and no questions asked, I suppose they have them even here."

"No. We find the best hotel in town, and that's where we stay."

"Michael . . . "

I said: "It's very simple. We are supposed to register the moment we arrive, fill out the police forms, and hand in our passports; it's mandatory . . . "

"That's why we have to make other arrangements . . ."

"No. We tell the desk clerk that we had an accident in the car, dropped it into a gorge or whatever, that we left all our baggage in the trunk, including our passports, and that the first thing in the morning we'll hire a car and go get everything sorted out. In a really good hotel we'll get away with it. In a really good tourist hotel . . . it's everything for the customer."

"Are you sure, Michael? I wish I could be . . ."

I said: "It doesn't really matter how sure I am. If it doesn't work, what happens? They won't let us register. So, we say okay, we'll mosey over to the police station and fix it. And *then* we go find a fleabag."

She always liked to think these things over before committing herself. But she nodded, finally, and said: "All right, I think we'll get away with it."

There was a little moment of silence, and then: "I'm beginning to think: The hell with it." She turned her eyes on me and said gravely: "And that means you're bad for me, Michael, doesn't it? Doesn't it?"

I said, and I was absolutely sure of it: "It can't make one iota of difference whether we sleep in comfort tonight, or in a fleabag hotel with cockroaches everywhere. So let's be comfortable."

"But first, we find a store so that we can look presentable. We'll never even get into the hotel if we look the way we do now. They won't even let us pass the door."

The schoolteacher came to our rescue again. He told us there were several stores in Sarajevo open till nine o'clock at night. He seemed to think that in a People's Republic that wasn't really very correct; but they needed the foreign currency and that made it all right.

We pulled into the depot at seven-forty, and fifteen minutes later we had found a very American-style department store where they had no problems with currency, not even a form to fill out; and we spent an hour there getting to look civilized again.

I bought an excellent denim leisure suit made in England of all places, a new polyester shirt from Austria, some new socks and underwear, a battery electric shaver and other toiletries, and a new pair of shoes from Bata, rather than go through the hassle of getting all the mud off the ones I was wearing.

I used their can to get rid of nearly two days growth of beard, and when I was through, I found that Christine had bought herself a very fetching ivory-colored pantsuit with a dark blue blouse, and had somehow contrived to fix her hair and her makeup. I hardly recognized her, and when I complimented her on it she said: "What I really need, my darling, is to soak for an hour in a good hot tub."

"Soon. Any minute now."

The girl at their tourist information booth gave us some maps and pamphlets and timetables, and we found that there was a plane to Belgrade at seven in the morning, a connecting flight to Athens at eight-fifteen. It was perfect. She also told us of a first-class hotel just around the corner, the Kosovo, and we stopped off at a bar and had three cups of very strong Turkish coffee and two glasses of cognac each before we braved the stern disapproval of the night clerk, faced with arriving clients who had no baggage and no reservations—and no passports.

But we had worried for absolutely nothing; there was just no trouble at all. I explained that our car had gone over the edge of a cliff, and he interrupted me, smiling: "I'm afraid that this is a very common occurrence, M'sieur."

I said: "We need a tow truck to get it back up again, and at this time of night . . . It will have to wait till the morning. Can we register now and give you our passports then? They're still locked in our suitcases, in the car."

"It is a little irregular, M'sieur, but I am sure that in an emergency such as this it will be all right."

I was sliding over a few of the oh-so-useful twenty-dollar bills and saying confidentially: "I expect you'd like a deposit; we have no baggage . . . "

I don't care whether it's right or wrong, but if you're a tourist with money, in a country that needs the exchange, it's *always* made easy for you.

He murmured: "Quite unnecessary, M'sieur, but . . . if you would kindly sign the register?"

"And would you send some brandy up to our room? The best of the local brands, a bottle?"

We signed in: "Monsieur and Madame Roger Soubise. Reason for entry into the country—tourism." Three or four minutes later we were shown into truly marvelous rooms, all hung about with brocade drapes and crystal chandeliers, with a bathroom as big as my Hollywood apartment, and ten times as sumptuous, with those huge white bath sheets, again, hung over a towel rack warmed by hot water, and a four-poster bed in a bedroom that looked as big as a football field.

We soaked together in the enormous tub for half an hour, made love a couple of times, and then got dressed up and went downstairs for a dinner I was certain was going to be the best ever; I was already ordering the crisp, iced Romaine, the steak *bien bleu,* maybe some mushrooms, some asparagus with a butter-lemon sauce, and then a plate of cheeses to follow, with a great deal of a full-bodied red wine and some local brandy to finish it all off.

We walked arm in arm down the splendid baroque staircase, and through the foyer—where the desk clerk bowed at us politely, recognizing quality when he saw it again—and down a long white corridor toward the dining room. . . .

And who did we almost bump into, but Harry Slewsey. I just could not believe my eyes.

He was standing there with a glass in his hand, looking at us, grinning delightedly, dressed in a far-too-elegant tuxedo with—so help me—a red carnation in the buttonhole, and who has buttonholes these days?

I felt Christine's hand clench my arm even before I saw him, and there he was, that big white smile and the hail-fellow-well-met attitude he always put on when there was trouble brewing. He put down his glass and came toward us with his hand outstretched and said delightedly: "Madame . . . ! Michael! How utterly fabulous! What on earth are you two doing in this neck of the woods? You're supposed to be . . . elsewhere."

I know Harry a lot better than Christine ever will, and I was seized with the *certainty* that the most horrible calamity was about to come our way. But he took my hand in his hearty shake and pumped it up and down, and said: "The wilder the surprise, the better it always is! And you couldn't have come to a better place at a better time . . . "

I said: "Surprise? I have the greatest mistrust of coincidences, Harry. How did you know we'd be here?"

He spread his arms out in a gesture. "Know? Michael, how could I possibly know?" He said shrewdly: "Did you plan on being here? I can't imagine you did."

"Well, you've got a point there, I suppose. So what the hell goes on?"

He was looking at me but talking to Christine, knowing that she was the one to convince. He said: "Purely fortuitous, Michael, and I can't tell you how pleased I am."

I looked at him, and there was the wide, open gesture again; he even slapped my back. "Don't be so professionally suspicious, Michael! It doesn't suit a man of your charmingly simple character."

He turned to Christine, and his attitude changed altogether; it was supposed to mean he knew he was dealing with someone a little smarter now. He said, very carefully: "Madame Andress, it is unexpected and quite enchanting. I am giving a party here tonight, a few good friends from all over the world, and of course you are both invited. It's a *good* party, it really is, so come. . . . Let's join the festivities."

She said, very calmly: "Mr. Slewsey, there is nothing in the world I would enjoy more than a really good party."

He was fairly bubbling over with bluebirds. "Then take my arm, Madame . . . "

He led us down the corridor to a sign that said, in a variety of languages: The Zagreb Room, and we went inside and found one hell of a party going on—fifty or sixty people in their Sunday best all milling around and having themselves a good time.

I thought: All right, you bastard; before we get liquored up for the night, I'm going to find out just what the hell you're up to.

Chapter Thirteen

It was just a party, after all—albiet a very good and expensive one, the kind I like—and there was really no reason why a world traveler like Harry, a man who'd throw a party at the drop of a hat, shouldn't give one here too; maybe he was right about my professional suspicion. But I thought it very unlikely.

With *everything* Harry does, you have to look for the reason hidden under the reason, and the reason under that one too, and you're still only halfway home.

His guests were a very mixed crowd, as might be expected—some of them very elegant in tuxedos, some in business suits, some in the most casual clothes ever. They were American, Italian, French, and German, with a smattering of Serbs or Croats, and a few English couples—one of whom I recognized as the number-two man at their ministry of labor, together with his current mistress, a rather dim-witted, red-headed girl with a penchant for getting her picture in the papers.

A dozen waiters were moving among them, the old-fashioned European kind of waiter with white gloves and the deferential air, filling champagne glasses and carrying trays of canapés; and there was a string quintette of elderly gentlemen (an equally elderly lady on the double bass) squeaking out something from the *Peer Gynt Suite.*

There was an enormous buffet table, loaded down with slices of roast beef, lamb, pork and ham, plump prawns in a crystal bowl of ice, little Swedish meatballs, a damn great bowl of caviar decorated with lemon wedges, tiny cocktail sausages on a bed of parsley and dill, some barbecued ribs, veal birds, and everything else that might delight the senses of ordinary mortals . . .

We headed straight for the table, and as I loaded down

a china plate, I watched Christine attacking it all mightily too. I'll never know how she keeps that marvelous figure —it has to be a freakish kind of metabolism—but whatever it is, it's greatly to be envied. There was a smile of pure amusement on her face, just as though she knew that Harry and I were going to have a stand-up row before very long and was rather relishing the idea; I don't suppose his unexpected presence pleased her very much, either.

Harry was slapping me on the back again, grinning like a Cheshire cat and telling me how glad he was we were there, and I said: "Harry, come off it, you're not here just by chance; so why don't you tell me what the hell it's all about?"

He gestured again, very broadly, his eyes wide and innocent. He said: "Michael, didn't you know? This is the tenth anniversary of the founding of my magazine, and I just happened to find myself in Sarajevo . . ."

"Doing what, Harry?"

"And you didn't know that either? They just dug up some seventh-century remains that prove conclusively that the Avars were never exterminated, as everyone believes, by the Servians, but that they simply joined forces to wipe out the Illyrian barbarians. . . ."

I said: "Harry, I just can't see any money coming your way from seventh-century Balkan history."

He seemed hurt. "Michael, it's one of the greatest archaeological finds of the century! The papers are full of it."

"And that's what brought you here."

"The story broke while we were in Paris. I came on down here the first moment I could. And the anniversary rolled in; so I made a few phone calls, chartered a few planes—you know how I like to do things . . ."

"Indeed I do."

He gestured around the room. "And this is the result. So enjoy it; you have to learn to relax once in a while."

"And is the redoubtable Mrs. Bentley here too?"

He took a slice of coulibiac of salmon on a fork. "Redoubtable is quite the wrong word, and yes, she's here, somewhere around. She may have stepped out to do a little job. Try some of the coulibiac. The pastry has a little too much lard in it, but the salmon is wonderful. They have superb salmon here, did you know that?"

"All I know about Sarajevo is that it started World War I. It's liable to start another if I don't get some straight answers soon. Oh yes, and that it has one-hundred mosques."

"Including the three regarded as the most beautiful in Europe. Ah . . ." He turned, beaming.

A large black man in a brightly-embroidered gown, a little black-and-gold pillbox on his head, was bearing down on us with a glass of champagne in each hand. He looked at Harry and said: "Mr. Slewsey, may I say that you are undoubtedly the world's finest host outside of Africa. Allow me to offer you my congratulations on the auspicious occasion." His English was impeccable, Oxford accented.

Harry said: "Your Excellency, permit me to present Mr. and Mrs. . . . " He was suddenly seized with a fit of coughing, waiting for me to make sure he got the name right. I shot out a hand and said: "Roger Soubise," and Harry recovered and said: "Forgive me. Roger and Madame Soubise, from Paris, his Excellency M'Buto Segoto, minister without portfolio from Zaire."

The minister took Christine's hand and bowed over it, switched immediately to French, and told her he was ravished. He picked up the two glasses, emptied one into the other, contrived to spear four prawns on one little silver pick, and waddled off.

Harry said, watching him pensively: "Poor fellow, he's going to be assassinated next week, and he knows it." He shrugged. "There's nothing he can do about it, and he knows that too. He's made himself one of the richest men in Africa, and it's all finally caught up with him. Ah, well."

I said carefully: "Harry, I believe the bit about the archaeology; I believe the bit about the anniversary. Now tell me how you knew we'd be here."

For a long time he said nothing. There was an almost mischievous look on his face, and he snapped his fingers for a waiter to refill our glasses. Christine was watching him obliquely.

He said at last, turning to her: "All right. I made a guess. Intelligent deduction is my viaticum. I never go anywhere or do anything without it. And I suspect that Madame Andress can reason it out. Let me give you a hint. . . ."

I said, interrupting him: "Harry, stop playing games, for God's sake! We didn't know ourselves that we'd be here until a few hours ago! And that opens up all kinds of questions, and I don't like the answer to any one of them."

He was still smiling at Christine. He said imperturbably: "The hint is that a little peasant cottage near the coast was mysteriously destroyed by fire the night before last, and fragments of half a dozen hand grenades were found there. The police are very upset about it. Can you take it from there?"

Christine was right, then; I had never quite believed it.

She held his look. She said: "There was a gullible bandit looking after us there who thought he was employed by the police. When he lost us he went to them for help in searching the forest and to make sure his so-called pardon was not going to be jeopardized. And you, no doubt, have informants in the police department."

He said gravely: "At the very highest level."

"And what happened to the poor man?"

"It just took the police a few minutes to get over their surprise. And then . . . they locked him up, what else? They've been hunting him for years." He looked back at me now, and his voice was mocking: "You should have figured that out, Michael."

"That was only one of the possibilities. I wanted to hear it from you."

He was very wary now, still smiling. I thought: *You sonofabitch, if you clap me on the back again, I'm going to punch you in the nose.* He wanted to change the subject, but not too fast, so he said: "I assumed you'd make for the nearest airport, which is here. It was a guess, of course, but I had to be here anyway. I just . . . *hoped* that things might turn out the way they did. Satisfied?"

"No."

"You should be. When you hear what else I have to tell you, you'll be truly delighted we met. The opposition, it seems, also made the right deduction. I've been keeping an eye on them for you. Isn't that nice of me?"

Christine said sharply: "They're here?"

He shook his head. "I don't think Helder is, though I've an idea I can guess at that. But the Verignana woman is in this hotel—where else would she stay in Sarajevo—in Room 232. She's been there all day and hasn't left the room once. Waiting for her legmen to report, no doubt."

I said: "And Helder?"

"Only a guess. I don't like guesses."

"Coming from you, Harry, I'll buy them."

"All right. I suspect that Helder will be in Belgrade. Because there are really only two routes you could have taken: one, via Sarajevo, here, where the lovely Veronica has those legmen all over town; and the other, via Belgrade itself. That's where Helder will be."

I could almost feel the steam rising off Christine. She was getting more and more furious at every word, though there was a patient, even friendly look frozen onto her face. She was very calm and self-controlled, but her voice was like ice: "Then, if you know about the cottage, you must know that Helder got what he was looking for?"

It was the question I had wanted to ask myself; the teamwork was beautiful.

Harry said slyly: "I know he got *something*. I don't know whether they were decoys or not. I don't suppose Helder does either. Were they?"

She said carefully: "Mr. Slewsey—at this stage of the game, at any stage of the game—the intrusion of outsiders, however well intentioned, is terribly dangerous. I must ask you to stay out of it." I had expected the claws to show, but she was keeping them well sheathed.

He was well aware of how deeply he'd offended her by his interference, and Harry never likes to offend anyone . . . at least, not openly; there was something going on that smelled like a sour Camembert.

But he just shrugged and said apologetically: "I was aware, of course I was aware, that I was risking your displeasure, Madame Andress. But at least you are warned that they are waiting for you here. I'm sure that's helpful."

"It is indeed. And will you excuse us now?"

He said, protesting: "But there's no way out of here until tomorrow morning. In a crowd like this, you're perfectly safe, you must know that. So why don't you relax and enjoy yourselves?"

She was still keeping all doors open. I half expected her to say something like: Your party is beginning to stink, Mr. Slewsey. Instead, she just shook her head: "You're very kind. But no. Good-night, thank you."

He looked at me, a very sly, even satisfied look on his face; I knew what it meant. I took Christine's arm and we wandered off. As we moved across the foyer, I said to her: "A council of war, *now*."

"Yes, I know. Let's go to the room."

"We don't have as much time as we thought we'd have."

"I know."

Now the anger began to show, the claws coming out for action. "I can't believe he's up to . . . what I think he's up to."

"He is. And it's worse than you think. Believe me."

We went up the stairs to our room and locked ourselves in, and she sat down on the bed and said: "*Merde!*" She looked at me and said: "All right, Michael, you know him far better than I do. What's he trying to do?"

I began pacing, and she watched me. I said: "Let's put it all into some sort of coherent order by taking a look at the Harry Slewsey scenario; it's fascinating. First scene: Someone mentioned the raising of the association's insurance fees, largely on account of Helder's successes. What kind of money are we talking about? Hundreds of thousands?"

She shook her head. "No. The insurance on our merchandise alone is over the million mark. In a year, the association pays out—and yes, largely on account of Helder—six, seven, maybe eight million dollars."

"Good, it strengthens the argument. So if Harry could arrange, through me, to put Helder out of business *permanently*, they'd be grateful, to say the least, right?"

"Very true."

"That establishes his financial reward, without which he won't touch anything. Second, and now let's go back to Bluebeard's cottage. Helder kept on telling us how half convinced he was that you were the girl. I don't believe he had to say that even once, certainly not two or three times, ramming it home like that."

"Go on . . ."

"He just wanted us to *believe* he wasn't sure. He was being very smart there, but he also mentioned a source of information *that liked to play tricks,* and that was a very small mistake that wouldn't have mattered a bit if it stood alone. Because look what else we have. Helder knew all about me—my name, my profession, everything. Where did he get his information? The same source that likes to play tricks?"

She murmured: "A leak somewhere, at a high level, without a doubt . . . but there has to be more."

"There is. Harry said, in answer to your question, that he knew Helder got *something* in the cottage. If his police spy told him that, it presupposes that Bluebeard told the police."

"Well, he would, wouldn't he? To bolster his story that he thought he was working for them? Against a pair of diamond smugglers?"

"No. I won't buy that for one minute. The moment Bluebeard found out he'd been fooled . . . for God's sake, Christine, he's not the kind of man to talk and talk and go on talking! He'd shut his mouth so damn tight they wouldn't be able to pry it open with a crowbar! It was Helder who told Harry that he'd got . . . *something.*"

She was very thoughtful. "It's a little thin, Michael, but . . ."

"And how did he know Veronica was here? Okay, a few large bills would get him a look at the hotel register, but would she be registered here under her own name? Even in Paris she was Claire Aprise, remember? God alone knows who she is here."

"It's persuasive, but it's all circumstantial . . ."

"And we're not in a court of law."

"Then tell me the why, and I'll believe you. I won't believe that one of the world's leading magazine publishers is suddenly going to embark on a life of crime."

"No. I agree, that wouldn't make any sense at all. But there's a clincher. And it's your own fantastic reputation."

Her eyes were clouding over, hiding the wheels that were spinning back there; she knew what I was getting at.

I said: "Helder is known to be a good man. You are known to be better. Harry will have worked out the odds, down to the last detail. And he will have found them unfavorable unless he does one thing. He *has* to give Helder a helping hand. If he doesn't do that, you make the delivery, and Helder loses out and waits for the next time. *Not* put permanently out of business at all. Which means, quite simply, Harry doesn't hit the association's jackpot."

She said flatly, and her voice was tight with anger: "So he's throwing us to Helder."

"No. He's throwing Helder to us. He's convinced that if we come together, one of us is going to get . . . put away permanently. And he's betting it will be Helder."

She got to her feet and began striding around, furiously. She said, gesticulating: "I'm convinced, I'm convinced, and I still can't believe it. . . . "

"I'm sure of it. I believe that he went to Helder in the early days, right at the beginning, and said something like: 'I know you're after the diamonds, and I don't give a damn whether you get them or not. But in exchange for your side of the story, I'll throw a few tidbits your way.' That's all it would need."

"Helder would never agree to that."

"And Harry, of course, might ask for a small cut. Which, to give him his due, he would never expect to get or even care about. I'll go a step further and say that if he *did* get a cut, you know what he'd do? He'd turn it over to a charity, a pious gesture to ease whatever conscience he has; that's the kind of man he is."

"A man in his position, working with Helder?"

"Not really working with him. Just offering him a little hint here and there, hoping that I'll get desperate when he gets too close, and either make sure that he ends up in jail, or . . . or kill him."

Her anger was going, the conviction coming, the game being played again.

I said: "It might not even have been Helder who got to that young pilot, what's his name? Colbert. It could just as well have been Harry, and it doesn't really matter one bit. They *both* knew we'd be in Vaganovo; they had to know."

She was frowning, working it all out. I poured us cognac, handed her a glass and said: "Will you buy all that?"

Her mind was already made up. "Yes, Michael, I'll buy it. It's the only thing that makes any sense at all. He's devious, isn't he?"

"The most devious sonofabitch you ever laid eyes on."

"And he's probably already told the Verignana woman that we're here."

"I'm sure of it."

I went to the door and unlocked it, and looked back and said: "Lock the door behind me, don't open it to anybody except me. I won't be more than a few minutes."

She said sharply: "Michael! She may not be alone!"

"I know it."

"Then . . ." Instinctively, she lowered her voice: "Why don't you leave them with me?"

"Because they know I'm not damn fool enough to walk in on them with the merchandise in my pocket. Besides, if anyone's going to bleed all over the carpet for them, it's going to be me, not you."

"That's a specious argument. . . . "

"Yes, it is. Keep my cognac warm. I'll be back."

She came over and kissed me, and I said carefully: "And I'll tell you something else that you may not find easy to believe. In his own mind, Harry will justify everything he's done. Openly, frankly, even honestly. He'll *justify* it. He wants a story from me about the way Helder operates, and if you're so good at your business that Helder can't even get to first base . . . where's the exposé? He'll call it merely stirring up the pot in the name of heightened interest."

Her beautiful eyes were very solemn. "Even if you were to get killed in the process? He must know how dangerous Helder is."

"He also knows my capacity for staying alive, and he's betting on that too. If anything happens to me, or to you, then Harry will be brokenhearted. *Genuinely* brokenhearted. Maybe for as long as half a day."

I opened the door, and she kissed me again. "Be careful, Michael."

I went into the corridor, waited for the sound of the key turning in the lock, and walked on up the stairs to the next floor.

Two thirty-two was just around the corner, and I

tapped lightly on the door and waited, and she answered, in Italian: *"Un momento . . . "* It sounded as though she were on the far side of the room. Another voice then, also in Italian, and it was a voice I recognized: "Who is it?"

I said very clearly: "My name is Michael Benasque, and I would like to speak to Signorina Verignana."

I wished I could have seen the look on his face. I couldn't hear a thing, but I knew they were whispering in there, wondering what the hell was going on, and possibly were worried about it; when the door opened, it was Veronica herself. She said, very calm and controlled: "Come in, Mr. Benasque."

The little French kid who had beaten up on us down at the beach was very sensibly in his preferred position, at the far side of the room, the two-two with the silencer on it pointing where it was supposed to point. He looked very angry because something was happening that he didn't understand.

The phone on the bedside table was off the hook, and Veronica motioned me to a chair and murmured: "Excuse me . . . " She picked up the phone and said, looking at me intently: "Mr. Benasque just invited himself into my room, I'll call you back in a little while . . . No, I can take care of it, there's no problem . . . all right, darling, I'll do that."

Darling. Helder, then. Good.

She put the phone down and sat opposite me, the two of us facing each other like strangers who don't quite know how to begin a polite conversation.

She looked very different now, not really dressed up at all. I reasoned, therefore, with no immediate plans to leave her room, she was just waiting for reports to come in from the legmen, as Harry had said. But she still looked extraordinarily beautiful, in the rare, classical manner. She wore a pair of silk knit slacks in a strange kind of olive-green color, with a blouse of the same material, a shade lighter, that was sort of tied loosely very low down over her shoulders with a ribbon; I think they're called lounging pyjamas or something—very fragile and sloppy and quite exciting. She wore gold sandals, and that thick mass of auburn hair was just hanging loosely down over her bare shoulders, shining nicely.

She looked very wary, and when she saw that I was studying her, she said: "I'm not really dressed for formal occasions, forgive me."

I said: "I think you look marvelous, but why don't you get rid of that unpleasant little bastard with the gun. He riles me."

"No, Mr. Benasque. Whatever you have to say can be said in front of him."

"I think not. It's very, very personal."

She hesitated, but she turned to him and said: "You can wait outside, in the corridor."

He didn't like it a bit, and while he was wondering how he could phrase a protest, I said carelessly: "If he's worried about you, let him wait in the bathroom, so he's close by if you have to start screaming."

She said tartly: "Well, I hardly think that's likely, but . . . in the bathroom, and close the door."

Good. I didn't want him prowling around the corridor and maybe taking it on himself to investigate the floor below. When he had tucked his little gun away and was gone, she looked at me with a hint of suspicion and said: "But then, this isn't really a social occasion, is it?"

"Unhappily, not quite. I wanted to talk to you about a man named Malcolm Reevers."

It startled her.

In a moment, she got to her feet, went to the dresser and picked up a bottle of Scotch, standing there nicely with the light behind her and sort of gesturing with it at me. "Will you join me?"

"Thank you. Straight up, please."

She splashed whiskey into two glasses, handed me one of them, sat down again and said: "Who told you about Malcolm Reevers?"

"The association, of course."

"Isn't that a little like putting ideas into your head?"

"On the contrary. They were very careful to let me know that he'd met with a traffic accident. More like making sure I didn't get any similar ideas."

"And just what else do you know about him?"

I shrugged. "I believe the figure he sold out for was half the value of the merchandise. But I'll admit, it seems rather a lot. I'm not quite so demanding, and the value is far more this time, isn't it?"

She was no fool. She said calmly: "And your courier sent you to me?"

"My courier is fast asleep, resting up after a hectic chase all over the country. She thinks I've gone back to the party downstairs."

"I see. You're not a professional CA, are you?"

"The new boy on the job."

"And venal."

"Almost the only weakness I have is a desire to get rich."

"And what exactly are you proposing?"

I said apologetically: "Well, I'd rather not talk about precise figures at the moment. We're really establishing a matter of principles, aren't we?

"Perhaps. But let's not be too sure about that."

She gulped down her Scotch and got up to pour herself another, a big one; so I finished off mine too and held out my glass for a fill-up. We both began pacing around the big room, like caged animals; it must have looked a bit comic.

She said: "Well, we have established one thing then, haven't we?"

"Oh? What's that?"

"You're suggesting that the stones we have are not the real ones."

That, of course, was where the danger lay; but I was counting on that suspicious nature her dossier was so full of. I said: "That's exactly what I'm saying. Not suggesting. Telling you. You see how frank and open I am?"

"Two sets of stones. And neither of them real. Just how many decoys are there?"

I said: "I can't really be sure about that. More than the usual number, I'm told. In fact, to my own inexperienced eye, it seemed there were decoys all over the place. Very good ones, too."

"And the real ones are . . . where?"

"I said frank and open. Not stupid."

"I can call . . . my man in very easily. It will take him just a few moments to find out."

"Quite wrong. I don't even know that myself. I will know by some time tomorrow."

She started thinking hard again. She stopped in front of the big mirror over the dressing table and looked at herself, touching that glorious hair and setting it just so, and she said: "What we have here is quite a challenge to the imagination, isn't it?"

"I don't think so. It's pretty simple, really. Just an exercise in . . . venality."

"No. When you tell me that all we have is imitations, my immediate reaction is to assume that we have the real thing. And that what you're doing is . . . trying to sell us a set of decoys. It's a nice try, I must admit. But I could be wrong. If so . . . we won't find out till it's too late, will we? *Unless* . . . we take a chance on you."

I said cheerfully: "That about sums up the situation. That's why I don't want to be too greedy."

"Except for one thing."

"And what's that?"

"Arthur decided that in this case, Christine would not be carrying decoys with her, sending the real stones with the girl. It's too important a delivery. And he's always right about these things."

I tried to look as happy as I knew how. I said: "Exactly."

Her eyes were so suspicious now! But she said clearly: "We have always known who it is you're traveling with. It is *not* the girl."

I shook my head, smiling at her. "We fooled everybody. Helder, you . . . hell, we even fooled Harry Slewsey, and technically, at least, he's my boss."

That did it. At the mention of Harry's name I could see her whole world crumbling for a brief moment. She recovered very quickly, but it was too late. She took the bottle again and filled her half-full glass, and in a moment, when she had fully recovered, she said: "That's very interesting. Only I wonder if I can believe *anything* you've told me?"

I shrugged. "Tell Helder. He'll believe what he has to believe."

She took a long, deep breath. "All right. If we *were* to

take a chance on you, how much money are we talking about?"

"I'll talk about that with Helder, no one else."

"He's not here now; you can make a deal with me."

"No. He is the one who controls the money, and that's all I'm interested in. Unless I can talk to him, then I'll have to be satisfied with my salary. Oh well, it was worth a try."

I finished my drink. She was at the bottle again, waving it at me. "Don't go. Have another; we don't have to rush into negatives or positives."

"All right."

As she poured: "Are they in the hotel somewhere?"

"I don't think so. I'll know tomorrow. And if I'm going to talk with Helder, I have to see him tonight."

"But that's impossible. Not before . . . well, daylight at the very earliest."

It's a hundred and fifty miles from Belgrade to Sarajevo, with no planes at this time of night. He'd have to drive over some of the most hair-raising roads in the country. It was just about the right timing. I said dubiously: "Daylight is cutting it a bit fine. . . ."

"Not before six in the morning."

I said: "All right. I'll have to settle for that, but I have to be . . . somewhere else in the early morning."

Now she was hooked. "Where exactly?"

I hesitated. Then: "Are we getting into a deal?"

"Possibly."

"Okay. You know the baths at Ilidza?" She shook her head, and I said: "Twenty kilometers down the road toward Mostar. There's a sign; you turn south over the railway line. You can't miss it. That's where I'll be at six."

The suspicion was creeping back again. "I rather imagine your courier watches you like a hawk."

I grinned at her. "I'm a hell of a man with sleeping pills. And there's one other thing."

"Which is?"

"Tell Helder that yes, I'm prepared to haggle. But I'll be bucking the association; they'll be after me for the rest of my life; you know what happened to Reevers. So I will want a hefty cash settlement. Otherwise, I might just chicken out."

"I'll tell him."

"And I have to get back; I've been away too long already."

She put down her glass and stood very close to me, slipping both hands under my jacket and shirt and running them over my chest. "You could stay for a while, if you'd like that?"

I'm not the kind of man the ladies get hysterical over at first sight; I always have to argue like hell for my pleasures; and I knew just what she had in mind. But I wanted to keep the door open, too, so I put my hands on her shoulders and turned her around very gently so that her back was tight to me, slid the top of the pyjama thing down over her shoulder and ran my hands over that statuesque jellied mousse, looking at our reflection in the mirror—a pleasing reflection indeed. I said: "I have to take a rain check, you must know that. We can't have her getting suspicious."

"Christine?"

"If that's what you want to call her."

"Yes, of course. Well, it was just an idea. When I first saw you, on Giles' yacht, I couldn't help thinking how good you must be in bed."

"You did? I didn't know that you even noticed me."

"Oh, but I did. You won't believe the things I was thinking about you."

"That's nice. . . ."

I pulled up the top again gave the mousse a final loving pat, and went to the door. I said: "Tomorrow morning at six. We'll have an hour to talk, no more. Preferably a lot less."

"All right."

She was already moving toward me, a goddess. She took my hand and said earnestly: "Can I really believe all this, Michael?"

I said, just as earnestly: "Frankly, it doesn't matter if you do or not. Tell Helder. He will. He'll *know*, you'll see."

As I slipped out, I saw her glance instinctively at the telephone. I couldn't help thinking I'd done a damn good job of work.

I went quickly back to our room—there was a matter of great urgency now—and said to Christine: "I'm going to tell you exactly what went on, every single thing, but first . . . she's on the phone now to Helder in Belgrade, and the next thing she's going to do is get hold of Harry Slewsey. So, you have to find Harry right away, get him up here where he can't be found, tell him some fascinating lies to keep him busy . . . and wait for me. We'll be moving out in a hurry, so make sure you have your purse and passport with you. I have to hurry . . . "

She was fantastic; she didn't even ask a single question, although I could guess how important it was to her, in more ways than one. She said: "Don't worry, I'll hold him here . . . "

We were already moving to the door; when she went to find my scheming boss, I hurried out into the parking lot at the back and chose a car that had a film of dust over it, as though it had been there for some days and might be there for a few more before the owner came looking for it—or at least, for the few hours we needed. It was a Peugeot, the big one, and I spent a precious five minutes getting the door-lock picked, only to discover it had a steering-wheel lock, the one problem that can't easily be overcome.

Five more minutes, and I'd hot-wired a ten-year-old Alfa with Italian plates on it. I left it there, ready to start up again in a hurry with a twist of the wires and a touch of the starter button, hurried back into the hotel and up to our room.

Christine and Harry were there. She was saying: " . . . and what you *can* find out for us is how long Helder is remaining in Belgrade—if indeed he is there, which we can't be sure about—because we were planning on making a detour to throw them off, all the way up to Trieste for a main-line flight. . . . "

He was taking in every word of it, his eyes bright and very serious.

I said: "I'm sorry, I have to break this up, Harry, something astonishing has happened . . . Christine, we have to get to Ivancici in a hurry, the contact's screwed up the schedule, and if we don't get him before he leaves . . . on the road there, we have to hurry . . . "

Harry said: "Ivancici? What the hell's Ivancici?"

I said quickly: "No time, Harry, we'll let you know, maybe, when we get back."

I said to Christine: "It's about half an hour of fast driving up the road. I've got a car ready, only we have to hurry, for God's sake. . . . "

She was already gathering up her purse, with a kind of automatic reflex and hurrying with me to the door, and Harry said, bewildered: "Michael . . . you can tell me . . . "

"No *time*, Harry, for God's sake . . . "

He was behind us when I slammed the door shut, and behind us all the way down the stairs and out into the parking lot. At the car, he at last said: "Michael! I'm coming with you!"

I shook my head. "No, Harry, emphatically no. I don't like the way you've been interfering and neither does Christine. You're not coming."

He said sternly: "I pay your salary, Michael. . . ."

I contrived to look embarrassed: "Yes, yes, I realize that, but . . . I promise you, I'll let you know when we get back. Some of it, anyway."

He looked genuinely hurt. "Michael . . . "

"I'm sorry." I helped Christine into the front seat, and as I held my door open, I said again: "I'm sorry, Harry, but this has to be kept absolutely secret."

He was already in the back seat.

He said sternly: "Your boss, and you can't say I don't pay you enough."

I sighed. "Okay then . . . "

He was grinning now. "And who knows? I might just turn out to be very useful."

I patted Christine on the knee, and we set off at high speed on the road to Ivancici. Harry still wanted to know what was happening, but I contrived to sound worried and told him to wait till we got there. I said: "Just before Ivancici, we take a shortcut through the forest, a third-rate road, but we'll save a precious few minutes."

He said suspiciously: "Where did you get the car?"

"I borrowed it."

"You mean you *stole* it?"

"Uh-huh. This is far too important to worry about little things like that."

"So *tell* me, Michael!"

"No. As a matter of fact, I hardly believe it myself; it's going to solve all our problems, put us back in the groove again."

"Who's the contact you mentioned?"

"You know I can't tell you that. Be patient, Harry."

"Very well, if you say so. But it had better be good. I'm leaving a lot of important guests back there."

"It'll be worth it, you'll see."

The map had called it a secondary road, and I'd never been on it before. It was like a goat track, but we kept up a very good speed, and when we'd left the town some twenty miles behind us, I slowed down and started peering out of the window.

In a little while we came to one of those shrines, a tremendous drop to the bottom of the gorge below it. I stopped and said mysteriously: "Is that the Virgin Mary there? It has to be."

Harry said impatiently: "Well, of course it is! What else would they put on a shrine, a plaster cast of the president?"

"This is it, then."

We were a long way from anywhere here, no farms, no houses, no *nothing* within more than fifteen miles of us. I got out of the car and held the door open for Harry, and he clambered out and said: "Will you please tell me what the hell goes on? There's nobody here . . . "

I said: "Just one man, all by himself."

I slipped quickly back into the driver's seat and yelled: "See you, Harry!" and sped off into the night, my foot on the floor, the rear wheels spinning up masses of gravel.

Christine yelled: "Darling, for God's sake, watch the edge of the road . . . !"

"Sonofabitch."

I'd rarely felt happier in my life. I said: "Even if he were to run all the way, which he won't, he can't reach a telephone or get to Veronica for three or four hours and by that time . . . we'll be in Belgrade."

"Where Arthur Helder is waiting for us."

"No."

It was time now. I slowed down and told her almost everything that had happened with Veronica.

I said: "At this moment, Helder has found a car and is driving furiously down this same road to meet with me at a place called Ilidza, where he will no doubt take Veronica along in case some soft soaping is needed. It's nice to know where the opposition is, for a change. The plane for Athens leaves Belgrade at ten minutes to six in the morning, and we'll just make it nicely if we push a bit."

She said, puzzled: "Helder's on his way to Sarajevo?"

"Yep."

"On this road?"

"Yep. Take a good look at the map and tell me where to turn off, a place called, I think, Zvornik? There's only this road for about a third of the way there."

She was pulling out the map, switching on the little map-light, and we were tourists driving through the mountain night. She said in a moment: "No, a couple of miles beyond Zvornik, we turn right at Loznica. And it looks like a dubious sort of road."

"He's not the kind of man to drive right past us without seeing who's at the wheel; we have to take it."

"It's quite a detour."

I put my foot down again, and it was time to tell her the rest of it. I said: "The lovely Veronica wanted me to spend the night with her."

She sounded very calm: "I'm not surprised. You're a very attractive man."

"I am? Well, I'll be damned."

"And why didn't you?"

"Because I'm in love, dammit . . . "

"And is that the reason you gave her?" I could detect the note of jealousy there now, in spite of everything.

"No. I told her I had to get back before you got suspicious. She imagines you must be watching me like a hawk."

"With women like her around, that's not imagination."

I had to tell her *everything*. I said, trying not to feel guilty: "I made a sort of pass at her when I turned her down, just to keep the door open in case we ever need it again."

"A pass? You mean . . . physically?"

It was getting worse. I said: "Well, she really was asking for it, and . . . well, I thought, at the moment she's convinced she can twist me around her little finger, and I didn't want . . . "

"What sort of a physical pass?"

Oh well. I said: "I just squeezed her a little bit here and there . . . "

"And was it enjoyable?"

"Dammit, I didn't do very much. I just . . . well, squeezed."

She sighed. "And that was exactly the right thing to do. I hate you for it."

I leaned over and kissed her quickly, and she said again: "Will you watch the road . . . ?" But her hand was on my knee, and she was stroking me gently, just to say that everything was forgiven.

I said: "Don't worry about the road. My cargo is far too precious to jeopardize, in any way."

She took my arm now and snuggled in tight, and I concentrated on some fast driving. We hit Belgrade at five-twenty in the morning.

And, thirty-five minutes later, we were on the plane to Athens.

Chapter Fourteen

Athens . . . It's always been one of my favorite cities, though it's growing too fast these days and getting crowded as all the Lebanese move in from the ruins of their own once-beautiful capital; when you walk around Syntagma Square, all you hear these days is Arabic.

But the ambiance is still there, and the fine old ruins everywhere, and the sidewalk cafes full of people taking it easy and just getting to know each other. . . . It's a great place for lovers.

The pilot had told us we were coming in to the airport, so would we please stop smoking and fasten our seatbelts. I was conscious that Christine was looking somber, if not downright sad and lonely too.

My hand was in hers, and I asked her quietly: "What's troubling you, Christine?"

She turned those huge eyes on me. "It's the end of the road, Michael. I always hate the end of the road."

"We're not there yet. When we are, it will be just another job done."

"And will I see you again, Michael?"

There was almost a panic in me, and I felt the hair rising on my scalp at just the thought of it. I said urgently: "For God's sake . . . "

What could I say? "We're together now, for . . . for as long as you like—forever."

"Are you sure about that?"

"Of course I'm sure! Aren't you?"

"Yes. Yes, I suppose I am."

She didn't sound in the least convinced, and it scared me, but before I could answer, she said: "The first thing we have to find out about is the girl. She must have arrived here. . . . My God, is it Thursday already? Then she got in three days ago."

I suddenly realized how completely we'd been out of touch with anything but each other. I said: "Christine?"

She looked.

"Please don't talk about my leaving you? It hurts me."

She held on tightly to my arm and laid her cheek on my shoulder; her eyes were wet.

I said: "I love you, and that's all that matters. Not only *in* love with you, I love you too."

"All right. Something's happened to both of us; let's try and make it last a long, long time."

"Forever. Have you ever been married?"

"No. Have you?"

"No. It must be very exciting. For the right people, I mean. Like us."

She squeezed my arm again, and we were touching down in the bright morning sunlight, just a few white puffs of clouds in a blue, blue sky. We walked down the steps, and it was already hot and pleasant. The terminal building was crowded with limber young Swedes with backpacks of red, blue and yellow nylon, and pretty girls in tank tops and bare feet, shouldering huge blanket-rolls, and lots of Japanese in business suits, with Nikons, snapping pictures of everything in sight. I noticed that Christine, with an instinctive reflex, was carefully keeping out of their shots, not taking any professional risks.

I took her arm, and we went through customs and immigration with no problems at all. As we stepped outside into the bright sunlight, I had that strange feeling that someone was watching us. I started looking around for a suspicious face, but what the hell is a suspicious face, I'd like to know? Was it the old fisherman with the crate of lobsters on his shoulder? The young black-haired kid with three days' growth of beard and a guitar slung over his back? The thick-set businessman with the red tie, staring at Christine with an oafish grin on his face? Or perhaps even the slovenly airport cop who was lounging there, his stern eyes on us? *Someone* was watching; I could feel it. But it was none of these.

It was Brett Howard. His presence here could only

mean trouble. My heart was thumping wildly. I fancied I could even hear Christine's too.

He was staring at us, but he turned away as soon as he caught my eye; so I looked away too, and he wandered over, with his eyes on the taxi schedule behind us, stopped close by, lit a cigarette, and said quietly: "A white van at the curb, a Ford, get into the back of it, quickly. Wait for me."

We hurried out of the building, arm in arm, and as we went to the van, I said: "So it's not the end of the road after all . . . "

We climbed inside it, and the driver looked round at us briefly then looked away. We waited. In five impatient minutes Brett Howard came in and shut the door carefully behind him.

He said furiously: "Jesus Christ! Where the hell have you two been?"

Christine sighed. "It's a long story, Brett. Let's get the delivery over and I'll tell you."

His eyes were very hard. "The merchandise is okay?"

She nodded. "Yes, of course it is . . . "

"Not a goddamn word out of you in three days. Vasileos is fit to be tied . . . "

She said sharply: "Yes, I know that! And he ought to have more sense! Doesn't he realize he's being watched?"

I said mildly: "Brett. How come you knew we were on this plane? We didn't know ourselves until we left Belgrade. Seems to me that everywhere we go, there's always someone there who knows we're coming."

I expected a certain belligerence, but he was just shaking his head, shrugging it off, worried about something else. He said: "I'm not here to meet you. I'm here to meet the girl."

I heard Christine catch her breath: "But she was due in three days ago . . . "

He nodded. "That's right. I guess you didn't hear what happened in Paris?"

She was startled. "No. We've been out of touch with everything."

"Jesus . . . " He ran a hand through his hair. "A regular firefight, a gun-battle on Rue de Rivoli. It hit all the papers everywhere, goddammit."

I had a feeling of terrible alarm now. "And the girl?"

"The girl's okay. Wounded, but okay."

"For Christ's sake, Brett . . . !"

"Okay, okay, I'm telling you."

He took a long, deep breath, and said: "A bunch of Algerians and the Cosmos Gang, working together. They came down the street in two cars, spraying machine-pistol bullets everywhere and . . . you won't believe it, it was crazy. I got one of them, right in the gut, the National Guard got three more, but the others got away. They didn't even get near the safe-box. Her CA was right beside her, a good guy, Chuck Adams. You know Chuck?"

"Yes, go on . . ."

"First sign of trouble, Chuck knocked the girl to the ground, dragged her under cover, but she still took two bullets—one in the arm, just a flesh-wound, the other here . . . " He was clutching at his right thigh. "Caught her on the inside of the thigh, a ricochet up from the ground, like to have torn her guts out, but it got deflected by her hip bone. And I'll say one thing for the girl, she's a real gutsy broad, I'll tell you. She was okay. She insisted on getting the vault open again and replacing the merchandise, and then we got her into the hospital. She came out yesterday afternoon, with half her goddamn side in a plaster cast and went ahead with the BM like nothing had happened, same schedule via Rome. She took the seven o'clock flight out of there this morning. She is due in any minute now, and that's why I'm here, with all the cops and the escorts and the razzmatazz, and who the hell walks into it? You do. It's great, isn't it?"

He said unhappily, not nearly so arrogant now: "And there's one other thing, Christine."

It looked as though he didn't know quite how to put it. He was embarrassed, awkward, and when he began, at last, his voice was surprisingly gentle—maybe a nice guy after all.

He said slowly: "The first sign was a single shot from a balcony on a building opposite. I'm afraid they got the Doberman, Christine, a clean shot right through the neck. Broke his spine. He's dead."

I heard her gasp, and she clutched at my arm.

Brett went on: "That was the one I got, a hundred and

fifty feet and I drilled him right through the belly. That shot was the signal. The two cars came round the corner, one from Rue d'Alger, one from Castiglione, and one of them, Christ, it even had a flat tire—a real amateur night show. The Guard was like to go crazy; you never saw so much shooting. It's a miracle they didn't wipe out half the population."

Nobody spoke for a while. Christine was wiping at her eyes, and she said at last: "If the girl is due in soon . . . how soon, Brett?"

He checked his watch. "Twenty minutes, if it's on time."

"Then we'd better get out of here in a hurry and leave you to it . . ."

"No. We've got to change things around now."

He thought about it for a while, then said: "I'll tell you what we have to do. The opposition is here somewhere—they have to be—but we're ready for them. The place is lousy with security. But I don't want another shootout on my hands, not with you in it anyway; so we'll get the girl on her way first, and with all the fuss, draw the opposition off your tail. Then, once she's on her way, you go straight to Vasileos' villa—you know where that is?"

"Sounion?"

"That's the one. I'll give you my driver; he knows it. Vasileos is there now. I checked a while back and told him to sit there and keep out of sight; so that's where you go. Okay?"

"Okay."

"I'll go with the girl, because I'm the one they're most likely watching. I'll go lay all this on, and you sit tight here and wait for me. I'll be right back."

He looked at Christine and said: "I'm sorry about the dog, I really am. I know how much he meant to you."

"Yes, yes . . . Thank you, Brett."

"Stay right here, under cover, I'll be back in a few minutes."

He was gone. I held Christine and said: "I'm sorry too, my darling."

With no one else there—only me—it didn't matter, so for a moment she let herself go, and I let her cry herself dry. Then she wiped at her eyes, took out her little compact, did her face, and said, quite calmly now: "I'm sorry. I was very fond of that dog. I'd raised her since she was a puppy. Her name was Mia, a beautiful dog. Brown and gold, she used to prance all the time on the tips of her toes, like a ballet dancer."

"They do that, Dobermans."

"Yes, I know. They're very highly strung. . . ."

Brett came back, closed the door carefully, and sat down on the wooden bench and said slowly: "Okay, this is what happens now. The girl's plane is on time; it's landing in five minutes. We'll get her through quickly, and in about ten minutes from now you'll hear the sirens, the escort starting up. Give them three minutes to get clear, then you move into the car right behind us. It's a black Cadillac; the driver's my own man, and he knows where to take you. You just drive out unobtrusively; there'll be two motorcycle cops ahead of you, so you shouldn't have any trouble."

I was getting a little edgy. I said: "A Caddy, with two outriders, and we move out unobtrusively. Got it."

He turned those hard cold eyes on me and said: So help me, one of these days I'm going to break both your legs, you sonofabitch."

He turned back to Christine, who he could put up with: "Its flying a diplomatic flag, and a police escort for diplomatic cars is mandatory here; so the escort is accounted for. You go to Vasileos' villa; there's no one there except Vasileos and his bodyguard . . . " He turned his eyes on me again: "And don't try and tangle with the bodyguard, Benasque. He doesn't have my patience."

Back to Christine: "Any questions?"

She looked worried. "Only one man with Vasileos?"

"You better believe it. No one knows he's there, and that's the way I want it. I want a very low profile on that house. Lots of overt security at the DDP." He looked at me coldly and said: "That's the decoy delivery point, *Mike*."

I sighed. "What happened to Bruce? He's supposed to be here."

The cold look again. "Bruce? Who the hell is Bruce?" He didn't wait for an answer. "You mean the screwed-up sonofabitch with the beard? He got fired the first day of the operation, in Paris. He wasn't a good enough bodyguard even for you; you don't keep up with things too good, do you?"

To Christine again: "Okay, I'm leaving you now. You're on your own, try not to get into any trouble, because if you do . . . there's only one thing I'm sure about. And that is . . . you won't be able to count on your CA too much; I just don't think he's up to it. I'll be at the Grande Bretagne as soon as the girl's made *her* delivery; so why don't you go over there as soon as you've made yours? And you won't need Benasque any more, so leave him behind. I hate to mess up their nice foyer."

I said nothing. He just stared at me for a moment, and then he was gone.

Christine looked at me and smiled sadly, and said: "He's really not a bad sort of man at all, Michael. But I must agree . . . let's not have him for best man at our wedding, okay?"

I just held her in my arms for a while. The driver looked round at us and grinned.

We heard the sirens a little later, very close by, and I instinctively waited for the shooting to start, but then I thought: Well, Paris was the Algerians, the amateurs, and Helder wouldn't try anything here, not with forty or fifty cops scattered around the place expecting trouble. And there was none.

We waited the dutiful three minutes, then slipped out of the van and into the Caddy behind us. The driver didn't even look round. He just started the almost-silent engine, and we moved off slowly.

As we did so, there was a darkly-bearded man leaning against a post nearby and lighting a short and stubby pipe.

It was Bruce.

We were driving along the coastal road, the two outriders ahead of us, at a modest sixty miles an hour or so. The sea was a glorious cobalt color, with a few fishing boats bobbing in the surf here and there, long nets strung out on the beach, and the great gray limestone mountain towering up inland on our left. The weather was perfect, and I felt good.

We were sitting very close together in the back, my arm around her, and she said: "I'm supposed to check once in a while, and in all this time I haven't done it once. Except visually, here and there."

"Check what?"

"You still have them?"

"I'm going to feel naked when I finally get rid of them."

"Is it uncomfortable?"

"No, not really. You get used to it. But when Helder ran his hands over me in that cottage, I was sure he was going to find them."

"They never do, you know. Not unless they strip you down completely. It's a very old trick. Mustn't be overdone, of course."

"I'm glad. I was wondering how many scrotums you hal access to. Or is the plural *scrota*? I suppose it is."

"That wasn't a very nice remark, Michael."

"No, I suppose it wasn't. But I'm jealous too."

I kissed her, she kissed me, and if it hadn't been for the stolid driver up front, we'd have been making love right there. God knows there was room enough for an orgy. The car seemed as big as a basketball court.

We passed Glifada, with the huge white mass of the Astir Palace Hotel perched up on its little promontory overlooking the sea; and Vouliagmeni, where the lake is surrounded with high, pine-covered rocks and the sulphur water flows; and then Varkisa and Legonisi, with boats moored everywhere, some modest and some very expensive-looking indeed, and always the brilliant blue-greens of the sea and the soft colors of the limestone rocks.

We passed through Anavisos, where the farms began, and the tiny waterfront tavernas—the city far behind us now—and on toward Lagrena, where the underwater fishing is so good, just a few miles from Sounion itself.

The road was deserted, and we were both relaxed and happy, chatting away about nothing in particular. I said: "The delivery, technically, is over, when?"

She stretched out her long legs, luxuriating. "A very comfortable car, I must say. But it's not so . . . what's the word?"

"Stately."

"It's not so stately as my Rolls. How can they make a car so big? And the delivery is over, technically, in two stages. The first, when he signs a note accepting delivery of three stones 'reputed to be' and so forth. The second stage is when he's had a chance to test them, and that is usually twenty-four hours later, but in this case it's forty-eight, because of the close examination necessary for the flaw in the Queen, you remember the Thai Queen's face? And the Number Four, of course, with its unlikely number of facets below the girdle—that takes a lot of close examination. That's when he signs the second note, which the association has ready for him, and that's when they deposit my check in the bank, and we all live happily ever after."

"Till next time."

"Yes. I have a delivery coming up in August, and another in December. Would you like to be my CA again? I can insist on it, you know, in spite of Brett Howard."

"I'd love it. I'm planning on making you my whole career from now on."

"Good. The first one is from London to New York, and the second is from Amsterdam to Bangkok, and that will be a particularly nice one, another major delivery, just one stone, but it's fabulous. Have you ever been to Bangkok?"

"Nope. Never."

"It's fascinating. They have these canals, *klongs* they call them, and you sit in a flat-bottomed boat and just drift along, and all you can smell is honeysuckle and frying fish. It's a nice combination."

"And temples, they tell me, everywhere . . . "

"The most marvelous temples. You can buy rubbings of the temple carvings. I have a whole lot of them at my place in Positano. You know Positano?"

"Sure, it's marvelous."

"I'm at the very top of the lower road, a little pink and white villa. Lots of wisteria everywhere."

"Wisteria is marvelous too."

"You really must come and visit some time."

There it was again, the panic and the scalp-crawling. I said nothing for a very long time, and then, very carefully: "I don't want this to go up in smoke."

She didn't answer, and I said deeply hurt: "For Christ's sake, we were talking about a wedding half an hour ago!"

"Yes. And I started it, didn't I?"

"And I took you up on it. I want to marry you, Christine. God knows how we're going to live. We have different . . . different financial standards, I suppose you'd call them. Okay, if I have to be kept, I don't really mind too much. But you wouldn't like that, would you?"

"I'd love it."

She moved in closer and threw her arms around me and kissed me again, and then she was suddenly clutching at me and crying her eyes out, all for nothing, just the way she had done the first night we'd spent together and made love.

I held her very close and said nothing and wondered about her secret thoughts. She pulled herself together and pulled out the compact again, and said: "Crying is the worst thing that can happen to makeup, did you know that? I was wondering about . . . No, I must stop calling her *the girl*. I was wondering about Marie. A bullet in the thigh, the hip . . . it must be terribly painful."

"Will I meet her one day?"

"I'm sure of it . . . "

And I swear I heard the shooting before it started.

It was a sudden burst of machine gun fire from the bouldered hill beside us, dotted with beautiful, peaceful pines. And I saw the motorcycle cop on the left, ahead of us, throw up his arms and let his bike go haywire, slewing round in the road and skidding on its side. There was even time to see the blood. The other cop flung his machine around and headed for the drop down to the water and threw himself off it—or was hit too. I couldn't tell which. They were obviously getting the escort out of the way first. I shoved Christine hard down onto the floor, threw myself on top of her, and yelled at the driver: "Go!"

The great behemoth of a car was already surging mightily forward, with all the power of its four-or-five hundred horses, racing like a mad thing to a dangerous speed. I don't care what you say, with power steering and suspension made of jello, a hundred and twenty miles an hour in a modern domestic car just isn't safe.

I heard the roar of another car and struggled to a sitting position, more or less, to take a look. It was a little Lotus coming at us, following behind from a dirt turn-off —a bomb of a car with the exhaust cutting out as he topped the ton-and-a-half and went right past us as though we were merely cruising. He was spraying gunfire at us as he roared by, and the Caddy was weaving all over the place. I dived on top of Christine again, then I got up and saw that the driver had lost control completely. That goddamn power steering was doing whatever it wanted to do, which wasn't the right thing at all, and we were off the road and in sand, beginning to spin around. I leaned over the divider and grabbed the wheel and tried to get us on course again.

The driver just flopped over to one side, and there were holes in his head and neck as he fell down onto the seat. I clambered over and swung the great car back onto the road again, trying to keep it on an even keel and only just succeeding.

We ploughed over onto the sand at the other side of the road and up onto rocks before I could get it under control, the sheer weight of it holding us down on the ground. And then it was on all fours again and screeching back onto the tarmac.

The Lotus was already a mile ahead of us, and I could see the smoke coming up from its tires as the brakes got slammed on, and it was turning and coming back at us for a second pass, and I thought: Well, that's one hell of a fine car, but we're the ones with the weight. . . .

It's incredible how short a time it takes for two fast cars, both busting a gut and traveling toward each other to actually come together. I suppose we were both doing about a hundred and something when we almost hit. His gun was chattering again, and I just drove straight at him, making him see for the split second of the final hundred yards or so that I had no intention of doing anything else but hit him. The top of his car couldn't have been as high as the Caddy's radiator, and he must have known that if we hit he would be exterminated.

He swung his wheel hard over at the last minute, and so did I, and it was a very fancy maneuver indeed. I hit his rear end so hard that it simply disintegrated.

I saw a complete wheel assembly flying through the air, and I swung the wheel back again, God knows how many turns lock-to-lock, a madman's car, but it righted itself by the sheer force of its momentum. And in the rearview mirror I saw the Lotus bouncing over and over, high in the air and smashing down again. It exploded on the third bounce, when we were more than a mile ahead.

Our radiator was hissing; and the windshield was shattered, with four neat, round bullet-holes in it over to one side. I slammed to a halt, threw the gears into park, leaned over the back of the seat to look at Christine. I was sure I would find her dead.

She was getting back up onto the seat again, a look of shock on her face. I said stupidly: "Are you hurt?"

She shook her head. She leaned over and looked at the driver, on his side on the seat, the blood no longer running.

She said, and it was almost a whimper: "Oh my God . . . "

I said savagely: "One, possibly two dead cops back there, just doing their jobs, and a dead driver too, just doing his. . . . "

I wasn't sure what was the best thing to do. Christine was staring at him with tears on her cheeks, for a different and more valid reason now. I got out, went round to the near side, opened the door, dragged him out, and laid him down in the grass with as much reverence as I could muster.

It's a strange thing, the reverence. You have to wait till you're dead before you get it. And then, what does it really matter? But I crossed his arms over his chest before the rigor mortis set in. I didn't even know how long that would take, not being too comfortable around dead bodies.

He wore a dark-blue chauffeur's uniform of serge, with old-fashioned high black boots, well polished as befitting his station, and his white shirt—terribly blood-stained now—was carefully starched, with the collar turned and restitched to hide the fraying.

Who turns collars and restitches them these days? I'll tell you who. Impoverished chauffeurs with a wife and ten kids to support, chauffeurs who don't even have names.

They just get to be called "driver"; they don't have life insurance either, because it costs too much.

Christ, I was almost beginning to weep myself. I got back into the car and badly wanted Christine beside me, but there was blood on the seat; so when she started to change places, I said quickly: "No, stay there, my darling."

She knew at once and was grateful. I said: "We drive on to Sounion, if the car's still driveable, we make the delivery, and then we call the police to take care of everything else."

"All right, yes, I think that's best."

But a police car was approaching, coming from the direction we were headed in, from Sounion perhaps, its two-note siren sounding, the blue lights flashing. They stopped only briefly as they passed us, and a cop leaned out and shouted: "Mr. Benasque?"

He knew then, Brett Howard's work.

I said: "Yes, there's a body here, the driver; he's dead, and a small car full of them back down the road, and a man with a machine pistol a mile or so further on."

"Are you all right?"

"We're okay, we're moving on . . . "

He sped off, and he was already using the mike.

I said: "Well, that means at least one of the motorcyclists is still alive; he radioed for help. But the other one? And the driver? For what, for God's sake?"

She said, her voice very small: "For money, Michael. It's horrible. And we are part of it."

We drove off, the smell of leaking oil everywhere, the steam forcing its way out, a couple of cylinders missing, and soon the ocher-colored houses were a welcome relief from the desert we had come through.

As we entered the main street, I said: "Which way?"

She was looking all around. "I'm not sure. We'll have to ask. There." I pulled in to a gas station, and Christine leaned out and said: "Ermou Street, please?"

The attendant was staring at the car in shock. It was full of bullet-holes and beginning to sound like a Sherman tank. He pointed and said: "Three street, three, right-hand side . . . " He was indicating the left, so I said:

"Right? or left?" He thought about it and said, grinning, "No, is right, left."

We drove off and found it a moment later.

As we turned the corner slowly, Christine nodded: "Yes, this is it. I was here a few years ago. We want number one hundred and fifteen."

They were splendid houses, not obtrusively big, but set in very large gardens of mostly grass and pine trees and bright red sand. Number a hundred and fifteen was set back in particularly large grounds, very shaded and pleasant, an ocher-colored two-story building with a fine stairway of stone steps leading up to the front door. A gardener was at work in the shrubbery, a trowel in his hand. He came and opened the big iron gates for us, and I eased the dying Caddy in, and thought: *Thank God we're here at last.*

There was a blue and gray van there from the telephone company, its driver staring at the wreck of our car with something like shock on his face. The gardener came over and opened the door for Christine as I got down. He indicated the steps to us and touched his cap politely.

We went on up, and I pulled the iron bar at the side of the door that rang the bell. The door opened almost immediately.

It was Arthur Helder.

He wasn't smiling any more, not in the least trying to be charming. I saw him look over my shoulder with a kind of brief nod and swung round as the gardener hit me hard over the back of the head with something that felt like a piece of rubber piping filled with sand, and as I went down, I heard Christine scream once—a scream that was cruelly cut off almost immediately.

I wasn't quite out, just incapable and suffering, and I tried to struggle. There were two of them now, lifting me up bodily and throwing me onto the floor in the back of the truck. Christine's limp body landed on top of mine, just thrown in there carelessly, like a sack of produce; as if I wasn't mad enough already, the callousness of it raised my anger to the boiling point, and the feeling of impotence was almost more than I could bear.

I heard Helder's voice, angry but quite controlled:

"Come on, hurry it up; the place'll be alive with cops any minute now. . . . "

The voice seemed to come from a long way off, and I realized I was slipping back into unconsciousness again and fought it.

There were two men clambering into the back now, the gardener and another man, and through the haze I saw, first, the little toy gun with its silencer, and then the hard, cold face of the French kid. He spat at me.

It was the last straw. I yelled and reached out for his ankles and tried to throw him off his feet, just to have the satisfaction of driving my fist into his face. He tossed the gun round lightly in his hand, catching it by the long barrel, and swung it at me, hard. It caught me just below the ear, and everything went black.

Chapter Fifteen

What finally brought me back to consciousness, strangely enough, was a lot more blows on the back of my head, one after the other, a relentless pounding that seemed to be splitting my skull open.

Not quite so vicious this time, just a repeated thump-thump-thumping that was driving me out of my mind. For a moment, I wondered who the hell was trying to do *what*. But when I opened my eyes it was to find myself lying on the steel floor, flat on my back, my head bouncing up and down in perfect concord with the jolting of the truck.

We were going up a steep hill, quite slowly in low gear, and it was pretty obvious that there was no road here at all, just a steep, steep slope of broken rock, an impossible grade.

Christine was very close beside me, lying on her stomach, her head cushioned on her forearm, and her eyes were half closed, but she was conscious; I saw them fasten on me, and I tried to read her thoughts, but that's a trick that doesn't work very often.

I thought: What the hell, playing dead's not going to get us anywhere. So I rolled over on my side and started taking stock of the situation.

There were two of them there now, the French boy and one of the gardeners—only the gardener was carrying a Schmeisser machine pistol across his knee, and both of them had their weapons aimed straight at my head. And there was something on their faces that had a strange and very unpleasant effect on me; they both contrived to look like executioners, and I realized with something of a shock, that up till this moment I had been regarding all this as a game—a brutal one, perhaps, but nonetheless a kind of sport in which the winner would go his way and the loser go his, too. Even the beating back at the cottage had seemed part of it, not really changing the aspect because it had been only momentary, after all.

But now . . . now it wasn't a game any more. I was convinced that the loser wasn't going anywhere except maybe in a coffin.

Perhaps it was the memory of the driver lying back there by the side of the road, his turned-over collar all stained with his blood, of the cops who might or might not be dead (and I was sure that at least one of them was). And the gun battle back in Paris that had left the streets strewn with carnage. . . . The game had suddenly become a deadly thing, and it had me scared witless.

"Almost nobody gets killed," Harry Slewsey had said, quoting averages. But averages just weren't good enough. Averages comprise both the best and the worst, and I'd been thinking all along of somewhere near the top of the scale, because disaster always happens only to other people.

But now, we were right down at the bottom; and the future looked anything but promising.

I rolled over some more, and got on all fours, and hoisted myself up onto the wooden bench that ran down one side. Nobody else moved, and I leaned back and shut my eyes, trying to drive a splitting headache away, and when I opened them after a little while, I could at least see where we were going and who was around.

Helder was in the passenger's seat. The phony telephone repairman was driving, and all around us were stark yellow rocks, great flat slabs of it lying around everywhere. It was alabaster, a whole mountain of it, and we were on a track that might have been made by the machines that went up there to cut it.

There was coarse scrub, some stunted pine trees, and an air of desolation everywhere; I wondered how long I had been unconscious, and how far we had come. I could see the water a long, long way down below us, the sky above it an impossible blue, dotted with puffs of cotton. I could hear a distant helicopter circling, the only touch of human life on this great golden-white mountain.

I closed my eyes again, but the pain just wouldn't go

away. And I thought about Christine, worrying about her.

We must have struggled over those rocks for another half hour; I could hear them spitting out from under the wheels as the tires kept losing their grip, and then the track leveled out again, and the trees were more dense now, a fertile valley up in the skies. In a little while we came to a wall of ancient red brick and a better surface to drive on, and then there was a cool, paved square of granite, shaded with huge trees, a fountain set in the wall there.

The driver stopped and cut the engine, and there was only silence. Not just quiet, but absolute silence, with no breeze, no birds, no nothing. The sound of the helicopter came back once and then was gone again, a trick of the contours of the mountain. It was very far away, too distant to be of any comfort at all.

The driver got down and unlocked the back doors, and I helped Christine out. We both just stood there for a moment, wondering what was going to happen now. Our three guards stood around us, a deadly escort waiting for orders, and Helder was slapping at his clothes and sending up great clouds of yellow dust. He said mildy: "Are you interested in Greek archaeology, Mr. Benasque? A fine old place, this."

There was a huge wooden door set in the brick wall, and an old blue-and-white signboard that said, in Greek and English: Monastery of Ossios Matallas, National Monument No. 1674. The board was broken and hanging askew, and a smaller board beside it said: Closed to the Public, by Order of the Department of Antiquities.

There was a small stone fountain set in the wall beside it, a ram's head with water spouting out of its mouth. I took Christine's arm and stepped over to it, and we cupped the water in our hands and drank, and splashed it over our faces.

Helder said: "The finest water in the whole of Greece; it's supposed to bring eternal youth; isn't that nice? They call the spring Agiasmos; I'm told it means 'consecrated water.' Do you think that's important? There used to be baths here, too, but there's not much left of them now. Dates back to the tenth century, and it's been closed for seven years; isn't that a shame? Still, it gives us a suitable hideout where we can transact our business. I don't suppose *anyone* has been up here in all that time; so we shouldn't have to worry about our privacy being disturbed."

I said: "Oh shut up, for Christ's sake!"

The French kid, still toting his gun, had gone to the door and was hammering on it with the flat of his hand. It was twenty feet high, or more, and studded with huge iron bolt-heads. We heard the fastening being thrown back on the inside, and it swung open slowly, heavily, the iron hinges silent.

It was Veronica.

She looked at me first, just briefly, and then at Christine, studying her from head to foot, and then at Helder, and she said: "Thank God, Arthur, you were such a long time. I was . . . frightened, this place is . . . it's like a tomb."

He was very gentle with her. "I know. But it's all over now." He kissed her on the cheek, a rather perfunctory sort of peck, and said: "Let's go inside."

She didn't move. She looked back at me and said coldly: "I don't like to be made a fool of, Mr. Benasque."

Her hand came up so fast that I didn't even step back, and she struck me across the face, just an ordinary slap, but so hard it nearly knocked me off my feet. She turned abruptly, and Helder looked at me and almost sighed.

He grimaced and said: "Well, I suppose you know you had that coming. Malcolm Reevers, indeed!"

We followed her into the courtyard, just two of the men behind us now, the driver getting back into the truck and driving it through the gateway.

The enclosure was fantastic. It was all paved over at different levels with great slabs of stone. Down one side of the courtyard there was a two-story ruin of arched brickwork, a row of cells on the upper floor, and a long colonnade on the lower. The ruin was on our left, and on the right there was a row of low, red-tiled buildings and another fountain, with a tiny broken-down Byzantine chapel in one corner. In another corner, a flight of brick steps led up to a series of what looked like larger rooms. There were olive trees growing everywhere, and odd-angled corners and tumbledown archways, and tiny gardens filled now with straggling weeds.

We passed a square-cut stone doorway with an iron grill over it. Inside I caught a glimpse of a huge stone mill wheel, a place to grind corn in the distant past. The tall trees covered the whole courtyard with a heavy canopy, and it was cool and lovely in here. I thought what a shame it was that it had all fallen into such a state of disrepair.

But that's one of the problems in Greece; there are just too many worthy sites, and they can't all be kept up. This one gave the impression, indeed, that *no one* had ever been here in the past couple of centuries.

Veronica was leading the way up a narrow stairway to the upper floor, looking quite incongruous in jeans and sandals, with a heavy off-white sweater of raw wool, the kind they make in the north, its sleeves rolled up above her elbows. It was miles too big for her, and I thought it might be Helder's. All wrong; she should have been wearing a Grecian robe of white cotton, and then she would have looked like one of the goddesses come back to earth.

She threw open another door, and we went into a large, square room that was in moderately good repair—one wall taken up with low brick arches that gave onto the courtyard, all joined together with a three-foot-high brick wall, a small barred window on one side, and a series of arches with seats in them on the other. There was a fireplace niche in one corner, only a couple of feet or so across. Some charcoal was burning there, a modern aluminum coffeepot on it.

There was a long wooden table and half a dozen wooden benches, a ten-year-old calendar on the wall, an icon in another niche, a few rickety wooden chairs, and a very big but broken-down cupboard, more like a dresser, with a few items of clothing tossed carelessly onto it.

I heard the truck in the yard below us stop, and the door slammed shut with a sound of finality. From up here, I could watch it; the driver was filling a can with water from the fountain.

Veronica had gone to the little grate and was pouring two cups of coffee, one for herself and one for Helder. The Frenchman was standing in the far corner, his legs widespread and his arms half folded, and the other man was by the fire with his Schmeisser pointed at us.

Christine, looking cross and unhappy, had found a seat on one of the benches. Helder stood by the grate, sipped his coffee, looked at her thoughtfully, and said, not even deigning to glance at me: "Sit down, Benasque, you make the place look untidy."

I perched myself up on the high table, dangled my legs, and looked at Christine. She was just staring out into space, a veiled look in her eyes, as though she knew this was the end of the road and was forcing a sort of resignation on herself.

Helder said at last: "Well, are you just going to hand them over and save us all a lot of trouble? It's the easy way out, you know."

Her voice was very heavy: "You have them, Sir Arthur. You should have found that out by now."

He sounded tired. "Oh for God's sake, are we going to start that all over again? The stones in the briefcase were identical with the ones in your hairbrush, and that means they are both decoys; it means there's another set somewhere and I want it. That's all there is to it."

I said: "Where's Vasileos, Helder?"

He shrugged. "Vasileos is back at the villa, where else? The police must have been there a couple of hours ago, so don't worry about Vasileos. Weeping on his wife's ample shoulder, no doubt, but once we borrowed his house—we had no further interest in him. Where are the diamonds?"

I said: "The girl's got them. She landed at Athens airport . . ."

He interrupted me, a mixture now of weariness and anger: "Oh for Christ's sake . . . !"

He raised his voice and stuck a finger out at me, and said: "Let me tell you what it's all about, Benasque, because you're a fool! If you had lost your delivery, as you're trying to pretend, then you just would not have gone to Vasileos' villa; so whatever doubts I may have had in my mind *then*, are quite dissipated *now*. I know that one of you has them, and if I have to dissect both your bodies with a scalpel to get them, that's what I'm going to do. Give me your shoes."

"My shoes?"

"Put them on the table there and go and sit on the wall. It's a thirty-foot drop to the courtyard; so maybe you'd like to find out if you can drop that far without breaking your fool legs."

I kicked off my shoes and laid them on the table for him, and he turned to the French boy and said briefly: "Your knife."

The kid reached under his blazer and came out with a sheath knife, handed it to Helder and went back to his post. Helder pried off the heels and looked at them, and when he had finished, he said disgustedly: "All right, take your clothes off, both of you, down to the bare skin."

I was perched up there on the low wall, and it was indeed a thirty-foot drop. The driver of the truck was sitting on a broken piece of pillar, munching away on a sandwich, his gun lying on the ground at his feet. There was a silent movement in the branches of the tree that overhung the wall behind him, a towering chestnut.

I could see nothing more than a protruding leg, groping for a lower branch, and then a hand, and I turned back, my heart beating fast.

Christine had not moved, and Helder said again, very angrily now: "Well, do you want me to do it for you?"

He turned back to me and said: "All your clothes, Benasque, one by one on the table."

I took off my jacket and tossed it on the table, and he picked it up and felt it all over for hidden pockets, but where can you hide three fairly large diamonds in a denim leisure jacket? He dropped it and said impatiently: "Your pants, come on . . . "

I had trouble with the belt, and then with the zipper, anything to gain a little time, and I half turned back to the archway and as I fumbled I stared up at the sky and down again to the yard. The driver was lying down on the ground, being dragged into the bushes quickly, and then they were gone, and just as I turned back and got my zipper undone, Bruce was reaching out for the gun he had left lying there.

I had not heard a sound of any sort.

I tossed the trousers down onto the table, and as he fingered them all over, I looked at Christine. She had her dress off now, her face tight with fury, and was standing there in panty hose and shoes. She slipped her shoes off and placed them carefully on the table, and he took those apart, too, with his knife. The minutes were slipping by.

I glanced down into the courtyard again; nothing there now, nothing at all except the unattended truck.

No, that was not true . . .

There was a moving shadow under it, at the rear end, by the gas tank; and still, only silence.

How much more time did we have?

I heard Helder say: "The pantyhose too; I want you naked, dammit!"

I turned back, standing there in nothing but my underpants, and he looked at me furiously and said: "Get rid of them!"

I shook my head. As calmly as I could, I said: "I'll keep them on, if you don't mind. There are ladies present."

He came up to me with his fist balled, ready to hit me. I stepped back and eluded the first blow, but I wasn't fast enough for the second. It caught me under the jaw—a good professional left hook, followed by a right to the gut—and sent me sprawling to the ground. Surprisingly, it didn't hurt that much, but I doubled up, staggered to the wall and saw that the flames were just beginning to lick around the back of the truck.

It would only be seconds now, and it seemed essential to keep the others right where they were, on the other side of the room, far from the courtyard's line of vision.

Helder was moving in on me again; so I held out my hands in a placatory gesture and stopped him: "Okay, okay, anything you say." I started peeling off my pants, my thumbs hooked into the cord that was around my waist, one last effort. When I had them off I placed them carefully, chamois bag and all, on the table.

But he had seen.

For a moment, he didn't even move. He just stood there, looking at the stuff on the table, as though enjoying the last few minutes, and then he said mildly: "I'm sure that isn't really a very good hiding place. That's amateur stuff, wouldn't you say?"

I looked at Christine, and never have I seen so much dignity in a naked lady. She just stood there, with her arms across her breast, and she was looking at Veronica as though mocking her. Veronica was looking her up and down, one beautiful woman looking at another, trying to find some kind of a flaw there. And then, her nose was wrinkling suddenly, and she was frowning. She said sharply: "Something's burning . . . "

I saw Helder's eyes go instinctively to the little fire in the grate, but a wisp of pale blue smoke was spiraling up now from the yard below—just a faint touch of it, like someone maybe smoking a cigarette just outside the archway. As Helder strode toward the window, the truck blew up.

It was a tremendous explosion.

A flat piece of steel, perhaps the roof-panel, smashed into the brickwork of the archway, and then both Helder and Veronica were at the aperture, staring down at the truck, and I saw that he was clutching the little chamois bag, the cord dangling from it. I had not seen him pick it up, an urgent reflex action.

He said sharply: "Lefevre!" The French kid was suddenly beside him, no longer anonymous, a name now for his last few seconds of life. The other man was there too, his gun aimed down into the courtyard, looking for a target. I saw Christine reach for her pants, decorum above everything else, and when the door smashed open, Lefevre swung round and thrust his little gun out with both hands and fired three times. I swear the last shot went off after he was dead.

He slumped to the ground, with a single hole neatly through the center of his forehead, and there was Bruce with the machine pistol pointed. The other man simply dropped his gun and held his hands high above his head.

I saw the shock on Helder's face, the absolute fury on Veronica's.

I reached for the gun the other man had dropped and checked it out quickly, and Bruce said, his eyes hard on Helder: "Put them down on the table, please."

For a moment, Helder seemed uncertain, and then he looked at the dead body on the floor, and at the other man with his hands raised high, and he tossed the little

pouch down. He quietly said: "All right. There they are."
Christine had her jacket half on now, and she moved to the table to get them, and Bruce said sharply: "No! Don't move. Please . . ."
I thought: *Oh my God, after all this, he wants them for himself . . .*
But he was grinning that wide, friendly grin of his, and he said more quietly: "We have a line-of-fire problem, Madame."
He was gesturing with the gun: "In the corner, Sir Arthur, Miss Verignana."
Helder's eyes seemed to have glazed over, a sign of defeat, I thought. He went to the corner and stood there, and the look now was almost of resignation.
Not Veronica. She just didn't move, and Bruce looked at her and shrugged, not making an issue of it at all. He turned to me and said: "You know how to use the Schmeisser, Mr. Benasque?"
I nodded: "I know."
"Good."
He went to the table, picked up the little bag, fingered it for a moment, then went to Christine and handed them to her with an old-fashioned sort of comment: "I think these are yours, Madame?" She took them from him, and I wondered what she was going to say, but she said nothing, and instead handed them to me, as I was reaching for my trousers.
I said: "Well, that hiding place has been blown, hasn't it?" Bruce had his gun at the ready again; so I slipped on my pants and stuff and dropped the diamonds into my pocket. I looked at Bruce: "Now, what do we do with them?"
He grinned. "All figured out, Mr. Benasque. There's a nice little prison cell downstairs."
"Ah, the iron door. Is it locked?"
"A lock on it, but no key. It's open."
"Then we have to find a padlock, and that might not be easy . . . "
"The millstone."
"Ah, yes, the millstone. You think we can move it?"
He shrugged. "I'm sure three men can roll it. That's all that has to be done."

"Then let's go."

We gathered up the rest of our stuff, and the solemn procession went slowly down the steps to the courtyard, where the truck was still burning fiercely.

Christine and Veronica sat on broken pieces of pillar like distant friends, and I stood guard, while Helder, the gardener-type, and Bruce put their shoulders to the big wheel. It was more than six feet across, and it took them a good twenty minutes, sweating profusely, to roll it outside and get it just in the right position, four feet or so from the iron grill door. I opened it until it was practically touching the stone, on its edge like a great solid barrier, and said to Helder: "You and your lady, inside . . . "

For a moment, I thought he was not going to move, and he said at last, a touch of desperation in him now: "One more suggestion, Benasque. Let us go. I'll give you my word we won't do anything to try and stop the delivery. A gentleman's word."

I shook my head.

He said, worried: "If they find us here . . . Name your own price, Benasque."

"No."

"Any price at all. Enough to retire on for the rest of your life."

"Inside."

He shrugged. He stepped into the little cell, and the gardener followed him and waited. Helder looked at Veronica and even contrived a smile: a cold and rather phony one, but a smile nonetheless. "Come, my darling."

She looked at him coldly and then at me. She said: "No."

I heard Christine sigh, then she got up and moved behind Veronica, twisted one of Veronica's arms behind her back, took a handful of hair in her free hand, yanked that lovely head up, and just marched her into the cell. Veronica was screaming obscenities at her as she slammed the door shut. I leaned my shoulder into the top of the heavy wheel and shoved, and it toppled over onto its edge and wedged itself firmly against the grill. There was no way in hell they'd ever get that door open from the inside.

Bruce said, and he was grinning, again, wiping at the sweat on the back of his neck: "It's less than half a mile to the helicopter, just the other side of the hill. Fifteen minutes to the top, and ten minutes down to the bottom of the valley."

I took Christine's arm, and we left the Monastery of Ossios Matallas.

Chapter Sixteen

Vasileos' villa was so thick with police that there was hardly room to move.

There were seven of their cars outside, four officers on the street with walkie-talkies, four motorcycle cops sitting on their bikes along the road, a radio command car parked in the garden, and at least thirty officers milling around in the house.

He was a short, darkish man with a neat gray beard and black hair, his face still white, with bandages at his wrists and throat. He was still trembling, and he said, spluttering: "They tied me so cruelly; they were monsters . . ."

He had a little glass of *ouzo*. He drained it and took another and drained that, as well, before he remembered his manners and offered me some too.

But Christine, calm and serene and on top of everything once more, said: "First, Mr. Vasileos, I think the matter of the unfinished business?"

"Yes, yes, of course. This way, if you please."

He led us into another room, a study, lined with books in three or four languages, a grand piano, a small bar, and some splendid antique furniture. We sat together, the three of us, at a fine old refectory table with a silver bowl on it, and for a horrible moment I thought that the blood-red contents were a man's severed hand . . .

But the illusion quickly went as Vasileos took the little square of red velvet and laid it neatly on the table, and I placed the diamonds carefully on it. He stared at them, not moving, for a very long time.

He was motionless, not seeming to breathe, just looking at them, but at last he pulled open a drawer and took out a slip of paper and gave it to Christine and said politely: "Is that satisfactory, Madame?"

She took it and read aloud: "On this seventh day of June, 1978, received from an undisclosed courier, three stones reputed to be: the Thai Queen, the Astra Para- the Jonkers Number Four."

She gave him back the paper and said: "Yes, that is acceptable. We have to change the date, and we'll both initial it."

"Willingly, Madame."

He signed the paper with a flourish, slipped the stones back into their pouch, and stooped to lift up a corner of the carpet. There was a small steel plate there, a recessed dial in it. He turned the dial a few times, opened it up, and dropped the little bag in and closed it again. It seemed a very fragile sort of safe to house so much of value, and I suppose I looked at Vasileos with a touch of surprise.

He smiled thinly.

He said: "Monsieur Armand, in Paris, has a vault which is reputed to be the strongest in Europe. But mine . . . it is more impregnable. A shaft, M'sieur Benasque, cut into the native rock one hundred and eighty meters straight down. There, at the bottom, in one of the caves under Sounion, is *my* vault. By comparison, Armand's is merely a clothes closet to hide trivia in. It gives me . . . a certain satisfaction."

"And there . . . they will stay till the next time."

He nodded. "Yes, until I have sold them at, I hope, a very handsome profit."

I said: "When a few more lives might just be . . . scattered by the wayside."

His eyes were very dark and bright and alert, and he was smiling—a slight and perhaps even rueful smile.

He went to the lovely old oak dresser and set three new glasses in a row, poured *ouzo* into them, offered them to us, and said: "The last one was merely to repair the damage that had been done to my nervous system. Now, we can drink more calmly to celebrate. . . . What shall we drink to?"

I looked at Christine, waiting for her to answer; she looked tired to the point of exhaustion, even of sickness. I said: "Well, we celebrate a delivery, I suppose?"

He shook his head. "No. Let us drink to the mystique of the most precious mineral known to man."

He looked at me hard. "And it *is* a mystique, Mr. Benasque. For diamonds, men have given their lives, and women their souls. It's all part of a pattern, a moving pattern that only ceases to move when the diamonds are in their safe resting places. . . . Once they are taken out, the pattern moves again, inexorably. Men lose their lives, and women . . ."

The police were still clumping around the house, but it seemed now that they were merely waiting to be told, by *someone,* that they were no longer needed.

Vasileos went on, and he was dreaming now—the stuff his life was made of: "The Astra Para is perhaps the most perfect little diamond ever cut, and almost no one really appreciates it, or knows what its true value ought to be. The Number Four?"

He shrugged. "The Number Four is important only because of a purely mechanical idiosyncrasy, that extraordinary and quite unnecessary cut, the ruination, in my opinion, of a worthy stone. But the Thai Queen . . . " He was in raptures now. "You know its history, M'sieur Benasque?"

I felt like an idiot saying no, after all the hassle over it, but I had to.

He went on: "An Indian stone, of course; it couldn't be anything else. The first time it was stolen was in the year 1304, when the Sultan Alla-ed-Din looted it on one of his forays into India; and even then no one was quite sure where the gem had come from. Some say it was part of the same rough diamond that comprised both the Great Mogul and the Koh-i-noor, though discovery dates would seem to disprove that. And in the next three-hundred years, it was stolen—the ravages of war, you understand—no less than twenty-seven times before the French got their hands on it. The British took it from them, the Russians had it for sixty years, and then the French got it again. And each time it changed hands . . . hundreds, sometimes *thousands* of men died. And the lovely women who have pined for it . . . they are legion. Not just another bauble to sparkle at awoman's throat, Mr. Benasque, but one of the greatest diamonds in the world. A diamond of historic merit and immeasurable importance. One might even call it . . . a diamond of the greatest dignity."

I thought that was a nice little speech. And then, he killed it; he said with satisfaction; "And now, it is *mine*."

We finished off our *ouzo* with ceremonial flourishes, and there was a great deal of shaking hands and even some Greek embracing here and there, and we went back into the other room and found Bruce waiting patiently. I said to him: "You want to clean things up around here? Ive no stomach for it any more."

He nodded. "Sure thing, Mr. Benasque."

"You have to tell the cops all about National Monument 1674. Couple of people still there they'll be interested in."

"You bet."

"And then, Bruce? I suppose you'll be going back to California?"

"I guess so."

"I've got some writing to do. I don't know; I'll probably do it there, I guess . . . "

"Okay. So I'll see you there."

We shook hands, and his grin was the comforting kind that says: Till the next time.

I looked at Christine and wanted so badly to be alone with her. She reached out and touched my arm and said: "Why don't we stroll along the beach, Michael? There's nothing for us to do now, except . . . Well, it's all over now."

"Yes. Some of it is."

I took her arm, and we went down onto the sand and strolled along it, and the silence was unbearable, broken only by the gentle sound of the surf.

We walked and walked and walked, and the wind was ruffling that lovely yellow hair. We came to an upturned boat lying on the sand, and I sat on it and waited for her to say what she had to say.

She found a long stick and stood beside me drawing lines in the sand, lines that meant nothing at all, and she said at last, her voice very quiet: "I hate good-byes more than anything in the world."

I said: "I won't make it any easier for you, Christine. Or any harder either."

"No, I was sure you wouldn't do that."

The lines in the sand were something to concentrate on. She said slowly: "If I could only find a *reason*. But I can't."

"There is no reason."

"I know. And still . . . "

"Except that you're very . . . how shall I put it? Let-down? It's not good to make important decisions when you're exhausted."

"I know that too. Will you wait here until I have gone?"

"If that is what you want. Anything that you want."

"Yes. Yes, I was sure of that too."

She dropped the stick and stood there, staring down at the surf. I stood up and took her in my arms, and the tears were rolling down her cheeks again, and I held her tight.

It was hard to find the words. I said at last: "Somehow, I knew this was how it was going to be, without even being able to guess at a reason. Tell me, *why*, Christine?"

She shook her head. Her voice was a zephyr: "I don't know the reason. I don't even know if there is one. All I know is . . . it has to be."

"For God's sake . . . "

She laid a finger on my lips. "Sshh . . . One day we'll both wake up, in separate beds, separate cities, separate countries, perhaps half a world apart, and we'll both know then *why* it was inevitable."

"Or we'll know that it was not."

"Yes. Perhaps that too. I don't know, Michael."

Her hand was on my cheek when she said good-bye at last, and then she turned and walked back toward the villa, quite slowly, her head lowered; it seemed that once she stumbled.

I waited a long, long time, till she was below the villa, a tiny figure in the distance. I saw her look round and hesitate, as though remembering, and then she moved off again, up to the little ocher-colored building that stood on top of the secret vault hidden so far below it.

She did not look back again, and after she had gone from sight, I sat down on the empty boat and did nothing for the rest of the evening.

There just wasn't anything to do any more.

Except, maybe, dream.

"C.I.A., Mister Fletcher."
"Um. Would you mind spelling that?"
"Enough of your bull, Fletcher."
"Okay, guys. What's the big deal?"
"You are going to tape the most private bedroom conversations of the most important people in American journalism."
"You're crazy. What have you got on me?"
"Taxes, Mister Fletcher."
"What about 'em?"
"You haven't paid any."

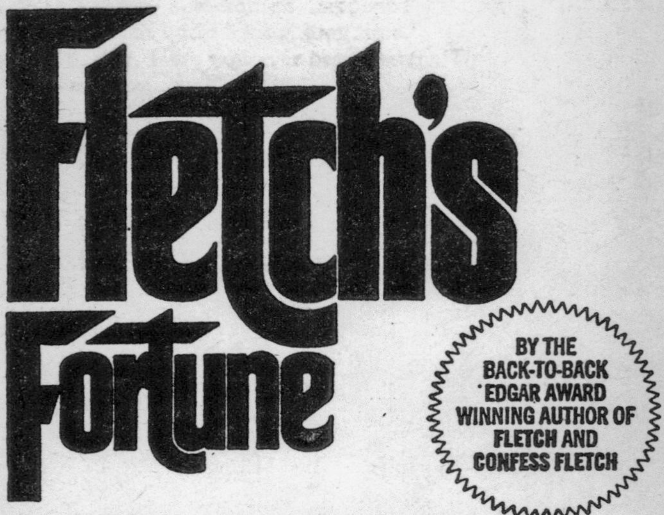

Snatched from bliss on the Riviera, Fletch was flown to the journalism convention with a suitcase full of bugging devices and a bizarre assignment: dig up some juicy scandals on Walter March, the ruthless newspaper tycoon . . . Then Walter March was found lying face up with a long pair of scissors stuck in his back. It was the crime of the century. And a hell of a story.

A blockbuster of suspense by
GREGORY McDONALD

". . . the toughest, leanest horse to hit the literary racetrack since James M. Cain."—PETE HAMILL

Avon/37978/$1.95

FF 7-78